THE BATTLE HYMN OF THE REPUBLIC

An Alphonso Clay Mystery of the Civil War

THE BATTLE HYMN OF THE REPUBLIC

An Alphonso Clay Mystery of the Civil War

by

Jack Martin

Fireship Press
www.FireshipPress.com

ISBN: 978-1-61179-203-4

BISAC Subject Headings:

FIC022060	FICTION / Mystery & Detective / Historical
FIC014000	FICTION / Historical
FIC032000	FICTION / War & Military

Address all correspondence to:
Fireship Press, LLC
P.O. Box 68412
Tucson, AZ 85737
Or visit our website at:
www.FireshipPress.com

1.0

Contents

Prologue
Appomattox Courthouse, Virginia
April 9, 1865

Robert E. Lee finished strapping on his sword, and carefully examined himself in the small mirror atop his pigeon-hole portable desk. The morning light of the mild spring day filtering in through the open tent flap was sufficient for him to make a minute examination of his appearance. Today it would be vital to appear dignified and in control – no matter how much his heart was breaking. His boots were polished to a mirror finish; his uniform spotless, lint-free and sharply creased. He noted the three stars on his collars – stars without the wreaths that indicated a general of the Confederacy; stars that were usually worn in that fashion by Confederate colonels. For the hundredth time, he wondered why he had not added those wreaths, and for the hundredth time he silently acknowledged the reason: colonel was the highest rank he had achieved in the United States Army, and for some obscure reason he would always be a colonel in his own mind. He looked at his face, determined to examine the kind of expression he would be presenting to the Federals, and received a shock: a tired old man stared back at him. Of course he knew the war had aged him; he lacked the energy he had brought at the beginning of the war, and even occasionally woke up at night with a strange, hollow feeling in his chest, gasping for air. But somehow he had continued to see himself as the virile, barrel-chested officer who had entered the service of the South with only a smattering of gray in his dark hair. Today – today of all days – he was looking like a tired, defeated old man. Which was what he was. Squaring his shoulders, he deliberately hardened his expression; he would not allow Ulysses Grant to see him as a broken old man.

Through the open tent-flap came Lieutenant General James Longstreet, Lee's senior corps commander, followed by Colonel Marshall, Lee's meek looking and efficient personal aide. Sighing, Lee asked Longstreet, "General, is there any chance at all of us breaking through to the west and joining General Johnston in North Carolina?"

Longstreet scowled; given his burly frame, dark beard crawling high onto his cheeks, and beady eyes, the scowl made him look very dangerous. "No, General, ain't no chance," drawled Longstreet. "No chance in the world. Meade's boys have scooped up Picket and his division, according to our scouts. Ain't going to be no help from there. And A. P. Hill and his boys couldn't shake Sheridan and his cavalry loose from the road west. At the last minute, Wright's VI Corps came up from Meade, and we ain't breaking through to the west. What with desertion and captures, Grant outnumbers us near three to one." Longstreet paused to light a cigar. "Hill tried his damnedest. He was out front, as always. A. P. is dead."

Lee felt his heart thump strangely. *'A. P. Hill dead? The general who always wore red-flannel shirts into battle, dead. The brilliant tactician who had lost his fiancée just before the war to the incompetent Union coward McClellan, and seemed to take every battle as personally as a duel, dead. The young officer who had tried to bury his heartbreak in Richmond brothels, and had come down with a roaring case of the pox, dead.'* Sad as he was, Lee was certain that Hill had a finer death this way than the death that would have faced him down the road.

Lee turned to Longstreet, who he always thought of as his "old warhorse." "There is no alternative. It is time to go meet with General Grant. Colonel Marshall, arrange for a flag of truce and saddle up some horses for you and myself."

Welling tears visible behind his spectacles, Marshall saluted and wordlessly left the tent. The moment he was gone, Longstreet spoke. "There is one alternative to surrender, sir."

Lee closed his eyes for a moment, as if in pain, and then opened them. "No more attacks, General Longstreet. No more piles of bodies."

Longstreet took a puff on his cigar. "I wasn't talking about an attack," he drawled. "Split up the army. Tell the boys to high-tail it off into the mountains in groups no bigger than ten or twenty, carrying only their guns. Sure, the Yanks will get a lot, but they will miss most; it'll be like herding fleas. Tell them to start up a real partisan war, like the one that brought down the Frenchies in Spain, during Napoleon's time. No more pitched battles, no more trenches. Strike and run, strike and run. Go where the blue-bellies ain't, and burn everything that helps them. The people of the North ain't going to put up with that for too long."

Lee sighed. "General, we did not fight our war for independence for that, to create an Ireland or a Poland, decades of isolated murders of Government officials followed by brutal retaliations and burnings. That is not the way of life we meant to preserve. We fought to preserve that way of life from the encroachments of the North, and despite everything we have lost – finally, irrevocably lost."

"Not if we made the South too hot for the Union to hold," growled Longstreet ominously.

Lee placed a hand on Longstreet's shoulder, and for one of the very few times addressed him by his nickname. "Pete, I have no doubt we could make a partisan war that after some generations would drive the Federals out of our land. However, our way of life would not be preserved; the way we will have won would guarantee that it could never return. I shudder at the mere thought of what kind of land the South might become. Far better to make our peace with Lincoln, and salvage what we may from defeat. Slavery will be gone, of course. Personally, I think that may be for the best. If the peace is gentle, we may preserve much of what made us the South." Lee released Longstreet's shoulder, took the gray planter's hat from his cot, and settled it neatly on his head.

"Forget officers like me for a moment," rumbled Longstreet. "I expect the Federals will try you and hang you. Jeff Davis, Joe Johnston, and Beauregard as well, at a minimum. The North is baying for the blood of those like you who were high-ranking in the peacetime army. They will want you hanged higher than Haman, saying that is the right punishment for 'traitors'."

"We were traitors," responded Lee mildly, almost sadly. "I broke my solemn oath to the country, given before God Almighty, to follow my country of Virginia out of the Union. If I hang, it will only be justice."

"If you hang, won't matter what you tell the boys. They will take whatever vengeance they want. Hell, I don't even want to think what someone like Nathan Bedford Forrest would do; saw him in action in Tennessee, and he don't follow the usages of war, to put it mildly."

"I am still in command," responded Lee coldly. "He will do as he is ordered." "Anyway, guess I better get ready," responded Longstreet grumpily.

"I am sorry, General Longstreet, but you must remain here. If anything ... untoward happens during the surrender negotiations, I need you to keep the army under discipline. I will only need Colonel Marshall."

Longstreet took another long pull on his cigar as he looked at Lee, the old man with whom he had argued, the old man whom he occasionally defied – the old man whom he loved like a father. "If you say so," responded Longstreet with a surly reluctance derived from his stubborn Dutch ancestors.

Lee squared his shoulders and marched out of the tent, looking as proud and noble as the day he had first taken command of the Army of Northern Virginia. Longstreet looked after him; saying nothing, he took another long pull on his cigar.

* * * * *

General John Rawlins tugged the heavy table toward the center of the parlor of the McLean mansion. The strain was too much for his weakened lungs; jerking a handkerchief toward his mouth, he began a gagging, breathless series of coughs that lasted for nearly a minute. When he was done he removed the cloth, and noted with melancholy relief no signs of blood.

"Leave that alone, John," said Colonel Ely Parker, a full-blooded Seneca Indian. "Wait for some enlisted men, or for God's sake let me do it." Without further ado the burly Parker easily shifted the heavy table to the middle of the room, and then began carrying chairs from the adjacent dining room into the parlor.

"My apologies, Ely," responded the still-gasping Rawlins. "I simply got carried away with the word from the pickets that Lee is coming,"

"Best to hold your horses for a while longer. Lee is a wily fox, and may have sent that word in order to make us lower our guard long enough for him to break out and join Johnston."

"No, Ely, this is the end of it. Finally the end. Lee is trapped, and must surrender or be slaughtered. I do not think he will want his army slaughtered, after all they have been through with him. Curious that the McLean family chose not to stay; they could have witnessed history."

Parker gave the grunt that passed with him for a laugh. "The McLeans are staunch rebels, and would not stay in a house being used by General Grant. I believe that they moved here, back in '61, from Fairfax County, the moment Fairfax came under Union occupation, because they could not stand the thought of being in a land ruled by Lincoln. I expect they do not see the irony in their new home being used to witness the end of the Confederacy."

The two friends heard the sound of horses pulling up in front of the house. Moments later Generals Grant, Meade and Sheridan strode through the door, leaving their cavalry escorts outside. The three Union commanders were a study in contrasts.

Ulysses Grant wore an unbuttoned private's tunic, to which shoulder-boards containing three stars had been carelessly sewn. The rest of his clothing was an extremely informal ensemble: shapeless blue trousers spattered with mud, unpolished and badly worn civilian shoes, the checked shirt under his vest possessing a surprisingly dirty collar and drooping tie. The only thing about his appearance to suggest he was the commander of all of the armies of the North was his eyes. Steady, steely, and somewhat sad, those eyes somehow communicated that he was in command of the situation.

George Meade, commander of the Army of the Potomac, wore the field uniform of a major general, as immaculate as the conditions of this final campaign allowed. His deeply-lined face and baggy eyes showed signs of suffering and disappointment. The suffering reflected the near-fatal wound he had received early in the war, and the stomach ulcers that left him in continuous pain and so frayed his temper that his men referred to him (behind his back) as the "damn old snapping-turtle." The disappointment came from the fact that in the last year of the war, Grant, impatient with Meade's cautious approach to combat, had gently taken away all his real authority over the Army of the Potomac on strategic matters, leaving Meade as little more than a glorified aide. Meade was an intelligent man, and knew that although he was the victor of Gettysburg, history would place him forever in the shadow of Grant; a man who before the war he had pitied as a failed drunk. This knowledge was as painful to Meade as his old wound and ulcers.

Phil Sheridan, commander of the Army of the Shenandoah as well as all cavalry in the area, appeared to be the most threatening of the three officers, despite being by far the smallest. Claiming to be five foot four inches, he revealed himself to be loose with the truth; in fact he did not quite reach five foot two. However, no one ever made the mistake of disputing his claimed height to his face. Short he might be, but his barrel chest and heavy arms, almost ape-like in their length, gave promise of great strength; while the glaring hostility with which his dark eyes darted about gave evidence he would not hesitate to use that strength.

"You shouldn't have called the cease-fire, Grant," said Sheridan with a notable lack of respect to the commander of all the armies of the United States. "I had them right where I wanted them. Right where I wanted them!" He smacked a powerful fist into the palm of his left hand, making a sound like a gunshot. "My boys could have put every last one of those bastard traitors into the ground. Into the ground!"

As Meade looked on, Grant responded mildly. "Couldn't kill the whole doggone Army of Northern Virginia."

"The hell we couldn't! It's not too late. Give me the word, and I'll make sure centuries will pass before the mere thought of treason doesn't make a disloyal bastard sweat blood!" Thus spoke the man who had promised to burn out the Shenandoah Valley so thoroughly that crows could not live there, and had delivered on that promise.

Grant produced a cigar from one tunic pocket and a curious mechanical lighter from another, then proceeded to light up. As he expelled his first large draw of smoke, he responded to Sheridan. "We won't be doing any of that now, Phil. Talked to Lincoln just before Petersburg fell, and he said something that stuck with me. Said when this is all over, the Rebs are going to be our fellow citizens, and we will need to let them up easy. I intend to let them up easy; that is, if they'll let me."

"Our 'fellow citizens' did not let us up easy," said Meade sourly. "Have you forgotten what they have done, just to my army alone? 25,000 of my boys dead and wounded at

Gettysburg, 30,000 in the Wilderness and the Crater. Sir, are you forgetting about them?"

Grant looked levelly at Meade, took another pull on his stogie, and replied quietly. "I will never forget them, or all the others, so long as I live. But I want their sacrifice to mean something. I want the country whole and at peace, with the crime of slavery gone forever." He shifted his attention to Rawlins and Parker. "Everything ready, gentlemen?"

"Just one moment, General," replied the pale Rawlins, who scooped up an ink pot, pen, and several pages of paper from a sideboard and placed them on the table that Parker had wrestled into the middle of the parlor. Throwing his crumpled hat into a corner of the room, Grant ambled over to the table, and settled himself uncomfortably into the chair facing the open doorway. Frowning slightly, he opened the ink pot, to see if there was an adequate supply. Just as he confirmed for himself the presence of ink, a breathless young cavalry lieutenant came flying through the open door. The beardless youth almost forgot to salute; remembering at the last moment, his hand went jerkily to his head.

"General Grant, sir it's him! He's here! Marse Robert in the flesh, and just one officer with him. My God, it's over, ain't it General? This Goddamn awful war is over!"

Grant saw that both Meade and Sheridan were about to visit their wrath on the excited, undisciplined officer. Stifling a smile, he said "Thank you Lieutenant. Please escort the General inside, then leave us. And thank you for your prompt attention to duty."

With a silly grin on his face, the lieutenant exited the parlor to do as he was asked. Some quietly muttered words drifted through the open door, and then Lee and Marshall slowly entered the MacLean family's parlor. Lee stopped, and looked around the room.

His gaze rested for some moments on the glaring Sheridan. His mind briefly went back to his tenure as Commandant of West Point, and a small, wry smile flitted across his features.

He remembered Cadet Phil Sheridan well. At one evening meal an aristocratic Southern plebe had mocked Sheridan for being the dwarf son of an Irish ditch digger. Sheridan had broken a dinner-plate over the young aristocrat's head, and then proceeded to chase him around the dining room with a bayonet until restrained by his classmates. The next day the unrepentant Sheridan was brought before Colonel Lee for discipline. Lee knew he should have proclaimed the little Mick's instant dismissal. But the highly honorable Lee had no patience with Southern aristocrats who mocked their social inferiors; and besides, something told him that there were the makings of a valuable soldier in Sheridan. So to the surprise of both Sheridan and himself, he only suspended the young plebe for a year, allowing him to return, graduate, and take up his commission. With the benefit of hindsight, Lee now realized that had been a grave mistake. Sheridan had gone from chasing an upperclassman with a bayonet to chasing Braxton Bragg off Lookout Mountain, chasing Jubal Early out of the Shenandoah Valley, and chasing the Army of the Northern Virginia off the only road giving it any hope of escape from Grant. '*I really should have expelled him*' thought Lee wryly.

Lee looked at Grant, who made no move to rise, and instead gestured to the other chair at the table, saying "General Lee, please be seated." Colonel Marshall pulled out the chair for his commander, and then drew silently back to the wall, positioning himself as far from the other Union officers as the parlor allowed. An uncomfortable silence reigned for some moments, until Grant decided to break the ice.

"General, we have met before; during the Mexican War. I was trying to get some badly-needed ammunition for my brigade from General Scott, and encountered you at that time."

Frostily Lee replied. "I have understood for some time that we must have met in Mexico. However, try as I might, I could not remember doing so."

Grant shrugged. "It is understandable. I was a very junior lieutenant, and looking very grubby. At the time Scott and his staff were congratulating you on personally scouting out the path to flank Santa Anna's army. It was your moment, and I made no especial effort to intrude."

Lee looked at Grant appraisingly for a moment, "It has bothered me that I could not remember. Ever since you...came to Virginia last year, I repeatedly tried to summon up some personal impression of you. Try as I might, nothing would come."

Surprisingly, Grant seemed uncomfortable with the way the conversation was going, and hurriedly came to the point. "General Lee, I understand that you are prepared to surrender the Armies of the Confederacy."

"Only the Army of Northern Virginia," responded Lee coldly. "I do not believe that I have the authority to speak for General Johnston in the Carolinas, or General Smith west of the Mississippi."

Grant shrugged negligently. "It's not important. We both know that when word gets out of your surrender, the other Confederate forces will submit within weeks, if not days. Everyone will know it is time for the killing to stop."

"All I ask is that my men be spared imprisonment, and permitted to go home on parole. The officers and generals, including myself, will submit to confinement, and await whatever fate Washington decrees."

Grant looked for a long moment at Lee; then taking his pen and a piece of paper, he began to write swiftly and legibly. While he wrote, he spoke. "None of your people are to be imprisoned; that includes you. If your men will surrender their arms and sign paroles agreeing to abide by the laws of the United States, they are free to go." Grant was silent for a moment, only the sound of his scratching pen filling the room, before adding "It is spring, and the planting needs to be done if families are to eat. Time to get the boys home; the boys on both sides."

Lee could barely keep his surprise from showing on his face. "It was my understanding that Washington is expecting a reckoning from my generals and me. Especially myself. Are you certain that you have the authority to grant such sweeping paroles?"

"I guess that I do." Grant had ceased writing, and slid the paper across to Lee. "You can read it for yourself. Upon surrendering their arms and horses, and signing written paroles, all of your men are free to go home, to be unmolested so long as they respect the laws of the United States. That of course includes the abolition of slavery."

Lee took out a pair of spectacles and put them on to read the document; the eyeglasses made him suddenly look a decade older. "This is extremely generous, General Grant. However, may I ask for one alteration? Unlike the Federal practice of horses being government property, in most cases the horses in my army are the personal property of those who use them. May this document be altered to permit those having horses to retain them?"

Grant gave Lee a hard look. "Horses have military potential; my terms as written do not allow for your men to retain them, and I am not inclined to alter the terms." Suddenly Grant's expression softened. "Never-the-less, I will informally tell the paroling officers to allow any man claiming personal ownership of an animal to retain it. Planting this year is going to be tough enough; the horses will help." He handed Lee the pen; after only a moment's hesitation the Virginian scrawled his signature. Grant drew back the paper and added his own signature, and it was done.

Lee stood up, sword clanking at his side. Glancing down at it, he starting to unbuckle his sword belt. "I understand that all arms must be surrendered, so it seems..."

Grant interrupted him. "General Lee, rifles and canon are what concern me. You and your officers may retain your sidearms. Such things have emotional value, and I would not injure anyone's pride unnecessarily." Grant then changed the subject in a surprising way. "General Lee, I expect your men have lacked adequate rations for some time. If you wish, I can supply your men with as much salt pork and hardtack as they need. Many will have a long way to go, and little to sustain them while they go. They should not go hungry."

Having ceased to fumble with his sword, Lee slowly responded. "I must admit that I had not been expecting such generous terms. You certainly did not grant them early in the war. 'Unconditional Surrender Grant' was the nickname the newspapers gave you."

"That was early in the war. Now the war is over, and like it or not, we are all one people again." Suddenly Grant stood up and offered Lee his hand. "General, let us have peace."

Slowly, Lee took Grant's hand and gave it a measured squeeze. Then he said "I must go and arrange for my men to take the parole. It will be hard on them, but your generous terms will make it bearable." Lee turned toward the door, motioning for Colonel Marshall to precede him. At the door he paused, turned and spoke one last time to Grant. "I really should have noticed you in Mexico." Then he walked out the door.

When the sound of horse hooves had died away, the Union officers could no longer restrain themselves. The morose, dignified Meade began throwing his kepi into the air repeatedly and catching it, yelling incoherent words of joy all the time. The smiling Parker was pounding Rawlins on the back, while Rawlins wheezed out whoops of joy. Even Sheridan managed a grim smile. Only Grant remained restrained, looking thoughtfully out the front door, wondering if what he had done was enough to keep a partisan war from erupting and poisoning American life for generations.

The word rapidly spread through both armies. Unrestrained glee was the reaction among the blue troops; their cause had won, and they had lived to see it. Sadness and muttered hostility was the reaction in the Confederate ranks. Still, the knowledge that they were going to live to see home again, and that there would be no retribution from Washington, kept their sullenness within bounds.

Among all of the soldiers, all the Johnnie Rebs and Billy Yanks, there was only one who was not thinking of his good fortune in surviving the war, thinking of being home for the spring. That one burned with an intense bitterness that things had not gone as planned, that his masters would not be pleased. But then he relaxed. His masters were people who took a very long view, and had a very much longer reach. They undoubtedly had alternate plans. Things would yet go as they should.

The one man smiled. A passing cavalryman saw the smile, and thought that the man was thinking of the joys of home. The cavalryman could not have been more wrong.

Chapter 1:
"I Have Read A Fiery Gospel Writ In Burnished Rows Of Steel.."

"And so, Madame, gentlemen, no part of the capital of South Carolina stands that was not made of stone or brick." Major Ambrose Bierce slouched in one of the comfortable wing chairs gracing the Secretary of War's office, looking deceptively at ease. In fact, he was growing increasingly furious with Lieutenant Colonel Alphonso Clay for placing him in this uncomfortable situation. For nearly two solid hours Bierce had spun tales to divert the people in the room, distracting them from the fact that Clay had not responded to their urgent summons. To cover for Clay, Bierce had spoken of the stirring march through Georgia, and of the fate visited on the once-beautiful city of Columbia. Bierce knew that he was instinctively a spellbinding storyteller; but he also knew that the patience of the woman and two men in the room was near the breaking point. He inwardly shuddered at the thought of their reactions if they knew just what kept Clay dallying at Willard's Hotel.

Secretary of War Edwin Stanton suddenly slapped the desk behind which he sat with a chubby hand. "Enough of this, Bierce! We have waited two hours for your friend Clay. Entertaining as your tales are, I have summoned Clay at the specific recommendation of General Grant. There is a threat to the Republic, and Grant feels that Clay may be the best man to counter that threat. I am not inclined to question the judgment of the General in Chief. Now, do I have to send a squad of Provost troopers to...” A polite knock sounded at the door. Without waiting for an invitation, Alphonso Clay entered the room and saluted. Always a bundle of nervous energy, the short, burly Stanton shot to his feet and rushed across the room and vigorously shook the young officer’s hand. Then he stepped back, and for a moment each appraised the other.

Stanton saw a short, slender, blue-eyed officer with wire-rimmed glasses, straight blond hair reaching to his shoulders, his placid, expressionless face marred only by a very recent scratch on his left cheek, still slightly oozing blood. Clay saw an intense, grim man who stared at the world through thick spectacles, occasionally tugging at his long, grey-streaked beard which was made to seem somehow even longer by his shaven upper lip. There was audible wheezing as he breathed, but his speaking voice was deep and clear.

“Thank God you’re here!” exclaimed Stanton abruptly. “Grant was not able to come to Washington; since Petersburg fell he has been hot on the trail of Lee. If Lee can join up with Johnston in North Carolina there is no telling...”

“My apologies for the delay in my arrival, Mr. Secretary,” interrupted Clay smoothly. “A personal matter of some importance required my attention. However, now I am here. If the urgency is so great, please let me know at once how I can be of assistance.”

“Certainly, certainly,” replied Stanton, somewhat taken aback by Clay’s polite insistence on getting to the matter at hand. “First let me introduce Chief of Staff General Halleck and Miss Elizabeth Van Lew.”

The balding, portly Major General Henry Halleck grunted in response to Clay’s salute, not bothering to return it. Instead, he absently commenced scratching at his left elbow with his right hand, staring at Clay with glassy eyes. Clay immediately concluded that the chief of staff of the army had sought to relieve the stress of his position with one of several opium-laced remedies, with rather too much success. Clay then turned to the middle-aged, painfully-thin woman who sat in the chair to Halleck's right. He clicked his heels and bowed slightly. The hatchet-faced Van Lew acknowledged him with a curt nod.

"Miss Van Lew is the reason you are here, Colonel Clay," said Stanton. "She is one of the most important heroes of the Union, but until this day she had to remain virtually unknown. It was only when the 25th Corps took Richmond day before yesterday that she could dare to have her exploits publicized."

Clay turned his expressionless face to the woman. "Indeed? I would be intrigued to know your story."

"I will make it brief, Colonel," Van Lew replied in the honeyed accents of Virginia, her sweet voice at odds with her sharp, angular features. "If you and Mr. Stanton will be seated, I will tell you why I believe the Union may be facing its greatest danger at the moment of its triumph."

Stanton returned to his desk, while Clay settled into the empty chair beside Bierce. As Clay sat, Bierce murmured out of the side of his mouth. "Feeling refreshed, Alphonso? Two hours; surprised you're still conscious." Clay spared Bierce a murderous glance, but said nothing.

"I repeat, I will make my history brief," commenced Van Lew abruptly. "The only reason I tell it you all is to convince you that my fears are well founded..Colonel, may I inquire if you are related to Cassius Clay, the Kentucky abolitionist?

Clay nodded slightly. "I have that honor. He is my cousin."

"I thought as much. There is something about you that reminds me of him. In any event, fifteen years ago he visited Richmond to give a speech advocating liberation of the slaves. It was a...tumultuous speech, as you can imagine, and not well received. By the end of it, death threats were being shouted from the audience. Despite the threats, he had made at least one convert. That was me. It was not so much the logic of his arguments, or the power of his rhetoric, but his complete certainty in his righteousness that convinced me. The recent cholera epidemic had taken my parents and my brother, and I had come into a substantial estate with several hundred souls in bondage. I freed them within a month of hearing your cousin speak, and determined to devote my life to his cause. I have done so ever since, providing shelter to those who escape bondage and arranging passage to the North. When the traitor secessionists tried to take my beloved Virginia out of the sacred Union, I felt it was my duty to do everything that I could to preserve the Union and bring an end to the scourge of slavery." The angular woman favored Clay with a wintry smile. "Being a woman, my options were limited. I gave some considerable thought to the matter, and determined that I could best be of use to the Holy Cause by gathering information for the Union – in short, by being a spy."

Clay was seldom impressed, and even more seldom allowed it to show on his face. This was one of those rare times. "Miss Van Lew, to undertake to spy in the capital of the Confederacy was foolhardy, to put it mildly. You were at incredible risk."

Again came the wintry smile. "There was risk, but not quite as great as you suppose. Despite my well-known views on slavery, my parents were extremely well-connected in Virginia society, and their old friends were able to shield me from inquiries to a certain extent. I believe the chief traitors took a certain perverse pride in tolerating my presence in Richmond. I suppose it was something like having a single village atheist; he emphasizes the piety of the rest of the community by his presence. I became Richmond's village atheist. In fact, I was occasionally invited to dine by Mr. and Mrs. Jefferson Davis, both of whom had known my family well. Traitors though they are, they both have impeccable manners, and those dinners were not disagreeable."

"You dined with Jefferson Davis while spying for the Union," murmured Bierce with wonder. "How did you get away with it?"

It was Clay who answered. "Major Bierce, you of all people should understand why, being such an enthusiast for the works of the late Edgar A. Poe. Surely you read his story, 'The Purloined Letter'?"

Van Lew nodded approvingly. "Just so, Colonel Clay. Like the letter in Mr. Poe's story, I displayed myself in plain view of the authorities. They could not imagine someone so vocally and publicly in favor of the Union Cause, let alone a woman, actually engaging in espionage. Incredible as it may sound, that is what I did. I slowly established contact with darkies working in the houses of all the major traitors – Breckenridge, Benjamin, Stephens, even the Davis' themselves. I gave them a choice, which was theirs alone to make: I would either arrange to smuggle them through the lines to the North, or they could spy upon their masters and provide me with information of military value, which I would then arrange to send to the North."

Clay's eyes widened slightly; to someone having such iron control, it was equivalent to his jaw dropping in horror. "Surely they understood the fate that would await them if they were detected in betraying their masters?"

Miss Lew nodded again. "Better than you or I. Yet not one chose to go North, not one!"

"Did they all evade detection?" asked Halleck, continuing to scratch at his elbow.

The wintry smile left Miss Lew's face. "One did not. A coachman for a cabinet minister. He was flogged to make him reveal who else was involved in his conspiracy. He refused to utter a word. I learned later from the captain of the guard at the city jail, who spoke of him with grudging admiration, that he was flogged at intervals, and asked again and again to betray his comrades. According to the captain, who had not the slightest idea that my life was in the coachman's hands, he would scream and cry, but never utter a coherent word. Not one word...before he died. The captain of the guard was a hard man, utterly devoted to the Confederacy, but as he told me of this, something like shame came over his features. As well it might."

Silence hung over the room for a long moment.

Finally, Van Lew began to speak again. "With the aid of these brave souls, and of courageous scouts who risked death at the hands of pickets for both sides, I was able to provide information of some little value to Secretary Stanton and General Halleck."

"Some little value!" exclaimed Stanton with an asthmatic wheeze. "The timing and amount of troop movements, for which we prepared. Scheduled arrivals of blockade runners carrying French and British munitions, which 'accidentally' encountered warships on the high seas. Even attempts to initiate widespread arson and other terrorist acts in our major cities, which were 'accidentally' thwarted every time."

"You have my deepest respect, Miss Van Lew," said Clay. "Fortunately, it would seem your work is done. Lee's army has fled Petersburg, and Richmond has fallen to the XXVth Corps. Grant is in hot pursuit of Lee, and it is only a matter of time until his army is either captured or destroyed. Once Lee's army is gone, the remaining Confederate forces will surrender quickly. This war is as good as over."

"The war may be over, Colonel, but there is no peace. My source with the Davis household has delivered to me truly disturbing information. She had helped pack into a carriage the luggage that the Davis's were taking with them to the railway station as they made ready to flee Richmond, the day before yesterday. My agent saw Jefferson Davis in a murmured conversation with a tall colonel she had never seen before. She was not close enough to hear the first part of their conversation. But as my agent moved closer, Mr. Davis, normally such a controlled man, suddenly burst out loudly. '*Is there no other course?*' The colonel replied '*No sir; it is our last throw. It will decapitate the Union, and throw its forces into utter confusion and despair.*' Normally an inexpressive, cold man, Mr. Davis seemed to be close to tears, saying harshly '*Then do it, and may God have mercy on my soul!*' Paying no attention to the colonel's salute, he then entered the carriage where Mrs. Davis and their children waited, and signaled the driver to make haste."

Clay pondered for only a moment. "You hardly need me to tell you the significance of what was said. Acts of terrorism and murder are to be unleashed, undoubtedly directed not only at Lincoln, but at the rest of the Government as well, and possibly at such important centers as New York. Still, the murder of President Lincoln, tragic as it would be, would not be sufficient to throw the Union in confusion at this late date."

"It might," replied Stanton. "Consider Vice-President Johnson automatically ascending to power." There was a moment of silence in the room; all had heard how Andrew Johnson had shown up roaring drunk at his inauguration in March.

Clay nodded to acknowledge the point, but then said "Still, no matter how...inadequate Vice-President Johnson might prove, he would presumably be guided to a certain extent by the other members of the government, and preserved from the grossest errors. No, there must be more than an attempt on the President's life involved."

"General Halleck and I would like you find out the details of this plot," said Stanton. "Will you accept the challenge?"

"Of course," replied Clay promptly, "providing you allow me the services of Major Bierce and any other resources I may need."

"Me?" blurted Bierce with surprise.

"You have some insight into my methods, and I cannot be everywhere at once. I presume you will accept the challenge of helping to save the Republic?"

Bierce emitted one of his unlovely, barking laughs. "Well, since you put it that way, I'm your man."

Clay turned his attention to Stanton and Halleck. "I would recommend heavy guards around the President. General Grant as well."

"The President will not permit more than a single guard when he goes about," interjected Halleck, still scratching that troublesome elbow. "Secretary Stanton and I have repeatedly begged him to permit a more substantial guard, but in vain. Not even when an assassin shot off his hat while the President was riding to the Old Soldier's Home, about six months ago."

"I've heard nothing about that!" exclaimed Bierce, abandoning momentarily his air of cynical ease.

"Lincoln ordered us to hush the matter up," explained Stanton grimly. "I kept begging him to permit more security, until he finally lost his temper with me, something he had never done before. "Don't you understand, Stanton?" he shouted at me. "When this war is done, so am I. There is not a thing on Earth that can be done to change that!"

"Strange man," muttered Halleck, glassy eyes seeming to stare off into the distance.

"And General Grant will permit no formal guard whatsoever," continued Stanton, indignation in his voice. "I have taken care to extract promises from his two closest staff members, General Rawlins and Colonel Parker, that they will find excuses to be with him wherever possible, armed with Colts. That was the best I could contrive."

Clay nodded slightly. "Proud, fatalistic men, the both of them. It would seem we must make haste to eliminate any threat. To start with, I will need a list of known Confederate sympathizers in Washington. They are unlikely to be directly involved, but may give us useful leads, if properly... encouraged."

Stanton had frowned uneasily at the way Clay had said "encouraged." Ignoring his own unease, he replied "The Washington police are useless for anything more than rounding up drunks and breaking up fights in the fancy houses. You will want to talk to Baker, Colonel Lafayette Baker. He took over from Pinkerton when..."

Stanton broke off speaking as he noticed a strange sound coming in through the open windows that faced Pennsylvania Avenue. The noise grew louder and louder, and swiftly resolved itself into the yells and cheers of hundreds of people. Muttering

"What the hell..." Stanton sprang from his chair and bounded over to the room's right window, leaning dangerously far out. The others in the room went more carefully to the left window, and witnessed an astonishing sight. A crowd of several hundred men and some women, shouting, laughing, and in some cases crying with apparent joy, were marching in a disorganized parade toward the War Department building, led by an army telegrapher. The amateur parade-master motioned the crowd to a stop directly under the windows to Stanton's office. Seeing the pudgy Secretary of War, the soldier made an exaggerated bow, then in a booming voice proclaimed, "Secretary Stanton, I have just come from the main telegraph office. My lieutenant is busy decoding a long message from General Grant. As soon as he read the first sentence, he ordered me to come straight away to you, and then to the President to communicate its import. My apologies for violating army regulations, but on my way here I could not help but share that sentence with these good people I encountered on the street."

"Soldier, you shared the contents of an army communication with strangers on the street?" replied Stanton, a dark look appearing on his face.

The soldier simply ignored the expression of gathering displeasure on the face of the Secretary of War. "Sir, the first sentence of the telegram reads, 'I have the honor to report that today at Appomattox Courthouse, Virginia, General Lee surrendered the Army of Northern Virginia to the forces commanded by myself.'"

Stanton gasped; then to the surprise of everyone in the room, the grim, hard-charging Secretary of War began to cry, shedding tears of the purest joy. Briefly removing his thick spectacles in order to wipe his eyes with a large, dirty handkerchief, he called out from the window. "Wait for me! We will go tell the President. All of us together!" As the sound of ragged cheering began in the street, Stanton bustled to the door. He opened it, then paused, saying "Miss Van Lew, gentlemen, please come with me. So often I have had to bring the President bad news. I would like you to witness me bringing joy for once."

A serious look on his face, Clay shook his head slightly. "With respect, Major Bierce and I should begin our investigation; the danger may not be past."

Stanton shook his head abruptly, as if being bothered by a large fly. "Whatever the Rebel plans, they will probably see that it is too late for anything they do to affect the outcome of the war. Still, should make sure. Do as you feel best." Stanton offered his arm to the angular Van Lew, who nodded to Clay and Bierce as she left the room, saying "Gentleman, a pleasure. I hope to see you again."

General Halleck stood, jammed his crumpled kepi on his head, and started to follow his superior. Just as he reached the door, he paused and fixed his glassy, far-away gaze on Clay and Bierce. Scratching again at his troublesome elbow, he began to speak. "Stanton has always been an optimist. Perhaps that is best when one has the kind of responsibility he has. It allows one to endure...setbacks. I am not an optimist. I do not worry about losing the war. I worry about losing the peace." He seemed to lose his train of thought for a moment, then recollecting himself, he continued. "Gentlemen, be more diligent, not less. If the threat is genuine and you fail to stop it, you will carry the burden of failing your country. As do I." Tears began to appear in the chief of staff's eyes. With an angry shrug, he shambled heavily out the door.

After Halleck was out of earshot, Bierce said jauntily "Well, looks like our chief of staff has been into the laudanum. I have seen the signs before. That could explain his blunders that have cost so many lives."

Clay shook his head slowly. "I rather think the blunders explain the laudanum." A faint look of pity came over Clay's normally expressionless features.

* * * * *

Bierce shuddered as he and Clay caught sight of the Old Capitol Prison. As its name implied, it had originally been the seat of Congress while the grand permanent Capitol building was undergoing its slow construction. Sorrowfully, the structure's days of glory had fled before the beginning of the Civil War. Congress had moved out while guards moved in, to watch hundreds of prisoners arrested as disloyal, some for good reason, some for no reason at all save some officer was unconvinced of their enthusiasm for the Union. The grimy brick building now exuded a miasma of misery and despair. Clay and Bierce stopped in front of the pair of sentries at the main entrance. Bierce glanced up, to see a pale woman's face pressed to one of the many barred windows, and to hear the distant babbling of someone ill with fever. Clay did not look up at all, but simply announced to the sentries "We are here to see Colonel Baker. His office said he would be conducting business at the prison, and we cannot wait on his return."

The slovenly guards looked over the officers insolently. Then, the elder of the two shrugged. "Hell, why not? Damn war's over. Go on in." They moved aside. Bierce opened the door for Clay and followed the senior officer in – only to come to a shuddering halt. The ground floor windows were completely boarded over, and the gloom of the interior easily swallowed the uncertain light of the occasional gas lamp. After the brightness of the street, Bierce's eyes had trouble making out anything in the shadowy interior. Bierce sensed rather than saw Clay's impatience. "Do not dawdle, Major, time is precious."

"Damn it, Clay, give me a moment; I can't see my hand in front of my face."

"I have no trouble. I will guide you." Bierce felt a strong hand with a surprisingly powerful grip on his sleeve, and found himself almost being dragged along by the impatient Clay, being led toward the sound of a loud, hectoring voice. By the time they had reached the speaker, Bierce's eyes had adjusted to the gloom as well as they ever would, and the fastidious young major almost recoiled at the sight that greeted him. A lean colonel with a scraggly beard stood in the middle of a large chamber that had once housed the Congress of the United States. The gas fixture that dimly lit his features gave a spectral cast to his face. He was flanked by two large soldiers casually holding Spencer carbines, and was addressing an audience of about a hundred prisoners, equally divided between men and women, dressed in grimy clothes and seated on the floor in a semicircle before him. Even in the darkness, it could be seen that some of the prisoners were lousy, and all indifferent to the beetles that scurried about the filthy floor. It was clear that none of the inmates cared to hear what the colonel was saying, and equally clear that the guards gave them no choice.

“With the traitor Lee surrendered there is no hope for your precious Confederacy, none,” said the officer, who had obviously been going along in this vein for some time. “Do you Reb traitors know that Richmond has burned, much of it burned near to the ground?” A few groans came from the unwilling audience, but most were silent. “And the beauty of it was that your own boys in grey did it; set fire to the warehouses and skedaddled. Idiots! As if there was anything in those warehouses we needed. Only reason your precious Richmond did not completely burn is the nigger soldiers of the XXV Corps arrived and fought the flames. I want you to think on that. Richmond is now occupied by niggers. Abe Lincoln has already gone there, and has sat in Jeff Davis’ chair!

“Now some of you may think that you can go right home, now that the war is about over. Let me disabuse you of that notion. The reason Stanton kicked out Pinkerton and made me responsible for the security of Washington is that Pinkerton had been mollycoddling you traitors and Copperheads. You are staying here until Stanton tells me what to do with you. Maybe he will tell me to let you all go tomorrow. Maybe he will tell me to hang the lot of you tomorrow. Maybe he will tell me to hang some of you and release others. Maybe he will not decide at all for a year...or two...or three.”

A gaunt man rose to his feet slowly. He wore a suit of clothes that might have been of an expensive cut, but in the dim light the suit was too grimy for an observer to be certain. “Colonel Baker, you have no authority to hold us for our sympathies alone,” he said in the cultured accent of an upper-class Southron. “You did not during the war, and certainly do not now that combat has ceased. The Constitution makes that clear. Aside from the legality, there is the humanitarian issue. Many here are sick with the diseases that are inevitable under such conditions. Just yesterday a young woman died of typhus. You must immediate release at least the women…”

He never finished the sentence. Baker gestured at one of the soldiers. With two swift steps the guard came up to the prisoner and delivered a roundhouse blow to the man’s jaw with the butt of his carbine. The speaker dropped to the floor as if pole-axed, a spray of blood and bits of tooth visible as he fell. Absolute silence fell in the chamber; none of the prisoners approached the injured man, or even seemed to look at him. Bierce sensed Clay was about to spring forward; the major placed a restraining hand on Clay’s shoulder and urgently hissed, “This is not our affair. We need Baker’s co-operation.” Clay relaxed slightly, but Bierce could still sense the waves of outrage coming off his friend like a physical force. Knowing Clay’s capacity for sudden violence, Bierce wondered if Baker would realize just how much danger he was in at this moment. Instead of violence, dangerously calm words came from Clay.

“Colonel Baker, I am Colonel Alphonso Clay; this is Major Ambrose Bierce. The Secretary of War has entrusted us with a vital assignment, which must take precedence over your… administrative duties. We must speak to you privately.”

Even in the dark the expression of sneering contempt on Baker’s face was clear. He seemed about to say something offensive, but then paused, visibly struck by a thought. “Alphonso Clay. I’ve heard about you. You’re Grant’s man, aren’t you?”

Clay bowed ever so slightly. “I have that honor.”

"Well, I can make some time for you. Got a little office I sometimes use here. Should be private enough. Follow me." Ignoring the injured man on the floor, he led his two visitors to a door near the front entrance. Throwing open the door, Baker revealed a small office with a bare wooden desk and several chairs, illuminated by weak light filtering in from one of the few windows in the enormous building that had not been boarded over. A slovenly guard had been lounging in a chair, boots on the desk. At the sight of three officers, he scrambled to attention with comical speed. Jerking a thumb toward the door, Baker grunted "Out. Close the door behind you." Squeezing past his superior, the soldier did as he was told.

Baker seated himself behind the desk, saying to his visitors, "Draw up a chair." He then rummaged in one of the desk's lower doors and produced a bottle of whiskey and a dirty glass. Without a comment to his visitors, he poured himself a shot and knocked it back in a single gulp. He then restored the bottle and glass to the door, and looked at his guests. "All right now. What is so Goddamn important that you had to track me down here?"

"We require your assistance, specifically your knowledge of Confederate sympathizers in Washington. Evidence has been uncovered of a potential plot to take the life of high Union officials, possibly the President himself."

Baker laughed, an unpleasant, ugly sound. "So you've discovered a plot against Abe. Well, good for you. Listen boys, there have been Copperheads aiming to kill Lincoln since the war began. Half the men in this Goddamn Southern town would pay to see Lincoln's blood. There are only two reasons they have not succeeded in taking his life."

"What are those?" asked Bierce.

"Number one, they're Goddamn cowards. All the brave ones went south to join Lee, and left only those who valued their hides more than their precious cause. And number two, I've been rounding up those who might just have belly enough to risk their own lives to kill Abe. You didn't much care for what I had done to that Copperhead in there, did you?"

Somewhat taken aback by the abrupt change in topic, Clay replied, "He gave no cause to be treated in such a manner. It was cowardly and dishonorable."

Baker laughed again, mirthlessly. "Oh, that poor darling Reb, abused by that beast Baker. That's what you think, isn't it? Well, let me tell you about that Johnnie. He's Courtney Delapore, of the Tidewater Delapores. Brought some of his family's money up to Washington just before Fort Sumter and started a paper. That paper attacked everything the Union was doing to stay alive. Found out about military plans and published them for Richmond to know. Encouraged young recruits to desert; some did. Some of those deserters were caught, and were shot. And yet Delapore could not be touched, wrapping himself in the First Amendment while he hopes and prays for every other scrap of the Constitution to be destroyed!" Baker then smiled grimly. "At least he couldn't be touched until I persuaded Stanton to sign the arrest order. Now he's mine, and I hope he rots in this hell-hole!"

"Well, that is neither here nor there," replied Clay. "Would you wager Abraham Lincoln's life that you have apprehended every last traitor capable of an act of assassination? With respect, to believe so smacks of hubris, in my opinion."

Baker looked as if he were about to make an angry reply. Instead, with a visible effort he reined in his temper. "Only a fool would claim to be absolutely certain of everything, and I'm no fool. Still, I have been damn thorough; would rather arrest ten innocents than miss one traitor."

"No doubt," replied Bierce. "Still, it cannot hurt to make '*assurance double sure,*' as the Bard said. The concern is not among the ones you have arrested, but among those outside this prison. The lines between here and what is left of the Confederacy are porous. Can you truly be sure that no threat has arrived recently that has escaped your attention?"

Baker again looked as if he were about to give an angry reply, but paused for a moment and grudgingly muttered, "I suppose it's possible."

"Do you know of anyone – anyone not already in your custody – who would be knowledgeable concerning the pro-Confederate community in Washington?" asked Clay.

"Hell, they all seem to know each other. One traitor can always smell another out."

"Anyone within your custody that might be especially knowledgeable as to Confederate sympathizers still at large?" added Bierce.

Baker paused for a moment. "That would probably be Delapore himself. He was up to his armpits in Copperheads, and is one of the most recently arrested. If some new Reb trash has found its way into town since his arrest, I would be surprised."

"Very well, we must make a beginning somewhere," said Clay briskly. "You will release Mr. Delapore into our custody. Say it was a demand on our part, due to his recent treatment; that will cause him to look upon us with some favor, and make it easier to secure his co-operation."

"Now just a Goddamn minute!" exploded Baker. "This man is my prisoner, and a dangerous Copperhead. I'm not about to hand him over to some fancy-dan..." Baker's words trailed off. He was staring at five gold double-eagles that had appeared on the desk before Clay as if by magic. One hundred dollars in gold; more than six months pay for a private. Tentatively, Baker reached out for the coins, and carefully picked them up, hefting each one individually; Clay made no effort to stop him. Thoughtfully slipping the bribe into a tunic pocket, Baker slowly murmured "I suppose I could cut an order for Delapore's parole into your custody on humanitarian grounds."

"That is very Christian of you, Colonel," replied Bierce. Clay glanced at him and smiled slightly; it was amazing just how much contempt and distaste the young major could load into such a simple statement.

*****

Teresa Duval lay stretched at full length on the bed in Alphonso Clay's expensive suite at Washington's exclusive Willard's Hotel. She stared doe-eyed at the ceiling, a satisfied smile gracing her beautiful face. Most who knew her would have refused to believe that she could be found in a single man's hotel room, luxuriating in post-coital bliss. The Teresa Duval the world thought it knew was a tireless, self-sacrificing nurse in the service of the Sanitary Commission, who dispensed medicine and pious religious sentiments to wounded Union soldiers with equal ease. In truth, the role of a nurse from New England was only one of several which Teresa Duval performed. She was naturally a brilliant actress, and in another life would have dominated the stages of the nation. Far from being a pious Christian from a middle-class New England family, she was a survivor of the Irish Famine, who had lived a bestial life in the slums of New York until the financier Jay Gould plucked her up from the gutter, gave her a veneer of sophistication and manners, and made her one of his most valuable agents. He had arranged for her to be assigned to Sherman's army, and directed her to send him coded telegraphs, apparently innocently addressed to her mother, giving advance knowledge of Sherman's movements and prospects. Using that advance knowledge, he was able to anticipate movements in share and commodity prices in the financial markets, and make hundreds of thousands of dollars at a stroke. Gould had also arranged for her to secretly be discreetly appointed to the Secret Service, with the understanding that whatever she learned of financial interest while serving the government would be immediately shared with him. A lesser woman would not have been able to perform all of these apparently contradictory roles without giving herself away immediately. Teresa Duval was no ordinary woman.

Now, she was content simply to stare at the ceiling and review in her mind the two hours she had spent with Alphonso Clay earlier in the day, the two hours for which she had waited so long. Despite her fears of disappointment, those hours had been everything for which she had hoped, exceeding even the pleasure she derived from the act of killing. Her reverie was interrupted by the rattle of a key in the room's lock. She smiled widely, anticipating a view of Clay. Clay did indeed appear as the door opened. Instantly her smile disappeared, to be replaced by a feral snarl, when she saw that behind Clay was Ambrose Bierce, who was half-carrying a filthy-looking stranger with a bloody mouth. She quickly slipped off the bed, and replaced the snarl of frustration with a look of efficient concern. She was certain that neither Bierce nor the stranger had noticed the snarl, but one look at the slightly amused smile on Clay's lips showed her that he had noticed.

"Miss Duval, I am glad you are still here; you have saved me the inconvenience of locating you," said Clay. "Major Bierce and I require your assistance. Our companion is Mr. Courtney Delapore, who as you can see is in need of some medical treatment. We have stopped at a chemist's shop to pick up the supplies you might need." Clay handed Duval a brown-paper package, tied with string. Duval took it to the bed and carefully undid the string. The open package revealed some bandages, medicinal brandy, some simple dental instruments, fine cat gut – and a small brown bottle of laudanum.

"Mr. Delapore, be so good as to lie down on the bed so I can inspect the wound to your face," said Duval. Briskly but not ungently she seized the man's jaw, moving it back and forth. Delapore moaned slightly, then made an obvious effort to silence himself; uttering not a sound when Duval inserted her fingers into his mouth to inspect the extent of his injuries, although beads of sweat popped out on his pale forehead. Finishing her inspection, she stepped back and looked appraisingly at the wounded man. "The jaw does not appear to be broken. As you are no doubt aware, you have a massive bruise on your cheek, and three of your teeth have been broken off at the roots. Mr. Delapore, if I did not know better, I would think you had been struck with the butt of a rifle."

"Mr. Delapore is undoubtedly uncomfortable talking for the time being, so I will speak on his behalf," interjected Clay. "Until today he was a resident of the Old Capitol Prison. He dared to speak up on behalf of his fellow prisoners, and suffered the injury you see for his presumption. Major Bierce and I were able to...persuade Colonel Baker to release him into our recognizance."

"The Old Capitol," murmured Duval as she looked at Delapore, eyes narrowing slightly. "One of the sneaking traitors lacking the courage to put on a uniform." *'English-loving bastard!'* she thought, as the image of a burning house flashed through her mind, with a corpse dangling from the tree in the yard where red-coated figures bent to an obscene task.

Seeing the subtle change in Duval's expression, Clay turned to Bierce. "Major, Mr. Delapore seems to have been improperly nourished recently. His injuries prohibit solid food for the time being. I would appreciate it if you would go down to the kitchens and order up something appropriate. Beef tea, mush, and fresh milk should meet the case." Bierce nodded his agreement; then pausing only to cock an ironic eyebrow in Duval's direction he left the room, closing the door softly behind him.

"You will need to remove the roots of the teeth that have been broken, and clean and suture the injuries, both within and outside his mouth," commented Clay. Beckoning slightly with his right hand, he added "Please come to this side of the room. I must discuss something that is of no interest to Mr. Delapore."

Duval glided over to where Clay stood, coming as close to him as was possible without actually touching. Hardly moving his lips, Clay spoke in a voice so low that the injured Delapore could not possible have picked up the words.

"I know what you are thinking. I know what can happen to Confederates under your care. This man is not to suffer a medical setback. Is that clear?"

Duval's expression hardened – hardened in a way that would have frightened anyone but Clay. "He is a traitorous, English-loving bastard; he does not deserve to live," she replied in a murmur as low as Clay's.

"Your private war is your affair alone. However, I need this man. If it is any consolation, I hope he will lead me to more dangerous and important traitors who intend harm to the Union."

Duval looked deeply into Clay's eyes, and saw that he spoke the truth. "Very well then." She turned abruptly and strode over to the bed where Delapore lay. Rolling back the sleeves of her dress, she picked up a wicked-looking dental tool, announcing in a loud voice "Mr. Delapore, I must remove the remains of your broken teeth and pack your gums, or your injuries might lead to an abscess that could prove fatal. This will be painful, but I will give you some laudanum to take some of the edge off of it. Please open wide."

Eyes closed, with obvious pain Delapore arched his neck and opened wide his mouth. Duval uncorked the brown medicine bottle and tilted it toward his mouth. Making sure her body blocked Clay's view, she did not tilt it far enough for any of the pain-killing elixir to actually enter Delapore's mouth. "Swallow, please," said Duval briskly. Due to the numbness in his injured mouth, Delapore was unaware he had received none of the drug, and painfully did as he was told.

"Now we will begin," said Duval as she inserted the horrid dentist's tool into the helpless man's mouth. At the first stifled shriek from Delapore, a warm glow spread over her body.

* * * * *

Delapore sat in a chair by the open window. He appeared wan and frail, and sweated despite the cool April breeze coming into the room. Gingerly he sipped a thin gruel of oatmeal and milk, trying to make sure it went down without touching the injured half of his mouth. Clay and Bierce sat in plush high-back chairs, watching the emaciated man eat in silence.

Silently the door to the room opened, and Duval glided into the room; she had been down the hall cleaning her hands and forearms of Delapore's blood. As she closed the door, Delapore placed the bowl on the side table and unsteadily rose to his feet, bowing slightly. In a muffled, slurring voice he said "Miss Duval, I am deeply grateful for the care you took of my wounds. I am sorry to have inflicted such distress upon you."

"It was my job, sir. Frankly, I was amazed by your composure during what must have been a painful procedure." '*Damn his eyes!*'

"A true gentleman must endure what the fates send," he enunciated carefully. "May I offer you this chair? To be truthful, I feel somewhat dizzy; and this is the only other chair in the room. I can recline on the bed, but it would not be seemly for you to do so." Frowning slightly, Duval took the just-vacated chair, while Delapore lowered his thin body onto the room's bed as if he were made of glass. Lowering his head slowly onto a pillow, he tiredly turned his attention to the two officers.

"Gentlemen, I am grateful you removed me from that place. I am not so naïve as to believe it was done for reasons of compassion. What is it you need of me?"

Clay smiled slightly; he appreciated Delapore's quick-wittedness in spite of his poor physical shape. "Indeed, Mr. Delapore. Although I was impressed by your standing up to a pig such as Colonel Baker, and angered by his ordering an assault on a helpless man, I do indeed have an ulterior motive."

The thin man on the bed sighed and closed his eyes. He then spoke in a low voice. "I thought as much. Let me anticipate you. I will betray no one into the hands of Colonel Baker. If that is the price of my freedom, I will not pay it; if it is the price of my life...I will not pay it. Pray give me a few moments to recover my strength, and I will return with you to the Old Capitol."

Bierce felt an odd surge of respect for the Copperhead before them. Traitor he might be, but he seemed to be a true gentleman, and Bierce always respected true gentlemen. He spared a glance at Clay; as usual, the Colonel's face gave little insight into what he might be feeling.

"I appreciate your intellect, Mr. Delapore," replied Clay. "You cut to the heart of matters, and save us all considerable time." Suddenly Clay was aware of Duval's lips beside his right ear, her whisper, barely audible.

"You and Bierce go for a little stroll, see the Executive Mansion. By the time you are back, I will have any information he possesses."

Clay turned and looked into her dark, avid, hungry eyes, and shook his head slightly. "We will save that option for a last resort," he replied in an equally soft whisper. He turned his attention back to the frail form on the bed.

"Mr. Delapore, are you truly a traitor, or simply a fool?"

The eyes of the man on the bed opened and focused angrily on Clay. "If it is treason to believe that the sovereign states had the same right to leave the Union that they had to join it, to believe that the right of habeas corpus actually guaranteed a citizen a right to a jury trial, that the Constitution clearly recognized a property right in slaves, to give succor to those who held the same views, then yes, I am a traitor." The fire went out of Delapore's eyes, and the eyes closed. In a tired voice he continued. "It would also seem that I was a fool to believe that the Government would respect the First Amendment."

Quietly, Bierce replied. "You may be a traitor and a fool; but are you a murderer and assassin?"

Once again Delapore's tired eyes became sharp. "What do you mean by that, sir?"

"You and your paper gave support to those who believed the same as you," said Clay in an oddly unemotional voice. "Among them were those who would smuggle information and supplies to the traitorous government in Richmond. Beyond that, we have reason to believe that hiding among such low characters are even more despicable beings, monsters in human form who plan to bring murder and chaos to the country for no good reason save revenge. Tell me, Mr. Delapore, would you take joy in the death of President Lincoln?"

Delapore started, and then swung himself into a sitting position, looking intently at the three people who faced him. After a long moment, he said, "My uncle's plantation was burned by General Wild's brigade; they killed my uncle and left his only grandson a motherless waif. I could tell many other such stories."

Duval felt an unpleasant sensation in the pit of her stomach. What the Rebel bastard had said brought to mind a similar, horrific event from her own past. With some anger she realized the strange sensation was something akin to pity, an emotion she had seldom felt. Angrily, she shook her head to clear the annoying thought, while Delapore continued to speak.

"I had reason to wish Abraham Lincoln dead. Yet what purpose would it serve now? Vengeance is an expensive luxury, and one the South can no longer afford. If he were to be killed now, and the South blamed, I tremble for what remains of the way of the life I loved. Besides...well, once late at night I was taking a short cut through the cemetery when I saw to my amazement the President, entirely alone, standing by a tomb and weeping. I remained in the shadow of a tree for near an hour watching, Lincoln's tears visible in the moonlight the whole time. Finally, he wiped his eyes with a large handkerchief and walked off in the direction of the Executive Mansion. When he was out of sight I went over to the tomb where he had stood; it belonged to his son, the one who died three years ago. It is hard to completely hate a man grieving a child three years after his death."

The room was now so silent that if a pin had been dropped, it would have sounded like a canon. Finally Delapore continued. "So to answer your question, no, I do not wish Lincoln dead; for several reasons, I do not wish him dead. Further, I find it impossible to believe that any true son of the South would stoop to political murder. The dishonor entailed in assassination would prohibit it."

"We will not argue the relative merits of our causes in the conflict that is rapidly coming to an end," replied Clay. "Suffice it to say that most on both sides behaved with honor, while there were dishonorable scoundrels on both sides as well. For all its talk of gentility, the south had its Mosebys, its Quantrills...its Nathan Bedford Forrests." An unearthly light briefly flickered in Clay's eyes as he mentioned the last name.

"And the North had its Turchins, its Wilds, and its Clays," replied Delapore. "Yes, I thought I recognized your name. The Devereaux family and their overseer died horribly, if I remember correctly."

Clay tensed as if he were going to leap at the emaciated Delapore, but with a visible effort calmed himself. "Point taken. Indeed, you prove my point. The best of causes can harbor... monsters. So, let me ask you to consider what might happen in the South should Lincoln be murdered at the very time the war is ending?"

"There is no longer any prospect of separation. All that would be accomplished would be creating an everlasting hatred, a hatred that would cause even greater oppression to be visited on the South."

"Nevertheless, there are those who might not see the situation as clearly as you. You and I may have chosen different sides in the current conflict, but we were both raised to hold dear the values of the South. I can respect your desire to protect those who hold your views, but could you respect yourself if you gave protection to an assassin?"

Once again Delapore's tired eyes closed, and he sank back on the bed. "Even assuming there was an assassin, I do not know him to be one. The people that I know who are sympathetic to the South confine themselves to talk, for the most part. Those few whom I suspect are more active, limit themselves to carrying messages or smuggling quinine across the lines; hardly murderers, but Colonel Baker would hang them without benefit of trial. I could not bear that burden on my conscience."

Bierce leaned forward in his chair. "Mr. Delapore, you must know by now that General Grant has paroled all of Lee's army, including Lee himself. It is only a matter of time until similar forgiveness is granted…irregular supporters of the Confederacy."

Without opening his eyes, Delapore replied "A man could hang during that short time. No, with regret, I feel unable to be of help to you." He opened his eyes, swung his legs off the bed, and rose unsteadily to his feet. "I am rested now, and ready to return to my companions."

Gazing at the emaciated Delapore expressionlessly, Clay spoke softly. "Many of your companions in the Old Capitol are in distress, their health deteriorating by the day. Is that not so?"

"That is so, Colonel Clay. It is especially hard on the children. Your…Colonel Baker has confined children of the women he has arrested with them."

"What if I could tell you that I could secure the release of all prisoners not actually charged with violent crime who are now confined in the Old Capitol?"

"If I co-operate by betraying those I know into your hands."

"If you co-operate. I emphasize that I am only interested in those plotting active sabotage or murder. I am operating under the authority of the Secretary of War, Colonel Baker's superior. If I ask Stanton, he will order the releases."

Swaying slightly, Delapore considered what Clay had said for some moments. Finally he spoke. "Suppose such people never existed? Suppose even if they existed, they are unknown to me? Suppose even further that I know whom you speak, but deliberately aim you in the wrong direction?"

"As to your final supposition, it does not concern me. The very fact that you raise it shows your honor will not permit you to so act. As to the rest, all I require is your best efforts; even if they lead to nothing, I will secure the release of your compatriots in the Old Capitol."

Still swaying, Delapore suddenly looked near to tears. "I do so wish to believe you, Colonel Clay. I fear I am a weak man. I fear returning to that place so much that I fear I am deluding myself as to your good faith."

"Mr. Delapore, there is no reason why you should believe him," said Bierce. "However, you must understand I have known Colonel Clay for two years now, and have never known him to go back on his given word."

Delapore suddenly sat down on the bed; a single tear flowed down his left cheek. His voice was calm as he said, "Very well. Very well. We have a bargain. I only wish I could be certain it was more for the others than for me.

"As you well know, there are many in Washington with emotional ties to the South. Relatives of those in the Confederate service, deserters from Lee's army, and the like. I cannot believe who you seek would be among them; their concerns would be for themselves or their families, not the Cause. There are also a number of paroled Confederate soldiers, released in previous prisoner exchanges, who have chosen to stay in Washington, having had enough of war and fearful of being drafted back into the armies should they return home. They live on day labor and handouts, and are in many cases pathetic; some still wear their Confederate uniforms for lack of money to buy other clothing, and this is such a common sight that just the other day I saw one in the full uniform of a Confederate artillery sergeant walking down Pennsylvania Boulevard, with no one giving him more than a glance. Such people are unlikely to have the fanaticism for the kind of horrid acts that you propose.

"Then you have some loud-mouthed braggarts who have spent the war proclaiming their devotion to the cause, while being careful not to risk their own skins. Most prominent among those is John Wilkes Booth and the sycophants who gather around him, at least when he is in town."

"John Wilkes Booth of the acting Booths?" inquired Clay.

"The same. Actually, an impressive actor. I have seen him several times at Ford's Theater. However, take my word for it, he is certainly no gentlemen. All of society talks of his relentless seductions and debauches."

"Sounds like my kind of fellow," interjected Bierce with a wolfish grin. Delapore favored the young major with a frown of distaste.

"It sounds as if you have a low opinion of those who oppose the Government's policies without putting on the grey," commented Clay. "Yet you yourself have not done so."

Delapore sighed slightly. "I do not expect you to believe me any more than Colonel Baker. However, I will say it one more time. My opposition to the Lincoln government is due to its violation of the freedoms guaranteed by the Constitution. To take up arms against it would be treason, and I am no traitor, unless you consider defending and aiding those who suffer from the excesses of military government to be treason.

"I truly think you have been misinformed concerning a plot, for whatever motive. For instance, Booth is a vain, sensuous braggart, not the sort to risk his neck in active treason. Proceed if it will put your mind at ease; you can interview him for yourself. When he is in town, he stays at the National Hotel. Sometimes he visits a boarding house run by, I believe, a Mrs. Surratt; her son and the son's friends admire Booth beyond reason, I have heard, and he enjoys basking in their admiration."

Delapore hesitated, and then went on. "There is one other individual that comes to mind; but I have never met him, and know so little of him that I hesitate to mention him. I have heard a few whispers about a man who calls himself Colonel Ephraim Waite, who comes and goes mysteriously. Those who claim to have seen him say he dresses in black, and pays well in old Spanish gold coins for information that would be of use to Richmond. I have no idea where he might be found in Washington, or even if he is more than a rumor. And that, gentlemen, is all that I know that could be of interest to you."

Clay sat for a few moments, apparently lost in thought. Then, he stood up. "Mr. Delapore, it is not much, but it may possibly be enough to lead us in the direction of the conspiracy, or even better, to prove that the conspiracy does not exist. Mr. Delapore, I presume you have a home to return to."

In a curiously unemotional voice, the emaciated man replied, "Yes, a townhome in Georgetown."

"Major Bierce and I will escort you home."

"I imagine your wife will be glad to see you," added Bierce, who had noticed Delapore's wedding ring.

Delapore looked at Bierce sadly. "My wife died two years ago while giving birth to a stillborn daughter."

Bierce grimaced, but did not make matters worse by attempting to apologize. The fact Delapore wore his wedding ring two years after his wife's death told him more about the man than he was comfortable knowing.

In a surprisingly tender voice, Clay said "Major Bierce and I will see you safely there."

Duval added "And I best go to my own room and get some rest. It has been a long day." She made a display of stifling a yawn.

* * * * *

"You are late, Duval," said Colonel Baker an hour later. He did not bother to rise from the park bench on which he sat, or to extinguish the cheap cigar he was smoking.

Duval hid the resentment she felt at this rude greeting. She looked across the small street separating Lafayette Park from the Executive Mansion, noting the lights flickering through the second-floor windows. "Is it a coincidence that you wanted to meet in a park bearing your Christian name?"

Lafayette Baker gave a nasty laugh. "It does amuse me. Besides, after dark it can be surprisingly quiet and unvisited. I prefer not to be seen talking to you; knowledge of our connection would limit your usefulness to me. Now, what is Clay doing with that traitor Delapore?"

Not for the first time, Duval felt regret that Allen Pinkerton had lost the political battle with his many enemies, and had surrendered his security empire to the unpleasant officer sitting on the bench. Pinkerton had not been the fastest rabbit in the forest, thought Duval, but he had not treated her with such condescension. She found working for Baker much less enjoyable than working for Pinkerton.

"Colonel Clay suspects there is a major plot in motion, possibly to murder Lincoln, possibly involving other acts of violence. He feels that Delapore's connections in the Copperhead community might have brought him some insights into who might be participating in such a plot."

Baker uttered an amused snort. "And just why did Clay think Delapore would be straight with him?"

Smiling in anticipation of his reaction, Duval replied sweetly "Because Clay promised to have Stanton release most of the prisoners in the Old Capitol."

Exclaiming an obscenity, Baker surged to his feet, dropping his cigar in his outrage. "He has no right! Those traitors must remain where they are!"

"So you can continue to demand from them and their relatives money in exchange for decent food and treatment," said Duval. She had no feelings whatsoever for the prisoners, but enjoyed seeing the coarse Baker's outrage at the threat to his extra-legal income.

"Keep me informed about everything Clay does; you know the channels to use."

"I will, providing my salary is promptly deposited to the account we have arranged. For some reason, the latest payment has not yet found its way into that account."

"You will be paid," growled Baker, who then stomped off into the darkness. When he was gone, Duval's smirk was replaced by a thoughtful frown. She did not think keeping Baker informed would hurt Alphonso, but wondered what she would do if it turned out it would. Pondering the future, she glided out of the park in the direction of Willard's.

* * * * *

The dining room of the boarding house at 541 High Street was cramped. On the other hand, it provided an intimate setting for the five men gathered around the dining table.

At the head was John Wilkes Booth, probably the most famous actor in the country. Short, athletic, vain, his handsome face radiated an air of confidence and command. The other four men at the table gazed at him with looks that were not far short of worshipful.

To Booth's left sat John Surratt and George Atzerodt. Surratt, the son of the owner of this boarding house, was a nervous, somewhat flabby young man whose hands were hardly ever still. Atzerodt was a lean, dark-visaged German immigrant, whose addiction to alcohol kept him from employment at anything more demanding than occasional day labor.

To Booth's right sat David Herold and Lewis Powell. Herold, a puffy-faced pharmacist, had dreams of following his hero Booth onto the stage. Powell, a massively-muscled giant of a man, was a paroled Confederate prisoner of war who had attached himself to Booth before he could go home, and who followed Booth with the devotion of a dog, and about as much intelligence.

The five men sitting around the dining table were as different as five men could be. In fact, they were united by only three things: hatred of the Union in general and Abraham Lincoln in particular; love for the Confederacy and the idea of white supremacy; and the belief that now only John Wilkes Booth could snatch victory for the South literally from the jaws of defeat.

Booth had been holding forth for some time, but his worshipful followers still listened with rapt attention. Waving his small cigar for emphasis, he returned to a point he had made several times before that evening. He did not mind repeating himself, as after all, that is what actors do.

"So, the idea of kidnapping the President and holding him until all Confederate prisoners of war are released will no longer work. Andy Johnson hates the Confederacy as much as Stanton, and neither would release a single corporal to save Abe's life. Therefore, we must decapitate the Government. Kill Lincoln, Johnson, Seward and Stanton at the same time. Make it clear the South will never be governed against its will."

"You them kill, others them replace," said Atzerodt in his thick German accent.

"Then we or those who follow us will kill them," replied Booth. "Soon, there will be no one in the North with the belly to take those positions. Furthermore, inspired by our actions, the South will rise up again; the North will simply not have the will to fight another war. We in this room will be the heroes of the entire South. Now, are we all agreed?"

An air of uneasiness went around the room; it was one thing to discuss assassinations in the abstract, another altogether to actually perform them. Still, Booth's followers were hypnotized by his actor's eloquence, and did not pause to consider the gaps in Booth's logic. A murmur of assent passed around the table.

"Very well. We will plan it for this Friday. Ford's Theatre is putting on *Our American Cousin*, a dreadful old wheeze of a comedy that Laura Keene's group simply will not let die. I have it on good authority that for some reason Abe will never miss a performance of that tripe. Well, Friday he will see it for the last time. I will check with the theater to make sure that he is coming; the Executive Mansion always lets the Ford brothers know when Lincoln means to come, so they can trot out patriotic fluff to decorate the box. I will kill Lincoln. George, you will kill the Vice-President in his rooms at the National Hotel." Atzerodt started, but nodded his assent. "Lewis, you will answer for the Secretary of State.

John and David, the two of you will handle Stanton; the Secretary of War may be guarded, so it might take two. We will all then make our ways separately south, where heroes' welcomes await us."

John Surratt responded with teenage bravado. "I can handle a slug like Stanton myself. I want the honor of performing the act on my own."

Nervously, the squeamish Herold chimed in. "Ah, Mr. Booth, that will be fine with me. It might be better for me to be with Lewis. He doesn't know this town near as well as me, and I can help him get down south."

Booth shrugged negligently. "That's all right then. We will meet here one more time on Thursday night. In the meantime, get reliable weapons and assemble whatever would help you on a quick trip south."

The door to the kitchen opened, and the tall, handsome Mrs. Surratt entered the room. "All right boys, time to pack it in," she said in a pleasant, husky voice. "I need to lock up, and Johnnie needs his sleep."

The meeting broke up agreeably; the conspirators liked the motherly widow, and took no offense at her peremptory order. Booth was the last in line to go out the front door; before he could step outside Mary Surratt touched his elbow and in a low voice said, "Your friend is here again, in the backyard. He would like a word with you."

Frowning, Booth nodded and reversed direction. As he stepped into the darkened yard, Surratt softly locked the door behind him. Peering about, he spotted a dark form near the outhouse. Carefully picking his way through the cluttered yard he walked over to the figure.

"Is the plan in place?" asked the figure without preamble.

"This Friday," replied Booth.

"Do they suspect what will be happening in Virginia, and in New York?"

"No. They will be as astonished as the entire North."

"Astonishment is hardly the word," replied the dark figure. "The country will enter complete chaos. Big changes will be the order of the day; far, far bigger than pulling Richmond's fat out of the fire."

The dark figure laughed softly, and was shortly joined by Booth.

Chapter 2:
"As He Died To Make Us Holy, Let Us Live To Make Men Free…"

John Wilkes Booth normally enjoyed his regular sessions with admiring theater cronies in the bar of the National Hotel, his headquarters while in the District. Nevertheless, he was not enjoying this particular session. Despite sharing the intimate details of his latest amorous conquests, he could not lift the glum spirits of the half-dozen hangers-on at his favorite table. Most shared his attachment to the Cause, and were despondent over Lee's surrender and the impending destruction of the last vestiges of the Confederacy. Booth found this intolerable; he was a man who demanded constant adulation, and was fortunate that good looks and genuine talent usually gave him more than his share of that commodity.

"Boys, why so serious?" Booth asked his audience. "I see nary a smile around this table."

"And why should we be a-smiling?" responded a heavyset, middle-aged man in a thick Irish brogue. "The Confederacy is done. Lincoln and the black Republicans will be having their way, freeing the niggers to drive down the wages of decent working men, and to lust after our women. Putting half-human apes over white men, it's not to be born."

A murmur of dejected agreement went round the table. Then another of Booth's cronies, a scrawny youth with the smell of stables about him added, "Damn Yankee Republicans should be taught a lesson. By God, I wish I could take them on one at a time, I would..."

"Would what?" interrupted a soft, cultured voice. Along with the others at the table, the speaker turned to see two Union officers: the short, slight, bespectacled Alphonso Clay and the tall, handsome, sardonic Ambrose Bierce, who smiled ironically.

"I believe Colonel Clay asked you a question," Bierce remarked. "I would advise you to answer him; he places great importance on polite behavior."

The burly Irishman answered for the scrawny youth. "You blue bellies may have won, but you can't make us like it."

Clay looked disdainfully at the Mick. With a contemptuous drawl in his voice, Clay addressed him. "I am not impressed by threats from a stay-at-home Rebel, a traitor lacking the sole virtue of being willing to fight for his convictions; from a disloyal Paddy who spent the war around tables like this one, cursing the United States while better men than he fought and died. Now, be off with you, you and your friends. I have business with Mr. Booth."

The Irishman surged to his feet and, uttering an obscenity, started to throw a roundhouse punch at Clay, who dodged the clumsy blow and buried his fist in his opponent's stomach. The large man was unprepared for such a powerful blow from such a slight-looking opponent, and vomited as he doubled over. In a blur of motion, Clay grabbed a fistful of his opponent's unwashed hair, yanked his head up and then with terrible force rammed the man's face down on the table, where the Irishman's nose broke with an audible crunch. Maintaining his hold on the now blubbering man's hair, Clay jerked the man's head up, allowing all his friends to see the tears streaming from his eyes, the blood streaming from his ruined nose. In a conversational voice Clay said, "You have fouled my boots with your spew. Kindly clean them off." Clay was vain about his appearance and clothes, and took pride in his expensive footwear.

Angrily several of the blubbering man's friends started to surge to their feet, but they froze at the sound of a soft click from behind Clay, as Ambrose Bierce cocked his revolver. In a friendly, jovial voice Bierce said, "Now boys, the fun is over. Why don't you take your friend and help him clean up, while the Colonel and I discuss matters with Mr. Booth."

"My boots are not yet clean," said Clay in a cold voice, giving his victim's hair an agonizing yank. Screaming, the man grabbed a large bandanna out of one of his pockets, and with a few hurried swipes cleaned his own vomit from Clay's boots, which in fact had only possessed a few small splashes. Clay released the man's hair, and the Irishman slowly straightened himself. Through his pain and humiliation, he felt such a rage at the little nancy-boy colonel that he was tempted to have another go, despite his injuries. Nonetheless, just one look at the pale, placid blue eyes behind the spectacles immediately dissuaded him; it was only later that he reflected on how strange it was that it was Clay's eyes, and not Bierce's cocked pistol, that held him at bay.

As the wounded man staggered toward the exit to the bar, his companions looked uncertainly at Booth. With a negligent waive of his hand, the actor said, "Go on home, boys. I will talk to our friends in blue. You need have no fear on my account." As Bierce re-holstered his revolver, Booth turned his attention to Clay and drawled, "You say you have business with me. Sir, you have me at a disadvantage; I do not believe I know either of you, and find it hard to imagine what business we might have."

Without being asked, Clay sat himself in one of the empty chairs at the table, quickly followed by Bierce. Clay stared expressionlessly at Booth for a long moment, before finally addressing the actor. "I am Colonel Alphonso Clay; this is Major Ambrose Bierce. I find it...interesting to meet you. You have the reputation of the finest dramatic actor in America. It is a shame, I must confess that I have never actually seen you trod the boards."

Frowning slightly, Booth replied, "You seem to be a man of sophistication. It is hard to believe you have never seen me in the theater."

Clay shrugged slightly. "My family has always tried to maintain standards. The theater tends to attract the…less principled members of our society."

Booth started as if he had been slapped. "I take offense at that slur upon my profession, sir."

Clay shrugged again. "Whatever our respective views on your livelihood, that is not why Major Bierce and I are here. It is our understanding that you harbor hostile feelings toward the American government, and associate with those who may harbor more than mere feelings."

The actor scowled. "I have never made any secret of my detestation for Lincoln and the Republicans, and their desire to put niggers on an equal footing with white men. No nigger could be my equal."

Bierce replied solemnly to the actor. "That is very true. In fact, I knew a black man who recently gave his life for his country and his friend. You could never in a thousand years become his equal."

Booth seemed about to reply, but with a visible effort confined himself to casting a venomous glance in Bierce's direction. Turning his attention to Clay, he said, "Be that as it may, what is the reason for two Union officers harassing me while I have a few drinks with my friends? The noble Lee has surrendered to the ignorant scrub Grant, and Lincoln looks fair to working his will over the prostrate South. I am puzzled as to the purpose of this conversation."

Clay looked expressionlessly at Booth while he replied. "The South is defeated. However, it has many supporters who may not accept that defeat. We have learned that some of those supporters here in Washington may be planning acts of violence as some sort of mindless revenge; perhaps here in

Washington, perhaps elsewhere in the North. Since you are a famous man, and a man well known to be hostile toward the United States, it is possible that someone with knowledge of such a scheme may be among your associates – of course without your knowledge of his unlawful intentions."

Booth took a long draw on his cigar, and slowly expelled a cloud of smoke at the two officers. Bierce waved at the air before him in irritation; Clay did not react at all. Then in an exaggerated drawl, Booth said "Whatever my personal feelings, my destiny is on the stage, not in conspiracy or politics. My father was the greatest actor of his day; my ambition is to be the greatest of mine. I know of no one plotting against Lincoln's life; and I will not help you harass my friends whose only crime is not to delight in the coming victory of Sambo over the white man. And if that is all..."

"There you are, John!" interrupted a fresh-faced, somewhat plump young woman of about twenty who had entered the bar and was bustling over to the table where the men sat. "I went to your room, but you were not there. And now..." The woman had reached Booth before taking a good look at Clay; her voice trailed off in some confusion. Then she exclaimed "Alphonso! Is it you?"

Clay's eyes widened slightly with astonishment. In a fluid motion he rose to his feet, bowing to the young woman. "Lucy? Lucy Hale? This is an unexpected surprise."

The woman giggled, and replied, "I am not surprised you hardly recognize me, Alphonso. We last saw each other before the war, when your father met with mine on those boring political matters. I was just a girl then; now I am a woman."

"She is indeed," interjected Booth, the hint of a nasty smirk on his face.

Without taking his eyes off Lucy Hale, Clay addressed Bierce. "Major Bierce, may I introduce you to Miss Lucy Hale, daughter of Senator John Hale of New Hampshire? Our families have known each other for many years."

Blushing prettily, she bustled over to Booth, placing her hand possessively on his shoulder; without rising, Booth negligently patted her hand. “I see you have already met my fiancée,” Lucy said proudly.

What little color there was in Clay’s face drained away. “Miss Hale, Senator Hale...approves of this union?” he asked, unable to keep a note of incredulity from his voice.

Lucy Hale blushed more deeply. “He does not know yet,” she replied, her eyes drifting away from Clay to lose themselves in contemplation of Booth’s beauty. “John knows that my father might not understand our love. He has asked me to wait until he can talk to some of his powerful and wealthy friends in New York. They will be able to convince my father that there is nothing dishonorable in our love. Until then I beg you not to let my father know of this. He means well, but he is always trying to control me. He does not realize that his little girl is now a woman, and is able to decide these kinds of things for herself.”

“I’m sure that you are,” murmured Bierce. Only Clay caught the note of sardonic amusement in his companion’s voice.

“If you insist, Miss Hale,” said Clay, a noticeable strain in his voice.

“I think our business is concluded gentlemen,” said Booth languidly. “Now, if you will excuse us, Lucy and I have things to discuss.” Clay and Bierce rose as one, muttered polite good-byes, and left the actor and the senator’s daughter to sole possession of the National Hotel’s bar.

Clay arose and strode out of the National, beginning to walk the two blocks to Willard’s at a pace Bierce found hard to match. The slightly-built colonel made no response to any of Bierce’s attempts to initiate conversation, so the lanky major contented himself with being his companion’s silent shadow.

As they entered the lobby of Willard’s they spotted Teresa Duval just reaching the bottom of the stairs. In her brisk if faked New England accent, she called out, “Colonel, Major, what a pleasant coincidence. I was coming down for dinner; perhaps we could make a party of it.” She reached the two officers and cocked her head ever so slightly as she gazed into Clay's eyes, pointedly ignoring Bierce. Bierce was not offended. In fact, he was secretly amused at the stiffly formal way Clay greeted Duval; Bierce knew full well why Clay was trying to conceal his discomfort.

Clay looked at Duval for a moment, then visibly seemed to reach a decision. "Miss Duval, we would be happy to join you in a meal. Before we do, I would like to consult with you on a difficult situation; a situation in which you may be of material benefit to your country...and to me. The dining room is rather too public; the lounge to our right seems to be presently unoccupied. Would you care to join us there?"

Intrigued, Duval nodded her assent. The three settled themselves into the quiet public room, and much to Bierce's surprise, Clay told Duval the details of their meeting with Stanton, and of their encounter with John Wilkes Booth.

"So, you think this Booth may be a Rebel spy," said Duval briskly after Clay had finished speaking.

"It is possible," replied Clay, showing the faint trace of a frown. "He is ideally situated to travel back and forth in areas close to the fighting without arousing comment; no one pays much attention to how actors come and go. Also, his is one of the two names which were all that Delapore could suggest. If there is a conspiracy, Booth may be in it, or certainly close enough to it to direct us to its leaders."

"That's not your only concern," Bierce said suddenly.

"What do you mean?" replied Clay crossly.

"Please, Colonel, we are not children," said Duval, and let out one of her silvery, chilling laughs. "You are concerned about Miss Hale following into the clutches of – dare I say it – an actor."

"I do not deny that I am concerned for her. When I knew her before the war, she was a charming, delightful child from a prominent family, with brilliant prospects. To have her fall into the clutches of a...theatrical, is too much to be born. Her father would be devastated."

"How old is Miss Hale?" asked Bierce.

"She will be nineteen in about a month."

"Then she is old enough to make her own decisions," replied Bierce with brutal indifference. "I have met nineteen year old women with far more knowledge of the world than I will ever possess."

"I am certain that you have," replied Clay. "Lucy Hale is not such a one. Furthermore, Senator Hale is an honorable and patriotic man, suffering from dropsy. My family has obligations toward him. If his only daughter were to fall into the hands of a man like Booth, traitor or no, I fear the shock would be more than his weakened heart could bear."

Bierce leaned back in his chair and looked intently at Clay, a faint smile on his face. "You could of course frighten Booth off, Alphonso. Handle it right, and he might remember theatrical bookings he had in San Francisco. Make no mistake, you are a scary bastard sometimes, and look it."

"Mind your language, Bierce," said Clay abruptly. "There is a lady present."

Bierce knew more about Duval than did Clay, and resisted the temptation to laugh in the humorless colonel's face. He turned to Duval, nodded his head in mock contrition, and whined, "Do forgive my coarseness, Miss Duval."

"You are forgiven, Major," said Duval with just a hint of levity in her voice. She then turned her attention back to Clay. "Colonel, I have not met Miss Hale, but I am familiar with the type. She will forgive anything that happened before she met her lover, but nothing that happened after. If this Booth is the kind of man you say he is, I should be able to, ah, arrange a scene that would destroy any feelings she might have for him."

Clay frowned. "That is out of the question. I could not permit you to be placed in such an indelicate position."

Duval threw her head back and emitted another of those silvery, chilling laughs. "Colonel Clay, I am disappointed in you. After what we have all done and what we have been through, you doubt my ability to handle myself in a tight place."

"I do not doubt that you *can* handle yourself, only whether you *should have to*. If Booth is what I suspect him to be, he could be more dangerous than your typical theatrical."

Duval started to laugh again, but stopped when she saw the look of concern on Clay's face. That look touched and worried her at the same time. She lightly reached out and laid her hand on Clay's arm. "You needn't be worried. I will scout the ground carefully before taking any action. You say he makes his headquarters at the National Hotel? A very public place, where he will be unable to do anything to me that I do not wish. Now, gentlemen, I believe that you owe me that meal."

The conspirators were meeting once again over the dining table at Mrs. Surratt's boarding house. The atmosphere was much more solemn that the last time that they had met; the awesomeness of what they contemplated had fully hit them. Even Booth's joviality was forced, although he was skilled enough an actor for his nervousness not to be apparent. Casually lighting a small cigar, he said, "By this time tomorrow night, we will be the heroes of the Confederacy." He expelled a puff of smoke, then slowly looked each of the conspirators in the eye. "Anyone not got the belly for it, now is the time to say." The German Atzerodt was sweating heavily, and seemed about to say something, but the immigrant looked at the mountainous Lewis Powell, who stared back at him like the barrel of a canon, and decided not to speak.

Hearing no dissents, Booth again spoke. "Good. I knew I could count on you boys. It will be as we discussed with just one change. John, I've decide that Stanton can live after all, I'm going to need you to go to Buffalo instead."

The landlady's son looked crestfallen. "Hey, Mr. Booth, I can handle old Stanton all by myself. You can trust me."

"I know I can, Johnnie, I know I can. Plans have changed, and I have an important assignment for you. Richmond has placed a number of spies in New York State; many of them are already under suspicion, and are being watched. After Lincoln,

Johnson, and Seward are dead, the beehive is really going to be kicked over. Lafayette Baker will have our comrades taken in, and probably hanged without trial. I need you to go to Buffalo, establish a safe-house where our friends can hide, and find some unguarded route into Canada that they can use one or two at a time. Sort of an "underground railway," only one for white men. Can you do that, Johnnie?"

Somewhat uncertainly, young Surratt replied, "I guess so, Mr. Booth."

"Good. Knew that I could count on you." Booth reached in to the side pocket of his frock coat, and his hand emerged clutching a thick wad of Union banknotes. "This should cover all of your expenses. Leave first thing in the morning; just tell your ma that you had to deliver a message for me up to New York. She'll understand." He then turned his attention to the others in the room. "The rest of you, best go get some rest. Tomorrow we make history, and save the South!"

With muttered good nights, the meeting broke up, young Surratt going upstairs, the others shuffling off to their various boarding houses. Booth himself was the last to leave. He paused on the sidewalk outside the boardinghouse, looking at the sky as he finished his cigar, contemplating with satisfaction what would occur on the morrow. Suddenly, he heard his master's voice behind him.

"You have done well, Booth."

Booth turned, grimaced, and threw the stub of his cigar into the street. "I still think it is a mistake to let Stanton live."

"That cannot be helped. I want John up at the border, just across from Canada. So, you are going off to rest?"

Booth smirked. "Hardly. I am going to have myself some refreshment; the next few days I am unlikely to have the time for personal relaxation."

"True enough. Booth, you will never change. Well, have a good time, but keep a clear head tomorrow. Both of our causes require it."

Booth nodded a farewell and strolled off into the night. Within ten minutes his unhurried pace had brought him to the National Hotel; despite wartime growth, Washington remained a small town in many ways. He entered the half-filled bar, took his seat, and signaled the bartender for a large whiskey, which was promptly delivered. Sipping at the smooth, amber liquid, he idly wondered if he could get a message to Lucy Hale; what she lacked in experience she made up for in enthusiasm and that might be just what the doctor ordered for the night before he, John Wilkes Booth, changed history.

"Mr. Booth, would you mind if I shared your table?"

Booth looked up sharply. Before him was a tall, raven-haired beauty; her tresses swept up in an elaborate coif. He looked her up and down, and liked what he saw; the gown was of the finest silk, with a décolletage which would have been scandalous had not her figure been so perfect. Not one of Hooker's auxiliaries, he decided immediately, or if she was, she was from the very highest end; her dress was very expensive and obviously new. "Of course," he said, easily, gesturing to the chair across the small table from him. "You have me at a disadvantage, miss. You know my name, but I do not believe we have met."

"Not face to face," responded Duval in a husky, alluring voice as she smoothly seated herself. "However, everyone knows John Wilkes Booth, the most famous actor in America, as well as the most handsome."

Booth smiled; he had been through many conversations that had started this way. "You flatter me, Miss...?" he asked with simulated humility.

"Lind. Jenny Lind."

Booth laughed with amused surprise. "The same as the Swedish Nightingale. Any relation?"

"I am afraid not, Mr. Booth. Just a coincidence." Duval leaned forward to lightly place her hand on Booth's, and in doing so revealed her charms to spectacular effect. "Mr. Booth,

I cannot tell you how much it means to me to meet face-to-face a man as famous, as accomplished, as *handsome* as yourself."

Booth's smile widened; this was going to be a better evening than he had imagined.

* * * * *

Lucy Hale's heart was pounding as she hurried into the lobby of the National Hotel. A messenger she had never seen before had brought her a printed telegram from John Booth. She was flattered; telegrams were still expensive items, the longer the more costly, and the blocked out letters had run on and on, to what must have been a shocking cost. That was so like the man, never considering the costs of a gesture. More exciting than the expense of the message was its content: a wonderfully flowery invitation to spend an evening in celebrating the joys of their bodies. She knew that she should have been shocked by the receipt of such a message that had been viewed by several strangers before it got to her. Secretly, she smiled, then giggled slightly before starting up the National's stairway. She was honest enough to know that she was somewhat plain and somewhat overweight, and to receive a message showing such a handsome man lusted for her body was something for which she had never dared to dream.

Lucy Hale was so eager that her quick ascent to the third floor left her hardly winded. As she approached the door to Booth's room, she remembered how the telegram had warned her of the inquisitive, blue-nosed occupants of the neighboring room, telling her that the door would be unlocked and she should enter quietly without knocking. Stifling a giggle, she gently opened the door; then froze in utter shock.

Booth lay face up on the bed, stark naked. That was not what shocked her; she had half expected to be greeted by that sight. What shocked Lucy Hale was the beautiful, naked woman who knelt on the bed in front of Booth, seemingly about to apply her mouth to Booth's...to Booth's... Lucy Hale's mind went blank for a moment, unable to complete the thought, unable to process the images in front of her. The woman on the bed raised her head and looked at Lucy, smiled lasciviously, and in the thick brogue of a cheap Irish crib girl said, "Well, darlin', Johnnie said another lass would be along presently. You're bein' just in time; strip off and hop in."

Booth struggled to get out of the bed, stammering, "Lucy, I didn't know...let me explain." However, Lucy Hale did not hear a word Booth was saying. Emitting a high but soft shriek, she turned and ran from the room, knowing already that there was nothing the man could say, nothing that she would care to hear from him, ever again.

The naked Booth stood looking at the door in some confusion, wanting to run after Lucy, not daring to go naked into the hall of a respectable hotel. Meanwhile, Teresa Duval briskly dressed herself. The dazed Booth turned to see Duval making the final adjustments to her gown while deftly slipping on her shoes. "Where are you going?" he blurted.

"My job here is done. Miss Hale will never be able to forgive, much less forget, the little scene she just interrupted. It is time for me to go."

"You ...you trapped me," said Booth in a wondering voice. Then with anger building inside of him, he stepped toward Duval, saying "You whore! You arranged for her to come! You're working for Senator Hale! You must have unlocked the door when I wasn't looking, so I wouldn't get the warning of a knock!" Booth lunged at Duval, grabbing for her throat, fully intending to throttle her; however, there was a blur of motion, and somehow she was behind him, holding his twisted right arm behind him at an agonizing angle with her left hand, holding a wickedly gleaming razor to his neck with her right.

"Softly now, Mr. Booth, softly," she murmured quietly into his ear. "Be a good boy, and you will live to seduce many more foolish girls in the future. Pity; I could bleed you quiet, and leave you dead on this floor, you Rebel-loving scum. Sadly, I must leave you alive, so alive I leave you."

Booth was many things, but stupid was not among them. Duval's unconscious insult revealed her pro-Union bias.

"Low-born Yankee whore," he rasped, enough in control of himself to keep his voice low. "Bog-trotting Mick bitch! After tomorrow night, you won't be so uppity. Not you, nor any of your mudsill friends north of Mason-Dixon."

Duval laughed a silvery laugh. "Sticks and stones, Mr. Booth, sticks and stones. I'll leave you now, humiliated but unhurt; just take care that our paths do not cross again."

His agonized arm was suddenly released; simultaneously, the razor disappeared from his throat. Booth staggered slightly, and straightened his twisted arm with no little pain. He then whirled about to confront the traitorous woman, unsure what he would do but needing to do something to assuage his ego. The room was empty. He might have heard the rustle of a dress for a moment, coming through the half-open door, but he was not even sure of that. Part of him was angry at her quick escape from the room. A colder, more rational part admitted it may have been for the best that he had no opportunity to avenge himself on the woman.

* * * * *

Alphonso Clay knew that this Friday was going to be a busy day; so he made his personal business his first order of business. The blond colonel had left Willard's before 9:00 am and quickly strode the seven blocks that brought him to the Hale family townhouse. He had decided that he could not afford to wait for Duval to implement whatever plan she had in mind; he was simply going to have to break the news to Senator Hale as gently as possible, and hope that the sick old man would be strong enough to take the shock and determined enough to keep his daughter from Booth's arms.

Clay paused on the doorstep of the dignified looking Federal-style house, and reflected on how hard the ailing widower would take such news about his only daughter. Then he knocked resolutely. A neat, efficient-looking Irish maid opened the door. “What be your business, Colonel?”

“I need to see Senator Hale on an important personal matter.”

The young woman looked sourly at him. “The Senator is feeling poorly this morning, sir. I would not be disturbing him.”

In a commanding voice Clay replied, “Please tell Senator Hale that Alphonso Clay wishes to see him.”

From deep in the house a deep yet quavering voice boomed out, “Milly, did he say Alphonso Clay? Bring him in here!”

With a disapproving look, Milly swung the door wide and led Clay into the house. As they walked to the dinning room she murmured, “The Senator has been feeling very poorly. Don’t go and be exciting him; he’s a good man, and should stay in the world as long as God wills.” Then she stepped into the dining room and announced “Senator, Colonel Clay,” and withdrew, throwing a final dirty look at Clay.

A short, rotund man of about sixty struggled to his feet with visible effort and came to greet Clay. The small walk had seemingly winded the ailing senator, whose skin had an unhealthy bluish tinge; but the expression on Hale’s face showed nothing but pleasure.

“Alphonso, my boy, it has been far too long,” said Hale, pumping the young colonel’s hand with simulated vigor. “We haven’t seen each other since, oh, the summer of ‘63, just before Grant sent you to Knoxville. Come into the parlor; we have some catching up to do.”

“I am interrupting your breakfast…” began Clay.

“That doesn’t matter,” exclaimed Hale, leading Clay from the dining room to the parlor. “My appetite hasn’t been what it was, and I’d rather talk to the son of an old friend than eat any day of the week. I assume you’ve had breakfast. May I have Millie bring you some refreshment?”

“That will not be necessary, sir.”

“Then sit, sit,” responded the senator, directing to one of a pair of wing chairs facing each other. With a wheeze the older man settled into the other chair and smiled at Clay with obvious pleasure. It took an effort for Clay to smile back. Although Clay was a cold, self-contained individual, the cheerful politician who sat across from him, a New England abolitionist who had formed a political alliance with, and more improbably a personal friendship with, Clay’s slave-owning but Union-loyal father, was one of the bright memories of the younger Clay’s youth. It came close to breaking Clay’s stony heart to see that Hale was slowly dying, that he must know he was dying, and that it did not affect his sunny nature. That made Clay’s mission all the more difficult.

“Sir, my visit must be of necessity brief. I am still under orders, and cannot spare much time for social courtesies, much as I might wish to do so. I hear rumors that you may be spending the summer in Europe, and wanted to pay at least a short call before you depart.”

Hale made a sour face. “Yes, I will be sailing from New York in a little less than two weeks. Damn doctors insist on it. I have not been feeling as well as I ought lately, and they insist getting away from stressful work and a long, restful sea voyage followed by months of leisurely-sightseeing could put me back in the saddle. I’m still not sure I should go; just because the fighting is over, it doesn’t mean there won’t be important legislative work to be done in binding up our poor nation. I must go for Lucy’s sake, if not my own.”

Clay was surprised that the senator had introduced the subject of his daughter on his own. “How can Lucy matter to a decision involving your health?”

Hale’s frown deepened. “Lucy has reached that most difficult of ages, Alphonso. She thinks she is an adult, and certainly is one, physically. However, she has been keeping fast company. I fear she may commit...an indiscretion, an indiscretion that might ruin her life.” Hale paused and coughed several times. When he had recovered, he continued. “She is all

I have left of my dear wife. You know, I am not as young as I once was, and won't always be here to protect her. If I insist on her going to Europe with me, in Europe there will be lots of good families also on tour, many with decent, eligible young men; the sort that are all too rare around this town full of grifters and scoundrels. My only fear is that she will refuse to go with me..."

"Daddy, I wanted to talk to...why Alphonso!" Lucy Hale had swept into the room without warning, and was surprised to find Clay there. Clay was even more surprised at the changes that had overcome Lucy in a single day. The cheerful, light-hearted young society girl was gone, to be replaced by a serious-looking woman with haunted, swollen eyes.

Clay stood immediately, bowing slightly. "A pleasure to see you again so soon, Miss Hale." Turning to the aging senator, Clay lied smoothly. "I had the pleasure of encountering your daughter on the street near Willard's yesterday. It was that encounter that had reminded me how remiss I was in not paying my respects to you earlier." Then turning again to Lucy, he said, "You seem somewhat distressed, Miss Hale. May I know the cause?"

Avoiding Clay's direct gaze, Lucy replied, "It is nothing, Alphonso. Just hay fever." Then she walked over to her father and laid her hand affectionately on his shoulder, saying to the senator, "Daddy, I'm sorry I've been such a spoiled child about your European trip, wanting to stay here and flit about in society. The more I think on it, the better such a trip sounds. The ocean air would be good...for my hay fever. Besides, we have not spent all that much time together since Mother passed." Her voice suddenly went solemn. "Who knows when either of us would have the time do something like this again. Tell me, Daddy, is Paris as beautiful as they say?"

The ailing Senator looked both astonished and relieved. "I'm not sure; I've never been myself. I suppose we will find out together. And there are wonders to see in London and Rome as well. We will find out together if they have been puffed."

Clay allowed himself a tight, controlled smile. Still standing, he said, "I am certain you will both enjoy a sojourn in the Old World. I must really depart now on Government business, and may not be able to see you again before you set sail. Therefore, allow me to wish you both *bon voyage*; please write to me if it is convenient."

With a struggle, Senator Hale rose to his feet and warmly grasped Clay's hand in both of his. "We will certainly do so. God speed on your business, we will meet again on our return." Although the cheery smile had not left Hale's lips, Clay read subtle signs in the senator's face, signs that indicated Hale knew he would not be returning from Europe, at least not alive. "Lucy, escort Colonel Clay to the door. My...foot is bothering me, and I need to sit for a moment." With a heavy wheeze, Hale collapsed into his armchair, breathing hard, but still smiling.

At the door, Lucy Hale grabbed Clay's arm urgently and spoke to him in a low voice. "I have been wrapped up in my own selfish doings for too long. I have known Papa's health wasn't good, but today it was like I was seeing him for the first time. Alphonso, he is dying, isn't he?"

Clay considered lying to the young woman, but quickly decided that would be an injustice to her. He slowly nodded his head once. Tears filled Lucy Hale's eyes, but she did not actually cry. Instead, she said "Then I should make our time together count. There will be time enough to consider my own... pleasures."

Clay could think of nothing to add. Instead, he took the young woman's hand, kissed it, then wordlessly turned and strode in the direction of Pennsylvania Avenue. Lost in his own thoughts, he was not aware that Teresa Duval had fallen into step beside him. Playfully she nudged his left shoulder. Snapping out of his almost hypnotic reverie, Clay whirled about with his fist cocked for a powerful blow. Far from being frightened, a grinning Duval had assumed a defensive posture that would have done credit to a professional boxer. Lowering his arm, an embarrassed Clay stammered, "My deepest apologies, Miss Duval. My mind was elsewhere, and I tend to respond...automatically to something that seems a threat."

Duval offered up one of her silvery laughs. "No apology is necessary. I also tend to react swiftly; it would seem we are well matched in that respect – as well as others." Smiling disturbingly, she continued. "I take it you have been to see Senator Hale. How did he take the news of his daughter's liaison with Booth?"

Looking steadily at Duval, Clay responded, "The subject never came up. Miss Hale would seem to be abandoning Mr. Booth, and accompanying her father on an extended cruise. This was the best outcome under the circumstances. I suspect you had a hand in it."

"Why, whatever do you mean, Colonel Clay?" She batted her eyelashes at him like the most simpering of southern belles. After a moment, Clay emitted the barking sound that with him passed for a laugh.

"Very well, Miss Duval. You will tell me when it suits you, and not before. Whoever saved a decent old family friend from heartbreak, and his daughter from ruination, has my thanks – whoever she may be. Now, I must be off to see Secretary Stanton. I would imagine you need to be reporting to Colonel Lafayette Baker, so allow me to escort you partway." Ignoring Duval's guilty start at Clay's mention of her appointment with the head of the Secret Service, Clay continued speaking. "I need hardly tell you to be cautious with that man. He is a spymaster, and spymasters tend to be an ugly breed. Of course, some are worse than others. Pinkerton had his flaws, but underneath was a core of decency which Baker singularly lacks. I suspect you already know that."

"Do not worry about Colonel Baker. I have his measure."

Clay barked another laugh. "I imagine you do. Well, here is where we must part. Thank you again for the service you have rendered me."

Duval smiled in a vaguely predatory way. "Truly, no thanks are necessary. You owe me a debt, and someday I intend to call it in."

The corners of Clay's mouth twitched briefly into an almost smile. "I have no doubt. Until we meet again." Clay clicked his heels in the European fashion, turned, and swiftly ascended the steps of the War Department building.

"Oh yes, Colonel Clay," murmured Duval slowly as Clay disappeared into the massive building. "We will indeed be meeting again."

* * * * *

For some reason, the aide who normally guarded the entrance to Secretary Stanton's office was absent. However, the door to the office was open, and Clay strode in unannounced. Seeing five others in the room with Stanton, Clay briskly said, "My apologies if I interrupt, sir, but your aide was gone and the door open. I can withdraw until you are ready for our meeting."

"That is not necessary," replied Stanton from behind his desk, his wheezing more noticeable than usual. "I told the aide to take a long walk; good man, but don't want him hearing things he might have trouble keeping to himself. These gentlemen have an interest in your current...assignment, and I thought it best to have them here when we met. General Halleck you already know.

The balding general sat heavily in a chair to the left of Stanton's desk. He nodded vaguely at Clay, and began scratching absently at his right elbow, glassy eyes focused on nothing in particular.

Stanton looked at the larger of the two figures who occupied the sofa facing his desk. "Colonel Clay, let me introduce you to Senator Sumner of Massachusetts, Chairman of the Foreign Relations committee and an especial friend of Mrs. Lincoln." Clay bowed slightly to the elegantly dressed figure with the regal bearing. Clay noticed a certain vagueness about the expression on Charles Sumner's face, and suddenly remembered how before the war the abolitionist had been beaten unconscious on the very floor of the Senate by a Southern fanatic who disagreed with Sumner's views on slavery. The beating had nearly killed Sumner, and in fact had left him bedridden for over a year. Clay briefly wondered what such a terrible injury had done to the brain inside the leonine head.

Stanton then nodded to the emaciated, elderly man on the other side of the sofa, skull-like head topped with an obvious wig, who rested his clasped hands on a heavy walking stick. "Colonel, Congressman Thaddeus Stevens, Chairman of the Ways and Means Committee." Again Clay bowed slightly; the corpse-like Stevens responded with a barely-perceptible nod of the head.

A subtle change came over Stanton's voice as he introduced the remaining two men in the room, a change which Clay instantly interpreted as the sign of loathing barely contained. "Finally, I believe you may know my other two visitors already, from your time in New Orleans – Major General Butler and his chief of staff, Major Alan Phillips." The two had been standing by the window, appearing to idly watch the traffic coursing down Pennsylvania Avenue; only now did they face Clay.

"I do indeed know General Butler and his aide," replied Clay in a quiet voice; the Colonel made no effort to salute his superior officer, or even acknowledge him with a nod of his head.

"And I know this Goddamn spy from New Orleans," growled the shorter, rounder of the two figures. "Told lies about me to Lincoln, got me recalled from Louisiana. Stanton, why in the Hell are you involving this tin-plated informer in this matter?"

"Why are you still wearing the uniform of the United States?" responded Clay with ominous quietness. "You have hanged civilians without trial, not even a court martial; got rich off trade with the enemy; even stooped to steal the silverware in the houses you occupied. And when Grant and Lincoln gave you a chance to redeem yourself last winter by seizing Fort Fisher, the key to the South's last port, you utterly and completely bungled the affair. The papers said Lincoln has finally relieved you; why do you still wear a general's stars?"

"You might as well ask why Grant has promoted a baby-killer," replied the obese, cross-eyed Butler.

At the mention of the atrocity at the Devereaux plantation, the atmosphere of the room seemed to become electrically charged, as if a thunderstorm were about to strike. Stanton was no fool, and knew the escalating tensions must be stopped. He struck his desk savagely with a metal paperweight, creating a sound like a pistol shot. "Gentlemen, that is enough! Whatever past disagreements you may have had, you will behave yourselves in my presence! We are now concerned with the safety of the Republic in general, and the President in particular. Is that understood?"

Clay looked at Stanton and gave him a barely perceptible nod. While Butler muttered something savage under his breath, the lean, lantern-jawed Phillips smoothly said, "Of course the general agrees, Mr. Secretary."

"So, we have business," wheezed Stanton. "Everyone be seated and we will get to it." The standing figures settled into the remaining chairs. Stanton slowly looked at the various people in the room. "Fine. Colonel Clay, Senator Sumner and Congressman Stevens have come to me just this morning, bringing Butler and Phillips with them. Somehow, they had learned of your mission, and demanded to know the details."

"We have our sources," said Sumner in his deep, resonant voice.

"Colonel Lafayette Baker," replied Clay with no hesitation. The two legislators started, but did not contradict Clay. Clay turned to Stanton and added, "Of course I did not share details of my mission with Baker. I am not surprised that he could piece it together from the questions I asked him and from his... other sources."

"Colonel Baker has been of much use in the holy cause of abolition," said Sumner, who did not look at Clay, but rather seemed focused on some inner landscape known only to himself.

Clay replied in a neutral voice. "I would imagine you find Baker to incur great expenses, for which he would expect recompense."

"Baker is valuable, and worth the cost," murmured the stern-visage Stevens. "Neither here nor there. Point is, what are you doing to protect Lincoln?"

"The threat may not be only to the President," responded Clay. "It could well encompass members of the public, other high ranking officials – even senators and congressmen." At that comment, Sumner's right hand seemed to involuntarily go to his head and start massaging his temple, a vague look of fear coming over his handsome features. Stevens seemed utterly unaffected by the implied threat to himself.

"If traitors come after us, so be it. We are easily replaced. However, Lincoln is less so. Should he leave the land of the living, Andrew Johnson enters the Executive Mansion."

"Johnson is an honorable and loyal man," replied Clay. "He was the only Senator from a Confederate state who refused to follow his state out of the Union."

"He is a Democrat, a drunkard, and a bigot," interjected Sumner indignantly. "Why, he actually owned three slaves until the Emancipation Proclamation freed the poor souls."

Clay was silent for a moment, as he could refute none of Sumner's statements. Vice President Andrew Johnson had been put on the ticket with Lincoln precisely because he was a Democrat, and would be a visible symbol to Union-loyal Democrats that the Republican Party valued and respected them. As for Johnson's weakness for alcohol, everyone knew of the humiliating spectacle that the Vice President made of himself in delivering his inaugural address while clearly under the influence of John Barleycorn. Finally, Union loyalist he might be, but Johnson made no secret of his belief in the inferiority of the black man, and the undesirability of granting him political rights.

"No aspersion is being cast on your individual efforts," said Stevens in his unpleasant monotone voice. "Nonetheless, Sumner and I, and our friends in both Houses of Congress, would be happier if more...comprehensive steps were taken to guard against acts of traitors remaining in the field. We feel that in light of the unsettled state of affairs, a more...military approach is called for. Colonel, just before you came in we were just telling Secretary Stanton that we would like Lincoln to declare martial law and suspend habeas corpus throughout the border areas, including the District of Columbia, and appoint General Butler military governor of those areas until the situation is, ah, stabilized."

Stanton's face had gone red with fury. "Damn it, Lincoln just dismissed Butler from active command! A decision in which I totally agreed! You expect him to give what amounts to dictatorial powers to *that* man?"

"I don't give a damn what you think about my performance in the field, Stanton," growled the frog-like Butler. "No one can deny I know how to bring order and keep the Rebs down."

"In view of General Butler's...history, I feel very certain that the President would never consent to such an arrangement," replied Clay quietly.

"He will if he wants Congress' consent to his plans to reconstruct the Rebel states," rumbled Sumner. "Already many in Congress, including myself, think he is going far too easy on the traitors. Well, we control the purse strings, and he would do well to remember that. General Butler is sound on the issue of equal rights for the colored man; that is more than can be said for most of our generals. Further, in subduing New Orleans he showed that he has the nerve to do whatever needs to be done."

"By God, sirs, this is not to be borne!" exclaimed the apoplectic Secretary of War. "Very well, let us go now, this instant, to the Executive Mansion! I want to be there when Lincoln sends you off with a flea in your ear."

"It was always our intention to have you present at our meeting with Abe," responded Sumner with an airy wave of his large, soft hand. "It is well that you see for yourself that in this matter the power resides with Congress, not the Executive. However, we should do this first thing tomorrow morning. I visited with Mrs. Lincoln earlier today, and she said her husband is determined to go to Ford's Theater tonight, and has no time for us."

"Couldn't she persuade Abe to drop that foolishness?" rasped Stevens with irritation.

Sumner shook his head wryly. "Apparently not. The box has been reserved, and Lincoln dotes on his trips to the theater. She happened to mention to me that the original plans were to go with General and Mrs. Grant, but at the last minute the general cancelled; some nonsense about needing to go to Philadelphia to see their children. She thought her husband would decide to stay home, but instead he invited a staff major named Rathbone and his fiancée to replace the Grants in the presidential box. In any event, after he has had a night of pleasure, Lincoln may be in a better mood to accept some home truths."

With considerable effort the tall, emaciated Stevens struggled to his feet, relying heavily on his stout cane. "Gentlemen, the Senator and I have important engagements at the Capitol. We will meet at the Executive Mansion tomorrow morning." Sumner rose and offered his arm to the obviously crippled Stevens for support; together they limped out of the office. Butler turned his ugly, smirking countenance toward Clay, Stanton and Halleck, and rasped, "Best not fight this; that pair has both houses of Congress behind them. Soon I'll be stamping out the last embers of treason; by '68 the country will be ready to reward me with the Presidency. Then you will see some real changes take place in this country."

Stanton stood erect, somehow making his short frame take on the appearance of an Old Testament prophet. "Tomorrow you may indeed become dictator in all but name," he thundered, his usual asthmatic wheeze strangely absent. "However, today I am the Secretary of War, and you are a miserable cur! Now, leave my office before I have you thrown out!"

The furious Butler made as if to lunge at Stanton, but was restrained by Phillips, who deftly spun the ungainly general toward the open door, formally saluting before he followed Butler into the hall.

There was a long moment of silence, broken when Clay said to Stanton, "It was not wise to speak thus to Butler, given the powers he may have by next week."

"I don't give a damn!" snarled Stanton. "I used to be the highest-paid attorney in Pittsburg, and have lost money every day I've sat in this chair. The moment the price of remaining in this chair becomes crawling to the likes of Benjamin Butler, I'm back to making money." The asthmatic Stanton suddenly changed the subject. "So what is your opinion, Colonel Clay? Do we have something to fear?"

Clay did not answer immediately, but strolled over to the large window and stared down at the traffic on Pennsylvania Avenue. Without looking at Stanton, he began to speak. "I have always worshipped at the altar of the intellect. Sound reasoning, based on concrete evidence, is my god. Yet I know all too well there are things – forces if you will – beyond the brains of man to comprehend. So when I tell you that I have no evidence of any concrete plot against either the government or the citizens of the United States, yet my instincts are screaming that the danger is near, I am not inclined to ignore those instincts. I fear, Mr. Stanton. I fear a danger I sense coming like a runaway horse in the dead of night, invisible, but the power of the hooves all too audible."

"What will you do?" asked Stanton quietly.

Clay sighed. "I will start making the rounds of Washington's brothels." He turned to face Stanton, and smiled at the shock on the Secretary of War's face. "I mean I will be questioning some of the daughters of joy, even though just appearing in such places, even without availing myself of the services available, is degrading for a Clay. You must know that men of violence tend to frequent such places, and boast of their secrets to impress their companion of the evening. I had hoped to avoid the necessity, but in vain." Clay saluted Stanton briefly, then turned and strode from the room before the Secretary of War could say a word.

* * * * *

At a corner table in Willard's dining room, Teresa Duval leaned forward, staring intently at the gaunt, pale noncom seated across from her; the soldier clutched a slim leather-bound volume in both hands, as if it was a dangerous animal needing to be contained. "Well, Corporal Schatz, I assume you have digested some more pages," murmured Duval in a low voice. "Tell me something of its comments."

The corporal had trouble taking his eyes off the volume. "Miss, I do not believe I can continue with this," he commented in a high, German-accented voice. "Back in Saxony, back before the Prussians came and I had to flee for my life, I had heard of Friedrich von Juntz's *Unausprechlichen Kulten*. I laughed at things people said of it; superstitious peasants telling of wild tales. Now twice I have read some; and I think I do not want to read more. I think you can keep your ten dollars. I do not read more, and if wise you be, you will not ask another Deutscher to tell what it say." Schatz gave the volume a convulsive push across the table, and the book slid unerringly into Duval's hands.

Teresa Duval frowned. She had long wanted to know what was in the volume written by Clay's grandfather, the volume he had rescued from Wade Hampton's burning mansion six months ago in Georgia; the volume that Clay kept carefully hidden in his luggage. Duval's curiosity had been aroused, but the volume had been in German, a language that was not among her accomplishments. Luckily, she had found Schatz, and offered him half a month's pay to read the thin volume and tell her what it contained. Clay kept a careful eye on his possessions; so Duval had waited until the previous day to slip into his hotel room and extract the book. She had only given Schatz two hours to read it, knowing that she must replace it where it had been before Clay returned. Unfortunately, in that two hours Schatz had only finished a quarter of the thin volume. Although well-educated in his native tongue, he had found the prose unexpectedly difficult and confusing, as well as disturbingly ominous. Today, Duval had again extracted the book while Clay was out, and in the time allotted Schatz had completed another quarter. However, while he had appeared merely uneasy the previous day, today he appeared truly frightened. Duval knew Schatz to be a veteran of the Wilderness campaign, and wondered how someone who had survived that horror could be scared by a mere book.

Thinking the immigrant was merely trying to extort a higher fee she said, "If it is a matter of money..."

"Is not about money!" Schatz interrupted in an agitated voice. "Von Juntz may have been just a madman, and what he wrote a fantasy; but he believed it. *Gott im Himmel,* if he tried the things he writes about..." The corporal did not finish his sentence, but shook his head before resuming. "I hear there be only few copies of the book that the Church and Bismarck between them did not burn. I pray that is true. If wise you be, burn this one you will."

"Come, Corporal, you are an educated man. Surely you do not subscribe to superstitious nonsense. What could possibly be in the book that is so frightening?"

Schatz actually looked over his shoulder, as if he was being watched, then in a low voice replied, "Very well, miss, I tell you a little. Just a little. Hopefully you believe, but if you do not, if you delve more into these things, then God have mercy on your soul.

"I feel I know this von Juntz, even though he die before I was born. A proud man, an ambitious man, a man who dreamed big dreams and wished big things to do; Germany is cursed with many such. I can tell some things from this book, some things man who write it not aware he reveals. It seem he had studied much, and read much, and gone to out-of-way places in wilds of Eastern Europe, the land where the Turk, Russian and Austrian fight back and forth, where strange people and strange beliefs remain in that ruined and primitive land. You will laugh when I tell you what von Juntz wrote, for you do not read German. In my native tongue you can tell believe it he did, all of it. He believe there be beings of great power, beings not men, which could be summoned by sacrifice. That things be granted a man, if right sacrifice be given. You could tell he know it to be wrong, and some things he would not do, at any price, but you could also tell some things he tempted to do, feeling the good that might come outweigh the bad."

"What kind of sacrifice?" asked Duval, an amused look on her face. '*The things these contemptible peasants believed,*' she thought.

"I think I don't tell you," said Schatz, rising to go. "I can tell you will mock, and think me peasant. You could not believe any of things of which he write. You laugh would when I tell you von Juntz believed the dying could be saved by blood sacrifice to certain dark things; that he believed some of these beings could lie with man or woman, and bring forth offspring, children who be stronger and smarter than any man, children whose bodies so strong they never die, unless killed by violence."

Duval indeed started to laugh, but suddenly a flash of memory hit her. The memory of the night as a child she drowsed in an Irish field, and watched as the screaming herald of death, the Banshee, fluttered and drifted across the moonlit field toward her, until it had seized her chin and gazed with deathless eyes at her, issuing a final pitying moan before disappearing in an instant. How she then leapt up and ran home, only to find her father hanged from the front-yard tree and three English soldiers bending over her mother... Duval shuddered, and the laugh died in her throat. Instead she asked

"Do you really believe there is any truth in what von Juntz wrote?"

The corporal had jammed his kepi onto his head as if to go, but sensing her seriousness, paused to give her a serious answer. "I was in Wilderness from start to finish, in IXth Corps. In my company were 60 soldiers at beginning; at end, only seven of those still were alive and whole, of which I one. Many, many companies have casualties like that. For almost a year death with us every day; dead and dying surrounding those of us waiting our own death. When campaign start, I was free thinker, proud that I have no superstition of religion. But Miss Duval, if you live through something like Wilderness, the days and the nights, you...hear things from comrades. You laugh; then one day you yourself see something like what they say, or hear something like they say, and you laugh no more. I do not know if there is God and Heaven, but now I know there is Devil and Hell." With that enigmatic remark, he quickly marched out of the room.

Duval remained at the table for some minutes, staring at the thin black volume in her hand; thinking of the wounds and burns Clay had suffered recently which had healed so quickly and without leaving scars. A smile slowly came to her lips; she would need to give some careful thought as to how to use this latest information. Meanwhile, she needed to return the book to its hiding place in Clay's hotel room before he returned. As she gracefully rose and exited the Willard's dining room, she also began to formulate a plan by which she would place Clay under even greater obligation to herself.

* * * * *

Clay sat rigidly erect in the parlor of one of Washington's most discrete brothels, his discomfort obvious. Across from him sat the proprietress, who called herself Madame Sarah, a plump, smiling, motherly-seeming figure; motherly, that is, until one noticed her eyes, black and dead as those of a shark.

Amused at the seeming shyness of her guest, she commented “It seems that your companion is taking his sweet time. Are you sure that I cannot arrange something for your amusement, while we wait for the major to – shall we say, tire? I pride myself on catering to every taste; every taste except the French, men with men. For that you must go elsewhere.”

Thin lips drawn even thinner by disapproval, Clay responded. “Thank you, no. As I said, I am only interested in information. It is Major Bierce who is interested in... refreshment.”

Madame Sarah gave a motherly chuckle. “And as you told me when the pair of you arrived, you are interested in information on Confederate sympathizers. I sell services discretely to all who have the money and behave respectably. In return, my clients desire anonymity. To give information on them, even to Union officials, would be bad for business.”

“Even if that information could be of material use to the Union?”

There was another motherly chuckle. “I am strictly neutral, Colonel. Others can kill each other over causes. Within these walls, all are welcome who can pay the tariff.”

Suddenly they both heard a cheerfully off-key rendition of “Maryland, My Maryland” descending the stairs. Ambrose Bierce sauntered into the parlor, and addressed his uncomfortable friend. “Well, Colonel, thank you for waiting. Ready to go; or have you changed your mind about availing yourself of the charming wares above us?”

Casting a venomous look at Bierce, Clay rose, slapped a twenty dollar gold piece down on the table, and bowed ever so slightly to the madam. Then without a word he departed. Bierce grinned salaciously at Sarah, clicked his heels, and hurried to follow Clay onto the street.

Outside the early evening foot traffic was beginning to thin. Clay paused and took several deep lungfuls of the crisp night air, seemingly to expel some foul vapor from his body. A grinning Bierce came up beside him. "Why Clay, you act as if you've never been inside a fancy-house."

"I have not before this day. Only the need to serve the country would drive a Clay into such an...establishment. I am deeply ashamed that I asked you to...question the women upstairs, while I talked to the proprietress. That is disgraceful enough for a Clay."

Bierce emitted one of his unlovely barking laughs. "Clay, you are a caution. If you hadn't asked me to do so, I would have gone on my own. You have favored me with a rare opportunity to combine patriotism with pleasure."

"So were you able to learn something useful?"

Bierce immediately acquired a serious look. "The darling lass did indeed tell me some intriguing things, when I had directed our talk in the proper direction. Apparently she knows Booth, though she has not had the pleasure of servicing him herself. She tells me all the daughters of joy know him; he is a regular visitor at all the high-end brothels in Washington, spending money like a drunken sailor. She has talked to her friends in the trade; seems that lately when he is in liquor he has been boasting that he can save the South single-handed, even with Lee having surrendered. My lass says the girls don't believe him, but they smile and take his money."

"I do not like the sound of that," responded Clay.

Suddenly a grin lit up Bierce's face. "Well, there must be a hundred such houses in Washington, not counting the crib girls and the streetwalkers. Let us move on to another and see if I can pick up similar tales." Bierce looked with eager anticipation down the street where many of Washington's high-end "houses of assignation" were located. Just then, he started and the smile disappeared instantly. Clay noticed the change in expression, and followed the young major's gaze. In his own way, Clay was equally shocked; Teresa Duval had just glided into the well-lit area under one of the rare gas lamps of the disreputable street. She noticed the two officers at the same time, but did not start.

Instead she slid silently up to them and offered Clay her hand, which he automatically took.

"Why Colonel Clay, what an unexpected meeting," she said with a simper. "Whatever brings a man of such sterling character into such a part of town? This can hardly add to the Clay reputation."

"What of your own reputation?" asked Clay coldly.

Duval emitted a silvery, chilling laugh. "The difference between us is that you care for your reputation, while I do not. In any event, I can imagine that you are here for the same reason as I: to learn more about the Rebel-loving bastard, Booth."

"Indeed we did," responded Bierce. "Although the night is young, we have already learned that while Booth ruts like a stoat, he boasts to his paramours that he is going to reverse the results of Appomattox single-handed."

"Interesting," responded Duval. "I have already spoken to two madams, pretending to be a woman of means willing to purchase their businesses as going concerns, if the price is right. While discussing the, shall we say, business environment in Washington, I managed to direct the conversation around to John Wilkes Booth. Both said he could be counted on as a regular and well-paying client, and to disregard his wild threats when drunk against the Government, as they are merely the ravings of an egotistic Rebel sympathizer."

"The proprietress of the...establishment we have just departed would not answer my questions about Booth," replied Clay sourly.

"Perhaps you did not know the right way to ask them," responded Duval demurely.

A worried look had appeared on Clay's bland features. "Be that as it may, a disturbing pattern has been established as to Booth; I do not feel that we need to pursue further this... disreputable line of inquiry. I think we have acquired enough grounds to ask Stanton to order Booth's arrest. I believe I will suggest he be turned over to the tender mercies of Lafayette

Baker. Loath as I am to rely on Baker's methods, he will be able to quickly ascertain whether or no Booth is a serious threat to the nation. I suppose even such...animals as Baker have their uses in dangerous times."

"Stanton will probably have left the War Department by now," said Bierce. "Should we wait until tomorrow morning?"

"Delay could be dangerous," responded Clay. "I know where Stanton's private residence is; not far from Secretary of State Seward's. I am sure this war has accustomed Stanton to late-night calls on his time. He will make sure that Baker gives priority to the arrest of Booth."

"Should we try to hail a carriage?" asked Bierce.

"It is only four blocks, and the night is mild," responded Clay. "With Miss Duval's permission, let us walk."

With Clay briskly setting the pace, they swiftly covered the four-block distance, mostly in silence. As Clay turned a corner, he gestured toward a large brick structure on their left. "That is Seward's residence. We are almost at Stanton's..."

The front door of the brick structure was suddenly thrown open. A man dressed as a servant ran out of the house, colliding blindly with Ambrose Bierce. The startled Bierce grabbed the small man roughly by the shoulders, growling, "Here now, watch where you..."

The wild-eyed man interrupted Bierce. "Murder! Murder! They're murdering Secretary Seward! Help! Police!" He broke away from the major's grasp and ran off, presumably in search of the District's ineffective constables. Through the open door the sounds of a violent struggle came. Frowning slightly, Clay took command. "Follow me, Bierce! Miss Duval, wait outside!"

Smiling grimly, Duval muttered, "Not bloody likely," and followed the two officers into the building at a run. She did not notice a nervous figure on the corner opposite Seward's residence. David Herald gave the brick structure a long glance, concluded that Lewis Powell's attack on the Secretary of State had gone badly wrong, and took to his heels, deciding to leave the massive Rebel to his own devices.

Once Clay, Bierce and Duval were inside the parlor, it was clear that the commotion came from the second floor. Taking the stairs two at a time, Clay charged recklessly up the slippery steps, drawing his revolver as he ran. Bierce followed more slowly, clumsily working his own gun free of its holster; while Duval decided to forgo her favorite straight-razor and instead drew a small but deadly Sharp's pepperbox from a cunningly concealed pocket on her frock.

The second-floor corridor was dimly lit by flaring gas jets. On the floor lay a handsome young man, bearing a noticeable resemblance to the photographs of the Secretary of State. Blood poured from a bloody wound on his head; eyes focused on nothing, he babbled nonsense. From a room behind him came sounds and cries of a terrible struggle. Without hesitation Clay leaped the body of the wounded youth and hurtled himself into that room, quickly followed by Bierce and Duval. In the dim light of the room's single gas jet, a hellish, confusing sight confronted them.

A small, frail-looking old man lay on his back on a bed, a bizarre metal framework encasing his head and neck. Clay suddenly remembered reading that the Secretary of State had recently fractured his jaw in a carriage accident, and concluded that this was Seward. Over the prone figure hunched a gigantic man, slashing at the statesman's throat with a Bowie knife. In the blink of an eye the assassin delivered two vicious blows; the first was entirely stopped by the metal brace, while the second was deflected upward from the neck into the old man's cheek, cutting a gash through which teeth could be glimpsed. Clay was about to shoot the attacker when suddenly two figures leaped on the man: one, a wiry man in a sergeant's uniform, who grabbed the arm holding the knife; the other a teenage girl who raked her nails across the man's face while sobbing hysterically. The trio lurched about the room, making it impossible to get a clear shot at the assassin. Dropping his pistol, Clay lunged at the three figures just as Lewis Powell sent the girl flying toward the bed while simultaneously twisting his knife arm free and stabbing the sergeant in his upper body. Just as the noncom collapsed to the floor with a cry, Clay reached Powell and delivered a blow to his face with all the considerable strength that the deceptively slight colonel possessed. To Clay's utter amazement, the assassin shrugged off the blow, picked Clay up bodily and threw him at Bierce and Duval, who were knocked over like bowling pins. Snarling, Powell turned to the bed just in time to see the teenage girl roll the dazed and wounded old man into the narrow space between wall and bed, then turn with an answering snarl to face the Rebel killer, making it instantly obvious he would have to kill her to get to Seward. Powell turned back to the three new arrivals, who in various ways had lost their guns in the melee. He saw them stagger upright, Bierce a little more slowly than Clay and Duval, and begin to lunge for their lost weapons. With a cry of frustrated rage, Powell ran from the room with speed that was astonishing for a man of his size. In mere seconds his heavy footsteps could be heard pounding down the street outside.

"After him!" Bierce cried, and made to run after the fleeing assassin. Right as he reached the door, Clay grabbed his arm with an iron grip and said, "We dare not leave Secretary Seward wounded; he could die before help arrives. Besides, we cannot be sure that there was not a reserve assassin. Taking care of this situation must be our priority. Miss Duval, come help me examine Mr. Seward. Bierce, examine the sergeant."

Clay and Duval approached the bed where the crying but defiant teenager snarled, "Who are you? Are you here to kill Da too?"

"No, Miss Seward, I am Colonel Clay of General Grant's staff. Miss Duval here is an experienced nurse in the Sanitary Commission. We must get your father back into bed, and tend to his wounds." Numbly the brave youngster moved aside, shivering now that the danger was passed. Between them Clay and Duval extracted Seward from the gap and laid him gently back on his sickbed. The old New Yorker was a terrible sight. Semi-conscious from shock, his eyes rolled wildly, blood poured from the gashed cheek, some finding its way down his mouth, giving rise to periodic gagging coughs. Clay looked at Duval and said, "Can you stop the bleeding? He will die if it is not stopped."

Duval forced herself to frown, concealing the arousal that the sight of blood and pain always created in her. "I could, if I had some basic medical supplies; sutures, catgut, bandages and the like."

"The sergeant keeps a medical bag in the far corner," said Seward's daughter unexpectedly. At Clay's questioning glance, she explained, "He is an army nurse, sent over by Mr. Stanton when he heard of Da's accident. If he hadn't gone after that man, Da would be dead." While Duval swiftly retrieved the medical bag and began to rummage through its contents, the girl suddenly emitted a shriek. "Frederick! My brother Frederick! I was in the hall when Frederick saw the man take out a pistol. Frederick went after the man, and that awful man started hitting him over the head with the gun; hitting him again and again until the gun flew to pieces. I guess that was why he went after Da with a knife. Is Frederick...is he..."

"Your brother is badly hurt, but he is alive," said Bierce, as he tended to the moaning sergeant. He did not add that he feared the young man's skull was fractured, and that he might not live out the night. "This fellow here is in better shape; no vital organ was involved, and I have staunched the bleeding."

"Miss Seward, you have been unbelievably brave this evening," said Clay. "However, I must ask you to be brave a little longer. Can you summon a local doctor, as well as the police?"

Silently she nodded. Clay then went on.

"One favor I want to ask of you. When people ask what happened, please do not mention us. Give the sergeant the credit for driving off the assassin. His wound gives him the right to that credit."

"If you insist," she responded.

"I do. Our involvement tonight must be our secret, for reasons which I may not reveal to you, but which are sufficient.

Now, let me take you as far as the front door." Unspoken was Clay's desire to escort the teenager past her wounded brother. She flinched as they went past the young man, still lying on the floor babbling incomprehensibly. Thankfully, she seemed steady enough when she reached the front door, and she strode purposefully off without a backward glance.

Clay returned to the grisly sight, which had been the Secretary of State's bedroom, a pensive look on his face. Bierce had just finished bandaging the sergeant's shoulder; he looked up and asked "How is Miss Seward holding up?"

"Amazingly well," said Clay, a note of admiration in his voice. "The Seward stock seems to be sound. Miss Duval, how is the Secretary?"

"He will live, if infection does not set in," she replied as she wiped her bloody hands on the bed sheet. "I have given him laudanum to help him sleep; that is the best that can be done for him at this time."

"Please see what you can do for Frederick Seward," replied Clay. "I fear he may be fatally wounded, but we should do our best for such a brave young man." Duval nodded, and silently glided out of the room.

"This is puzzling," mused Clay aloud. "Important as the Secretary of State is, it is hard to see how his assassination could reverse Confederate fortunes at this late date. And where is Booth? My instincts scream that he must be behind this. It is not surprising that he had hired muscle, but I would expect him to at least witness his handiwork."

Bierce stood and nodded, his jaunty cynicism absent for a change. "Perhaps mere revenge was enough for these Johnnies. After all, Seward was one of the founders of the Republican Party, while Lincoln came to it relatively late..." Bierce trailed off; he had noticed that Clay had frozen as stock-still as a statue. Bierce had seen this a few times before, always when Clay was engaged in furious thought.

After a long moment Clay unfroze. "Booth must want to decapitate the Federal Government in a single blow; perhaps more, but that at a minimum. Seward was only a part. Booth is an egotist, and would naturally reserve the most important role for himself. He is an actor, and would want to preen on center stage…" Clay's voice trailed off; what little color there was in his face drained away.

Bierce's features had turned equally pale. "Didn't Senator Sumner say the Lincolns were going to Ford's Theater tonight?"

Both men darted into the hallway, Clay in the lead. As they shouldered past Duval, Bierce shouted "Stay here until help arrives; then have the Provost send every trooper available to Ford's Theater!" Not waiting for a reply, the officers were down the stairs and out the door.

There was no question of waiting for a carriage or trying to shanghai horses; Clay and Bierce simply ran for all they were worth, passing scores of pedestrians astonished at the spectacle of two senior officers apparently running a footrace. Bierce was long-legged and athletic; but he could barely keep up with Clay, whose short legs pumped like pistons. In less than a minute they had covered the three blocks to Ford's Theater. Clay grabbed the astonished doorman by his collar and shouted in a voice very much deeper that the one he normally used, "***Which is the President's box***?"

The rattled man pointed to a curving stairway "Up and last door on the left."

Clay threw the man aside and leapt up the stairs, taking them three at a time, Bierce doing his best to keep up. Through the doors opening on the main theater they faintly heard an actor declaim, "Don't know the manners of good society, eh? Well, I guess I know enough to turn you inside out, old gal; you sockdologizing old man-trap!" followed by a burst of laughter from the audience. And then, as they approached the last door on the left, they heard a sharp bang, no louder than a door slammed shut by the wind. Clay gave out a deep, inarticulate cry of agony and loss, and threw himself at the locked door. The Ford brothers had not skimped on quality in building their theater; despite his strength, Clay bounced off the heavy wooden door. Bierce caught up with Clay and gasped, "Again and together!" Their combined, desperate strength did the trick, and the door splintered into several large pieces. They stumbled through the wreckage of the door, to find a hellish tableau.

Abraham Lincoln sat in a large, upholstered rocking chair, eyes closed, head fallen to his chest as if he were asleep, a small trickle of blood coming out of his hair and down the back of his neck. Holding his hands was a plump Mary Lincoln, eyes crazed, screaming incoherent phrases to her unconscious husband. A dazed-looking major sat huddled in a corner of the box, blood flowing freely down his left arm, while a pretty young woman stared in horror. Clay darted to the front of the box, frantic to find Booth. He looked down on the stage, but could see no sign of the actor. However, some of the theatergoers were clambering up to the stage and running to stage left. Clay was about to leap to the stage and follow them when a frantic Mary Lincoln grabbed his arms and screamed, "Save my husband! Can you save my husband? He won't speak to me! Make him speak to me! He always speaks to me when I ask, but he won't speak to me!" Clay looked into the screaming woman's eyes, and saw madness, loneliness and despair all mixed up together. After a moment's hesitation, he decided that apprehending the assassin could be left to others, and that his place was with his Commander in Chief.

Suddenly a pair of hands grasped the edge of the box; a young lieutenant had made an impressive leap from the stage. Clay grasped the hands and easily drew the officer up into the box. Puffing, the young man saluted. "Lieutenant Charles Leale, sir. I am a doctor, and someone was saying the President had been shot."

"That is true, Lieutenant. If you can..."

"He has stopped breathing!" screamed Mary Lincoln who had darted back to the still form in the chair. "My husband has stopped breathing!"

Dr. Leale swiftly examined the President's head, then shouted, "Help me lay him flat." Clay and Bierce lent their aid; then to everyone's astonishment Leale placed his mouth over Lincoln's and began blowing puffs of air into the President's lungs. Laura Keene, proprietor of the company that was presenting the play, had entered the box, exclaiming, "What is that man doing to the President?" Behind her, a growing number of curious and horrified members of the audience were visible, trying to crowd their way into the box.

"Bierce, block that door and let no one else in!" shouted Clay. Without a word Bierce leapt into the doorway, drawing his revolver as he did so. The surging crowd outside recoiled respectfully. Clay now addressed Laura Keene.

"Dr. Leale is apparently very well trained. He is administering artificial respiration, the latest practice in reviving apparently drowned people and others who have ceased to breathe on their own." Clay then turned to the young woman who was trying to comfort the agitated Mary Lincoln. "Exactly what happened in here?"

The young lady was pale but self-possessed, despite the blood on her evening dress and the hysterical mutterings of Mary Lincoln. "It all happened so fast I cannot say. I did not even hear the man enter the box. There was a bang, not that loud, and just as I smelled gunpowder, I heard Mrs. Lincoln begin to scream. My fiancée – Major Rathbone – leapt to his feet and tried to capture the man, but the intruder slashed him with a Bowie knife." Clay looked to the major, propped against the wall, for confirmation, but the bewhiskered young officer was pale and in shock, and seemed hardly conscious of Mrs. Keene's efficient efforts to staunch the bleeding in his arm. It was clear he was in no shape to give immediate testimony. Clay turned back to the young lady, who continued her story.

"As the Major fell, the man stepped onto the railing of the box, and made to jump onto the stage. But as he leapt, the spur on one of his boots caught on the American flag that draped the front of the box, causing him to tumble wildly. I looked down at the stage and saw him struggle to his feet with difficulty; it looked as if he had broken a bone in his leg. He waved his bloody knife about and shouted something, but many in the audience had begun to scream, and I could not make out exactly what he said. Then, in obvious pain, he limped off the stage. Now you know what I know." She abruptly turned, and abandoning the calmer Mary Lincoln as well as Clay, knelt down to help Mrs. Keene minister to Major Rathbone. Clay turned to see Dr. Leale rise from the President's still form, absently wiping bloody fingers on his uniform tunic. He went to the near-catatonic Mary Lincoln, took her face gently in his hands, and murmured, "I have restarted your husband's breathing, and removed the clot at the site of the wound that was allowing pressure to build on his brain. Nevertheless, we must move him to somewhere we could make him more comfortable."

"The Executive Mansion," she said dully. "Call a carriage and let us take him there to recover."

Leale caste a furtive glance at Clay. With soothing words he guided the First Lady to a vacant chair, where she sat unresistingly. Then Leale stepped over to Clay and began to murmur in a low voice.

"Sir, you are the ranking officer, and must take charge here. However, I must tell you that in my opinion the President could not survive a carriage trip to the Executive Mansion, not with the unevenness of Washington's streets; a serious jolt could be instantly fatal." Leale hesitated, then went on to say, "I must further tell you that in my opinion the President's wound is mortal, and he cannot recover. The most that can be done is to move him to more comfortable and quiet surroundings where his final hours will be more peaceful and dignified. We cannot leave the President to die on the floor in a theater."

Clay's face had lost whatever small expression it normally possessed. After a moment's hesitation, Clay reached a decision. "There is a row of boarding houses directly across the street. Undoubtedly there will be a room in one of them that will serve the purpose." Raising his voice, Clay called out "Bierce, are there soldiers in the crowd at there?"

Over the buzzing commotion Bierce answered, "Half a dozen or so."

"Have them fashion a stretcher for the President. Tell them to tear up whatever wood or fabric they need to make it."

In an astonishingly short time it was done. Four pale-faced soldiers gently placed the comatose Lincoln on the improvised stretcher. Bierce cleared a path for them through the morbid, confused crowd with a combination of shoves, ominous gestures with his revolver, and surprisingly obscene yet creative curses. Alongside the stretcher walked Leale. Clay brought up the rear, gently guiding Mary Lincoln who had the appearance and shamble of a sleepwalker, leaving Major Rathbone to be tended by his fiancée and Laura Keene.

The somber procession emerged from the theater to find the street filled with people. Somehow, the word had spread like wildfire, and hundreds had come to see the wounded President. Normally, Clay despised such morbid curiosity seekers, but something about the earnest quietness of the crowd made it seem respectful, even reverential, forestalling his anger. Many removed their hats as the stretcher went by. Clay raised his voice and shouted, "We need somewhere nearby to take the President, so that he may receive medical attention!"

"Over here!" shouted someone from across the way. Clay quickly scanned the opposite side of the street, and saw that the speaker was a one-legged veteran standing in an open doorway, leaning heavily on a crutch. As the procession reached the door, the mutilated ex-soldier spoke. "There is an empty bedroom just off the second-floor landing." As the stretcher passed him, he automatically saluted the motionless form it contained. Clay paused to speak to the man.

"You can do a further service for your country. Make sure that no one but doctors, Secretary Stanton, or those personally approved by me comes through that door." The crippled man saluted again, then turned to the door with an expression on his face that made the nearest members of the crowd recoil back involuntarily.

The bedroom was spacious enough and reasonably clean. However, the single bed it contained was sized for a normal man, inadequate for Lincoln's 6' 4" frame. The soldiers had to lay him diagonally across the bed to give him sufficient room.

Suddenly Clay could hear an asthmatic, ragged sound working its way up the stairs. Preceded by the sound of his labored breathing, Edwin Stanton erupted into the room. He took one look at the silent figure on the bed, and made a choking sound. Then he rounded on Clay. "You bastard! You incompetent bastard! I tasked you to protect this Government. That meant the man on this bed! Now he's dying..."

At that phrase Mary Lincoln awoke from her trance, and began to howl inconsolably. Stanton looked at her with irritation, then spoke again to Clay. "Get out! I don't want to lay eyes on you again. Get out!!!"

Looking as if he had been slapped, Clay stiffly saluted the Secretary of War and left the room. He was followed by Bierce, who pointedly did not salute Stanton.

* * * * *

Dawn was approaching. Clay and Bierce stood vigil a half block from the boardinghouse where Abraham Lincoln lay dying, just beyond the far fringes of the crowd that stood their own vigil. There was nothing for them to do, no point in remaining, but neither suggested to the other that they leave.

Finally, after several hours of silence, Clay was the first to speak. "Say what you will about Stanton, it appears he is efficient. Look how quickly he established sentries and set up a temporary telegraph office. Look at the constant stream of messengers and couriers entering and leaving. I imagine he is directing the pursuit of Booth and his accomplices, alerting the military commands, recalling Grant to Washington, all without leaving that boardinghouse."

Bierce muttered an obscenity. “How can you speak well of that bastard, after what he said to you?”

“He said nothing but the truth,” replied Clay in an emotionless voice. “I was given a critical assignment, the most important of my life. I failed.”

“Hell, Alphonso, you didn’t fail. You gathered up all of the strings at the end. If you had just had one more minute, you could have stopped this.”

With a wintry smile, Clay replied “So your view is that the operation was successful, although the patient died. I am afraid I cannot take that view of things.”

Before Bierce could answer Clay, they both noticed a short, stout figure stepping out of the building where Lincoln lay. He looked around, spotted them, and pushing his way through the knot of onlookers strode toward them with the directness of a bullet. Edwin Stanton came to a stop before them, breathing heavily but saying nothing. Then abruptly he began to speak.

“One of my aides said he spotted you two standing here. Things are terrible in there; thought I would take a moment to come here and offer an unqualified apology for what I said earlier. It was my grief speaking, not what I really thought. You were closer than Colonel Baker, certainly closer than me. If you failed, how much greater is my failure? Besides, I heard from Seward’s daughter what you did; the Secretary of State owes you his life.”

A trace of irritation in his voice, Clay responded. “I had asked her to be quiet about the involvement of Bierce and myself.”

“Don’t be hard on her. My people tell me she was in shock; no wonder, for a sixteen-year-old who has seen what she has seen. No, we will keep your role quiet and give credit to the sergeant; poor bastard deserves some credit anyway. So Colonel Clay, Major Bierce, I offer you both my unqualified apology for my outburst, and beg your forgiveness.”

There was a long pause before Clay said, “It is granted.”

There was even a longer pause before Bierce finally chimed in. “Oh hell, never heard a general admit he was wrong, much less a Cabinet member. Guess the least I can do to pay for such a sight is accepting your apology.”

“Thank you, gentlemen,” replied Stanton gravely.

“I have noticed a number of doctors come and go during the night,” said Clay abruptly. “Do they hold any more hope than does Leale?”

Stanton shook his head angrily. “No. They all try to dress it up in pretty words, but I was a pretty fair lawyer, and am used to getting to the truth behind a witnesses’ evasions. It is a matter of time; hours at most.”

“Are the Vice President and the rest of the Cabinet safe?” asked Bierce.

Stanton nodded. “I’ve had guards placed over all of them. Grant too. Can you imagine? He was going to ride the cars down from Philadelphia completely unprotected, just his wife and himself. I told the district commander to smother that train with troops, no matter what Grant says.” Suddenly there was a high, keening wail coming from the boardinghouse where the President lay dying. Stanton frowned. “That damn woman! Mrs. Lincoln has been hanging about the room, alternately babbling nonsense or screaming like a banshee. Woman’s crazier than a March hare. In my opinion, she has been insane for years. How on Earth did Lincoln put up with it?”

Clay shook his head slowly, sadly. “Mary Todd Lincoln was not always that way. I know the Todds well; they are a family prominent in my part of Kentucky. Most of the men are cruel, most of the women high-strung. Mary Todd was different: intelligent, thoughtful, caring, a helpmate and asset to Abraham Lincoln. I have heard the same things you have heard. I do not know whether it was the strain of losing two of her children, or if the Todd blood finally began to show in her, but she has changed. You are probably right when you say she is losing her mind. Still, pity her. She must be aware she is losing her mind, and for such a proud, accomplished woman, that must be a fate worse than death."

"Be that as it may, you are welcome at any time to come in and pay your respects to the President; if that means anything to you, that is."

"I appreciate the offer," responded Clay. "I may avail myself of it, in a few minutes. I would just like to watch the sunrise, if I may."

"Well, I will go with the Secretary right now," responded Bierce solemnly. "It is probably not a good idea to crowd that little room."

Impulsively, Stanton reached out and shook Clay's hand. Then he and Bierce went back to the boardinghouse, leaving Clay to his thoughts and the lightening sky. He had not been alone for more than a minute when he heard Teresa Duval's voice.

"Alphonso, I'm glad I found you. Is it true what they say, that the President is dying?"

He looked at her, and noticed in the faint light of predawn that she showed some signs of exhaustion; yet the signs detracted not a whit from her unusual, exotic beauty.

"Too true. It will not be long."

Duval caressed his cheek with her left hand. "Poor dear. You blame yourself. Don't. It was that Rebel-loving bastard Booth who pulled the trigger, not you."

After a pause, Clay asked "How are things at the Seward's?"

Duval shrugged negligently; it was a matter of small import to her. "Old man Seward now has more doctors than hairs on his head. It may be touch and go, but I think he will recover. The sergeant should be fine, always assuming no infection sets it. It is the young man, Frederick Seward, who may not make it. His skull is definitely fractured. There was a time when I would have said he had no chance. However, ever since Bierce recovered from being shot through the brain, I am a bit more optimistic about such injuries."

Clay started as he remembered Bierce's seemingly miraculous recovery from his wound at Kennesaw Mountain the previous year. He remembered how hopeless the injury had seemed. He also remembered what he had read in his own grandfather's book, *Unausprechlichen Kulten*, about how those on the precipice of death could be drawn back from that precipice – provided the proper sacrifice was made to certain... entities. Blood sacrifice. However, not the blood of the lamb, not the blood of an innocent; only the blood of an evil creature, able to look upon hell and understand the meaning of what it saw, would do. He remembered how he had drawn from among Sherman's prisoners one of raiders who had been with Nathan Bedford Forrest at the unspeakable Fort Pillow massacre; taken him and had done...certain things. And Clay remembered how after those...things...had been done, done in accordance with the rituals described in his grandfather's book, Bierce's impossible recovery had begun. An idea was forming in Clay's brain, but he worried where he could find on such short notice someone evil enough to please the... entities.

"Alphonso, are you all right?" asked Teresa Duval. "You seemed a thousand miles away."

Clay forced himself to grimace a smile at Duval. "It is not important. However, there is something of extreme sensitivity upon which we must speak. I do not trust the street." Clay glanced at the yawning, unkempt entrance to an alley just a few feet from where they stood. "Let us go back here, where we are certain not to be overheard." Without waiting for a reply, Clay entered the alley; he did not look back, but could here the soft whooshing of Duval's dress. He turned right at the first opportunity, and entered a grimy, disused courtyard, faced only by blank walls.

"Now what is so secret..." Duval started to ask, before Clay's fist struck her jaw with a paralyzing blow. Her head snapped backward and struck a brick wall with scarcely less force, and she slid insensibly to the ground. Clay knelt and felt the pulse at her neck; it was faint but regular. He breathed a sigh of relief;

she must be alive for the ceremony. Clay drew a Bowie knife from beneath his tunic. His voice dropping an octave, acquiring a deep disturbing resonance that it did not ordinarily possess, Clay began to chant unknown words in an archaic language.

* * * * *

Teresa Duval slowly awoke from a nightmarish dream of banshee howls, corpses dangling from trees, and figures bent with obscene purpose over a woman who lay beside a burning building. Her eyes began to function in the strengthening light of dawn, and she could see that she lay on her side in a filthy courtyard. Seated across from her, his back against the opposite wall, was Alphonso Clay, a look of infinite sadness on his face, a Bowie knife held loosely in his right hand. From the ache in her jaw and back of her head, she realized Clay had coshed her. But she could not figure out why...and then it came to her. She remembered what the terrified Corporal Schatz had said about the contents of *Unausprechlichen Kulten*, about how one life could be saved for the sacrifice of another. With growing fury, she saw what Clay had intended: to trade her life for Lincoln's. Staggering to her feet, she hiked her skirts and drew out the straight razor which had served her so well so many times. True, she thought, Clay was holding the Bowie knife; to her mind, that would merely make what was to come more interesting. Crouching, advancing on the balls of her feet, she approached Clay from the side, until she was close enough to be sure that she could cut his throat to the bone with a sudden lunge, before he could respond with the Bowie. She paused before her final leap, puzzled. Clay showed no signs of assuming a defensive or offensive posture, no sign of even seeing her. He simply stared into space, that look of infinite sadness never changing. Hoping to get some reaction from him, she began to taunt.

"Buggering filthy bastard! You were going to slaughter me like a spring lamb, weren't you? Didn't have the belly for it, did you? Well, stand up, you betraying whoreson. I'm going to enjoy this. I am going to keep you half an hour dying."

Clay did not move, save to tuck the Bowie back inside his tunic. "I could not do it," he said, a note of wonderment in his voice. "I knew what needed to be done, what I must do; yet I could not do it. I do not understand it."

Without warning, Duval leapt forward, razor poised for a killing stroke. At the last possible moment, she checked the motion that would have severed the arteries in Clay's neck. She was aware of an unfamiliar burning sensation in her eyes; with some amazement, she realized they were tears – not the simulated tears she often used to great effect, but real tears. "Damn you, you were going to kill me. I loved you, God damn it, and you were going to kill me!"

Finally, Clay turned to look directly into her dark eyes. "Yes, I was going to kill you. The sacrifice would have been acceptable; I suspect there are few more evil than you on the face of the Earth. Why could I not kill you? Why did I condemn the President to a death I might have prevented?"

"You idiot," spat Duval, in a husky, breaking voice. "It is because you love me!" Then she attacked his mouth with her own. Her razor clattered to the ground, and for the second time the two of them engaged in an act that was more mutual rape than an act of love.

* * * * *

An hour later, Clay ascended the steps of the boardinghouse; the sentries recognized him, and had obviously been told not to stop him. He entered the second-floor room to find the motionless Lincoln attended by two doctors, Mary Lincoln, his dazed-looking adult son Robert, and Edwin Stanton; outside the door hovered a number of War Department orderlies who dared not enter unless Stanton asked them to. Stanton looked up as Clay entered, and answered his unspoken question.

"Any moment now." Mary Lincoln emitted a howl, but when Stanton looked at her with irritation, she lapsed back into silence. Stanton returned his attention to the dying form on the bed, and began to speak to Clay without looking at him.

"You know, I first met him before the war in Chicago, when we were litigating a patent case. I thought him the biggest scrub fool you could find in a month of Sundays, and could barely stand the sight of him. Then, when he appointed me to the War Department, I thought him a weakling being run by Seward; I would call him the 'original gorilla' behind his back. God forgive me. Only later did I find out that he knew what I called him, and did not care. During the war I began to see how sly he could be, and how clever; only later did I gradually come to see how great and noble. Only at the end did I come to realize he was the greatest man to ever lead this country, or likely ever to lead. And I never told him." Stanton turned to face Clay; there were tears in his eyes. "And now I never can tell him."

One of the doctors had been holding Lincoln's hand, while looking at his pocket watch. He suddenly snapped the watch shut, and quietly announced, "It is over."

Mary Lincoln began to howl incomprehensible words of grief. Impatiently, Stanton motioned to two of his aides who stood in the doorway, saying, "Take this woman away, and do not let her back in." Accompanied by the silently ineffectual eldest son Robert, Mary Todd Lincoln left the room of death in a halo of wails and tears. Stanton continued to look at the still form on the bed for a long moment before he spoke again.

"Now he belongs to the ages."

Even the articulate Alphonso Clay could think of nothing to add.

Chapter 3:
"He Has Sounded Forth The Trumpet That Shall Never Call Retreat..."

The inadequate, watery morning sunshine filtered feebly through the windows of the Secretary of War's office, illuminating the faces of men who showed various combinations of exhaustion, despair, rage and determination.

Edwin Stanton sat at his desk, clutching a still-damp poster announcing $50,000 for the apprehension of John Wilkes Booth. Also offered was $25,000 each for David Herold and John Surratt, making the total reward an unbelievable $100,000 – four years' salary for the President of the United States. Stanton's people had been busy; the top of the poster was graced with high-quality photographic images of all three men, obtained from diverse sources.

Lieutenant General Ulysses Grant sat in a wing chair to the immediate right of Stanton, fiddling with his curious mechanical cigar-lighter. Normally, Halleck would have sat there. However, the Chief of Staff and his troublesome elbow had been banished to a chair by the window. Halleck had tried to derail Grant's career early in the war, and knew that Grant was aware of that. Halleck was aware it was only a matter of time before he was also banished altogether from Washington to some obscure command. To his own astonishment, he realized that he found the prospect rather attractive.

In a chair to Stanton's left sat Colonel Lafayette Baker, who was occupied with scowling at Clay and Bierce, who lounged on the sofa in front of Stanton's desk. Baker was all too aware that the attacks on Lincoln and Seward did not speak well for his stewardship of the capital's security, and was furiously thinking of how he could shift blame, preferably to Clay and Bierce.

"So let me sum it up for you," Stanton suddenly announced, his voice surprisingly free of traces of asthma. "We are very sure that Herold and Surratt acted as accomplices with Booth; Herold was identified lounging outside Seward's house last night by someone who patronized the pharmacy where the bastard worked. And we have confirmed that Surratt was constantly in Booth's company the last few months; that, combined with the fact that Powell was taken at the boarding house run by Surratt's mother, pretty much nails his hide to Booth's ass."

"Are you certain Atzerodt and Powell are involved?" asked Clay quietly.

The Secretary of War nodded vigorously. "The killer at Seward's was described as a monstrous, powerful man; you can testify to that yourself. The Provost noticed such a man outside the Surratt boarding house, and decided not many could match such a...unique description so closely. Surprisingly, Powell allowed himself to be handcuffed quietly enough. The Provost troopers then ran him by Seward's place; the young girl went hysterical at the sight of him. Also, Miss Duval has been by the jail, and has identified Powell as the man who was trying to murder Seward. That is enough for me. As for George Atzerodt, several witnesses recalled a drunken Deutscher lurking around Vice-President Johnson's hotel. One of Baker's men remembered a German with a weakness for alcohol sometimes boarded at Surratt's, and went by to question him. When Atzerodt caught sight of the blue uniform, he started yelling that he hadn't done anything, even before Baker's man had a chance to ask a question. They are involved, and will swing for it."

"I understand Colonel Baker has arrested Mrs. Surratt and her daughter," said Bierce. "Is it really necessary to add to a mother's grief by imprisoning her and her child?"

"We need the son," growled Baker ominously. "If he has any particle of family feeling, he will surrender in order to free his mother and sister."

"What if he does not have family feeling?" asked Bierce.

Baker shrugged negligently. "Then a couple more Copperheads hang. Two more or less hardly matter, in this war with more than half a million dead."

"What is the prognosis for the Secretary of State?" asked Halleck, absently scratching his elbow.

"Major Bierce and I paid a brief visit to the Seward home before coming here," responded Clay. "He is still not entirely out of danger, but is at least able to sit in a wheelchair and talk for brief periods."

"Best keep knowledge of Lincoln's murder from him as long as possible," said Stanton. "Emotional distress could cause a relapse."

"I am afraid he already knows," responded Clay. "When we visited him this morning, Secretary Seward asked to be moved near the window, to catch some fresh air. After a few moments at the window, he whispered, 'The President is dead.' Before I could think of how to respond, he added, 'I can see the flag at the Executive Mansion is at half-mast. Someone is dead; if it is not Lincoln, he would have been here already, to check on my condition.'" Clay saw no reason to add that Seward had then begun to cry.

"Let's hope that Seward is tough enough so that this does not cause a worsening of his condition," said Stanton.

"Secretary Seward impresses me as tough enough," replied Clay quietly.

"What is being done to capture Booth?" Grant asked Stanton in his quiet voice.

"We've already traced him northeast into Maryland. Goddamn guards on the road saw two horsemen answering the descriptions given for Booth and Herold ride by bold as brass, and did nothing to stop them."

"Couldn't expect them to," Halleck suddenly added, scratching his elbow. "No word could have reached them as to the assassination; it would be unjust to blame them."

Stanton growled something under his breath, but did not openly contradict his chief of staff. "Anyway, we have cavalry patrols scouring the Maryland countryside, and patrol boats on the Potomac in case they try to slip into Virginia. Unfortunately, there are plenty of Copperheads in both states that would give them shelter. Furthermore, we cannot be sure of their ultimate destination. Are they going to make for Baltimore and try to take ship to Europe? Will they head into the Deep South and try to hide indefinitely? Hell, will they have the guts to try to cross the whole country and make for Mexico? We have to assume any and all of those possibilities. Right now all we can do is wait until they are sighted."

"Then what?" asked Bierce.

"If local troops can't corner them, we will send a flying squad of cavalry after them. Baker?"

The saturnine Baker grimaced as he replied. "I have assembled a reliable force, small enough to move quick, large enough to overcome any likely resistance. I have waiting Captain Edward Doherty and a company of the 16th New York Cavalry. With them will go Luther Baker, a cousin of mine; I trust Luther to make sure that Doherty and his men stay in line. Most importantly, they must not give in to rage and kill the bastard. We need Booth alive, at all costs."

Clay nodded. "It is unlikely that a vain, shallow theatrical like Booth came up with such a scheme on his own. It is vital that he live to tell us what he knows. Only after we are sure he is empty of information should the gallows be allowed to do its duty."

The pale, emaciated form of General Rawlins appeared in the doorway. "Excuse the interruption, but there is a visitor for General Grant. Sam, I think you will want to see him."

Looking irritated, Grant replied, "Well, who is it?"

Rawlins hesitated for a moment, and then said, "James Longstreet."

Grant seemed genuinely startled. He got up, replacing his cigar lighter in a tunic pocket, and said to the room in general "Well, if Lee's second in command wants to see me, I better let him see me." He began walking to the door, but suddenly found his way blocked by Alphonso Clay.

"Sir, with deepest respect, I cannot allow you to meet alone with a high-ranking Confederate officer, not until we know the depth of the conspiracy."

Grant's features clouded over. "Doggone it, Clay. Pete Longstreet is one of my oldest friends. He was best man at my wedding. No matter how this war has separated us, he would never do me harm off the battlefield. Now, out of my way."

Clay did not move. "With respect sir, I cannot."

"Colonel, do you wish to face a court-martial?"

"If it keeps you from harm, I would count it a small price."

Grant's face had reddened, and he seemed about to explode. However, with a visible effort he reigned in his temper. "Very well, Colonel. You and General Rawlins will be with me while I meet with Pete. Surely the two of you can handle one middle-aged veteran."

Clay hesitated only a moment before replying "That is acceptable, sir."

"Glad to have your approval," replied Grant in a dryly ironic voice. Turning to the rest of the room, "Mr. Secretary, gentlemen, please excuse me for a few minutes. I must go see an old friend."

Grant led Clay and Rawlins into the large outer office where an armed sentry stood eyeing the visitor suspiciously. James Longstreet was dressed in a neat but threadbare black suit, and held a somewhat tattered planter's hat in his right hand. He wore the clothing with the unconscious unease that those used to uniforms often display in civilian clothes. The formidable warrior whose motto was "Can't lead from behind" showed nervousness never displayed on the battlefield. He seemed unable to decide how to start.

Grant saved him the trouble by thrusting his hand forward. "Pete, I am glad to see you survived...all this. It has been far too long." Slowly, the massive Rebel took the much smaller Grant's hand as Clay tensed.

All that happened was that Longstreet said "I am glad you survived, too. Not only survived, but proved what I told those Goddamn fools; that you were the Yank general from which we had the most to fear." A deep, rumbling chuckle came from the massive chest, and he added, "Goddamn me, but I wished I had been wrong, and those idiot parade-ground soldiers had been right. I always could tell you had something in you; you did me proud." Longstreet looked at the disapproving sentry. "Sam, could we take a walk? There are things I would like to discuss, for your ears alone."

Grant shrugged. "So long as these two go with me. After what happened to Lincoln and Seward, Stanton insists I have nursemaids wherever I go."

Longstreet focused his beady stare on Clay and Rawlins. "Stanton's more than likely right. I recognize Rawlins from the newspaper descriptions. However, your colonel has me at a disadvantage."

"Alphonso Clay," replied Grant. "He is as discrete as Rawlins, and has my complete trust."

Longstreet bowed slightly to each of the officers, hesitating somewhat when he came to Clay. "Well then, shall we take a stroll over to where they will someday finish the Washington Monument?"

"Sounds fine to me," replied Grant. The four soldiers were silent until they had left the War Department building and had crossed the street onto the wasteland that was becoming known as the Capitol Mall. For some moments they stared as they walked at the scattering of massive blocks that would someday come together as a monument to the nation's founder. Grant was the first to break the silence.

"Pete, I heard how the yellow fever took three of your children, year before last. I'm sorry that...circumstances did not allow me to come to you. If it hadn't been for the war, I would have."

Longstreet grunted. "I know, Sam. I know. You were always a good friend."

"Is your wife...all right?"

"She is a strong one, that lady. Besides, the Lord left us two." He paused, and then said with an odd catch to his voice, "I heard your family thrives. For a while I resented it. But last year, when I was shot through the throat and had six months on my back to think about things, I realized that I was glad that you would not feel what I felt."

"You always were a tough bird, Pete," said Grant, attempting to lighten the mood. "How many times have you been shot now? Two, three? And you are still among the living."

A rumbling chuckle again came from deep in Longstreet's chest. "Three times, if you count Mexico. Once through the leg outside Mexico City, once through the arm early in the war, and once through the throat last year. Here I am, good as new; and I understand you never got so much as a scratch."

"Came close a couple of times, Pete, but that only counts in horseshoes." The two old friends chuckled, the tension of their first meeting after the war dispersed.

"So," continued Grant, "why this particular visit? Not that you are not always welcome, wherever I am."

"Same old Sam, always direct and to the point. Well, it's about this business with Lincoln and Seward. I know the South is being blamed throughout the North, people saying Southern sympathizers were behind it, which is obviously true. Anyway, hardly any of my boys have headed home yet. I need to know that what...has happened is not going to affect the terms you granted Lee, and that they won't be bothered none. Furthermore, me and the boys need to know that General Lee will be left alone."

"I gave my word, Pete. None will be touched, so long as they live in peace and respect the laws of the United States."

"Johnson and Stanton hate us Rebels. They might just refuse to ratify your terms."

"If they do, then I resign," said Grant simply.

Longstreet looked at Grant appraisingly. "And if you do that, the government descends into chaos. I expect you realize you are the most popular man in the North right now, and that the White House is yours for the asking in '68."

Grant nodded. However, the expression on his face was melancholy rather than smug. "I expect you are right, Pete. Johnson will have a heap of trouble getting people to accept him as President; he is going to need my support. In any event, you have my word. Your boys will be left alone. Now, is there anything I can do for you personally? Do you need a loan until you get settled?"

Longstreet chuckled. "It's going to be tight, Sam, but I'll manage. Soon as my boys are all on the road, me and the family are off for Georgia, to see what Sherman left of the old plantation."

"I truly wish it hadn't come to that," said Grant solemnly.

"No one wished it, but it did. Anyway, good to see you, Sam. I'm looking forward to seeing you in the White House in three years." The large Rebel chuckled, then suddenly gave Grant a bone-crushing bear-hug. Clay tensed as if to leap, but it was obvious it was a rough but genuine measure of the larger man's affection.

"Go careful, Sam. The dangers of the battlefield are nothing to those of Washington. Give my best to Julia."

"Pete, stay with us for the night. You can leave for Virginia tomorrow. Julia would really like to see you."

Longstreet shook his head slowly, a sad smile on his face. "Not yet, Sam. Too early for that; it would hurt your career. Maybe later."

"Well then, you go careful yourself. Take care of your family."

With a wave, Longstreet lumbered off in the direction of the train depot.

Grant stood looking moodily after Longstreet for a long moment, then without a word turned on his heels and began walking back toward the War Department; accompanied after a moment by Clay and Rawlins. When they had reached the steps to the War Department, Grant suddenly stopped and faced them. "Clay, Rawlins, before we go in there, I've something for your ears only. You remember that army doctor, Leale, who was at Ford's?"

Both Clay and Rawlins nodded.

"Well, he came by to see me early this morning. Seems he was afraid some blame might attach to you, Clay, for not stopping Booth. I assured him that none would, which seemed to put his mind at ease. He then went on to say something I thought you should hear. It seems Leale helped during the autopsy they had over at the Smithsonian; strange thing to have, since it was pretty clear how Lincoln died, but you know how doctors are. Anyway, it seems that Lincoln's heart was diseased. Leale is of the opinion Lincoln had less than a year to live before his ticker gave out on him. Said he wasn't too surprised; said that very tall, lanky men tend to get bad hearts, though no one knows why."

Clay thought of the President's consistent disregard for his own safety. "He must have known, somehow," Clay murmured, as if to himself. "He must have somehow felt it."

Grant spent some moments firing up a cigar. Expelling the first puff, he said reflectively, "Wouldn't surprise me if he had a premonition. Wouldn't surprise me if he preferred it this way; dying a martyr rather than a sick invalid."

Clay remembered what Stanton had said, how Lincoln had once shouted at him that when the war was done it would be the end for him. Solemnly he replied. "General, I fear you may be right."

Changing the subject, Grant said to Clay, "When we finally get on the trail of Booth and Herald, I want you and Bierce to be in on it. We need them alive; and I have a funny feeling that they might not make it back here. I would rest easier if you two were on the case. Go back to the hotel and get some rest; I'll tell Bierce to do the same. When the word comes, I want you both fresh and eager."

"Yes sir," said Clay saluting both Grant and his chief of staff. The two senior officers returned the salute, and proceeded into the War Department as Clay watched them go. After they had disappeared into the building, Clay turned and began walking in the direction of Willard's. He would follow Grant's order to go to the hotel, but he suspected he would be getting precious little sleep.

* * * * *

Clay opened his hotel-room door, and closed it without bothering to turn up the gaslight. He took a step toward the bed; then out of the gloom a fist slammed into his jaw, staggering him backward into the wall. In the gloom he could make out Teresa Duval standing before him, fists at the ready, eyes watchful, obviously prepared for a brawl.

"That was for the blow in the alley," she announced, carefully looking for his reaction.

Clay thoughtfully rubbed his jaw; for a woman, Duval had a powerful right. "I deserved that," he replied quietly. "However, I must object; not to the blow, but to your invasion of my privacy. You have a distressing tendency to come and go in my quarters; if nothing else, it could compromise your reputation."

Clay produced a friction match, struck it with his thumb, and lit the room's gas jet.

Duval gave one of her silvery, chilling laughs. "Colonel Clay, you do amuse me sometimes. Knowing what you know of me, you still think I give a fig for 'reputation'?" She stopped laughing, and looked appraisingly at Clay. "It is interesting that you would think of my reputation, not your own. Anyway, there are a few matters we need to discuss."

Clay gestured toward one of the room's chairs, and Duval gracefully seated herself. Clay then seated himself in the remaining chair, his face showing curiously little expression.

"We should discuss the relationship we now have," Duval began with brutal directness.

"I cannot marry you," replied Clay with equally brutal directness. "Despite my inexcusable failure to control…my animal passions, I do not love you; and few conditions contain more misery than a loveless marriage."

Duval threw her head back and laughed with uncontrolled amusement. Quickly recovering her composure, but still smiling broadly, she replied, "Oh, you do indeed love me, although you may not be able to admit it, even to yourself. But let that pass. I ask you, Colonel Clay, have I mentioned a word concerning marriage?"

A look of puzzlement flitted across Clay's face. "If marriage is not your object, then why did you…" The prudish Clay trailed off without completing the sentence. Duval laughed again, a quieter, more confidential laugh.

"You are fortunate, Colonel Clay, that you have touched something in me I would not have believed was there. You know more about me than any man…alive. Tell, me, what would you have expected me to do with an officer having your wealth and position?"

Slowly, Clay replied, "I would have expected you to have compelled him to marry you. Then, if he proved inconvenient in any way, I would expect his health to take a sudden turn for the worse, and for you to become a grieving, and wealthy, widow."

Once again, Duval laughed, but this time ruefully. “You see what I mean. No living man understands me like you do. And no living woman understands you like I do. I know the truth of your ancestry. I have read enough of Dr. Dee’s book and your grandfather’s book to guess the truth; a truth that probably no one alive would believe – but me.”

A dangerous stillness came over Clay. “What do you think you know? Who do you think would believe you? And believing what you think you know, why do you sit there, calmly unafraid?”

“Because we are alike, and we both know it, although your precious ‘Clay honor’ makes you loath to admit it. We both feel the thrill of the hunt; we both feel the unspeakable pleasure in the spilling blood. These instincts may come from different... causes; but we feel the same. The only difference is that you are sincerely ashamed of what you are, while I embrace it.”

Clay was now looking at Duval with something akin to horror. “I am nothing like you. No Clay is like you.”

“Really, Colonel? Shall we ask the Deveareux family about that? How about the Confederate raiders in that cabin outside Knoxville? Perhaps we should interview the good people of Columbia, South Carolina for their opinions – those that survived the fire.”

Features trembling with rage, Clay leapt to his feet. Fists clenched at his side, in a voice that had suddenly deepened an octave, Clay growled, “For such statements I would kill...”

“Exactly,” replied Duval, who remained calmly seated in her chair. “And I do admire how you can control such overwhelming rage – most of the time. As do I. We do indeed understand each other.” With the fluidity of a cat, she rose from the chair and faced the short colonel, eye-to-eye. “That is why I will use no wiles to make you marry me. I certainly do not need a piece of paper to justify to myself taking my pleasure with you. You are not one of the easily-manipulated cattle who are our natural prey. We will meet as equals. Perhaps a day may come when we will both want marriage; but when that day comes, it will not be because you want society to bless your liaison with me, or because I want your wealth and position. It will be because we both want it, for itself, and for each other, alone."

She reached up and gently caressed his cheek with her left hand; then quick as lightening delivered a punch to his stomach with her right. Howling with rage, Clay hooked his right arm around her neck as if to break it, but with a deft movement she had snaked her right leg behind him. Unbalanced, they both fell onto the room's bed, where the fight quickly turned into something else.

* * * * *

Out of breath from his dash up the stairs, Ambrose Bierce pounded on the door to Clay's room. After a slight delay he heard Clay's distinctive voice say from behind the door. "Who is there?"

"Clay, it's me, Bierce! Hurry up! Colonel Baker has received word from Maryland that a doctor has treated a man meeting Booth's description for a broken leg! We've got to get moving, while the trail is hot!"

After a pause he heard Clay murmur, "One moment. I need to dress." Bierce frowned; it was not like the fastidious Clay to be lounging around his hotel room in broad daylight in his long johns. Then the penny dropped, and Bierce grinned. He unashamedly put his ear to the door; over a rustle of clothing he heard Clay whisper, "I will count on you to watch for developments here in Washington; keep an eye on Colonel Baker if possible." Bierce stepped back before Clay opened the door just wide enough for him to slide through the opening and firmly shut it behind him. It was neatly done; Bierce could not catch a glimpse of whatever the room contained.

Casually fastening the top buttons of his blue tunic, Clay asked, "Are Captain Doherty and his men ready?"

"They are just outside the hotel, with a horse for each of us. Hurry; the doctor's farm is about thirty miles northeast of here, and with luck we can be there before sunset."

The two friends swiftly descended the stairs and jogged out the front entrance, where Doherty, about twenty cavalrymen, and a black-suited civilian waited on their horses. Doherty touched his hat, introduced the grimly silent civilian as Colonel Baker's cousin, and then gestured to the only two horses not carrying a trooper. "Best we could get on short notice, Colonel; they look good enough. With your permission, let's make tracks."

"Lead the way, Captain," Clay responded as he and Bierce smoothly mounted. Doherty spurred his mount into a trot, quickly imitated by the rest of the party; he was too experienced to exhaust his horse with unnecessary galloping, and a trot was fast enough to cover thirty miles before dark.

As they trotted, Clay asked the captain, "What do we know about this doctor?"

Doherty shrugged. "Not much, sir. His name is Samuel Mudd. He apparently only practices medicine on the side; his main business seems to be the tobacco plantation where he lives."

Clay pondered this for a moment. "He must have suffered severe financial losses when the slaves were freed. It would not be surprising if he were a Southern sympathizer. He might even be in league with Booth."

"If he is, we'll get the truth out of him soon enough," responded Doherty grimly in a gravelly New York accent.

Both officers being absorbed in their conversation, neither noticed the painfully thin figure of Courtney Delapore standing on a street corner beside a medium-sized man dressed wholly in black, who asked, "That colonel beside the captain is Clay?"

Delapore stared after the horsemen, and without turning toward his companion replied "It is. He has more authority than his rank would indicate. I would not be surprised if they are hot on the trail of Booth." Delapore finally turned to face his companion, an angry yet sad look on his face. In a soft voice that the occasional passerby could not hear, he said "Waite, you put Booth up to murdering Lincoln, didn't you?"

Colonel Ephraim Waite of the Confederate Secret Service laughed nastily and replied. "What do you think?"

"My God, Waite, what were you thinking? This isn't gathering information or smuggling supplies; this was cold-blooded murder of an unarmed man in front of his wife! On top of every other consideration, it is useless. The war is over; all you can do is bring dishonor on the South."

Waite made a disgusted sound. "It is not useless. It is just the first step in snatching victory from the jaws of defeat. Any act, regardless of cost or 'honor', is justified by that goal. Besides, I know something of the rumors surrounding your family, and why your ancestor had to leave England for Virginia in 1620. Don't talk to me about your precious honor."

Delapore flushed red with anger at the obscure reference to the terrible family scandal. Shame kept him from pursuing that argument. Instead he replied, "I may have lied to Clay about consciously helping the South; but I did not lie about my refusal to commit acts of violence. You above all know that I only agreed to help on the condition that it was only protecting people from Baker and his minions."

Waite guffawed. "It is too late to whine about that. I own you, Delapore, own you like a nigger. What do you think Clay, never mind Baker, will do to you if they find out about your connection with Richmond?"

"I knew nothing about the plot against Lincoln," protested Delapore, sounding unconvincing even to himself.

"Nobody will believe that. Don't worry; do as I tell you, and no harm will come to you. You will have the protection of the Confederacy. Even more importantly, you will have the protection of certain friends of mine, friends more secretive and powerful than ever the Confederacy dreamt of being."

"Who are these friends of yours?" asked Delapore in an uneasy voice.

"No need for you to know right now. When the time comes, you will learn their identity, and I guarantee it will astonish you. Go home and wait for my instructions. I have certain things to do." Without saying goodbye, Ephraim Waite began strolling down Pennsylvania Avenue, whistling cheerfully a tuneless melody.

* * * * *

The sun was just disappearing beneath the western horizon when the party of horsemen came up to a large, ramshackle farmhouse; even in the light of sunset it was obvious that repairs and maintenance had been long delayed. A corporal appeared at the door, Spencer carbine at the ready. Seeing the blue uniforms, the soldier visibly relaxed, and called over his shoulder. "Lieutenant Betz, Colonel Baker's men are here!"

A thin, clean-shaven officer appeared at the door. Saluting, he said, "Sirs, Lieutenant Karl Betz, 112th Pennsylvania."

Clay spoke for the party. "Colonel Alphonso Clay, on General Grant's staff. These are Major Bierce and Captain Doherty; our civilian companion is Luther Baker who, ah, represents his cousin, Colonel Baker."

"Your troopers can use the barn round back to take care of your horses; I expect they're winded. You officers and the... civilian can come in and meet the good doctor." Betz waited for Baker and the three officers to hand off their horses to various troopers and mount the steps, then led them into the house, telling the soldier with the Spencer, "Keep your guard up, Quinn. The war isn't quite over in these parts." He led the new arrivals into a short hallway; but before entering the parlor to the right he turned and spoke in a soft voice.

"I may be wrong, sirs, but I think Mudd is deep into this business."

"Any particular reason for your opinion?" asked Clay.

The young man shook his head. “I can’t say. He seems to be co-operating, but there is something about him not quite right. Talk to him, and judge for yourselves.” He led the new arrivals into the parlor, and made the introductions, “Dr. Mudd, Colonel Clay, Major Bierce, Captain Doherty and Mr. Baker have come up from Washington to hear your story.”

Samuel Mudd sat heavily in a wing chair. He was a middle-aged man with black hair and goatee shot through with grey, face marked by what appeared to be a combination of care and bitterness. His black eyes looked at the visitors intently, with what Clay believed to be ill-concealed hatred. A plump, frightened-looking woman stood to his left, her hand grasping his shoulder. He nodded curtly. “Gentlemen, I have told the young lieutenant all that I know. Must I go through this again?”

“Humor us,” replied Clay, walking over to look down on the doctor, and making no move to take one of the several chairs in the room. Clay instinctively knew the advantage conferred upon an interrogator by looming over a witness. The other Federals followed Clay’s example.

“At least allow my wife to go upstairs. The children are alone, and are frightened of the Yank...the soldiers.”

Clay’s eyes briefly lost their focus, and he murmured to himself, “The children.” Then slightly shaking his head as if to restore his alertness, he replied, “Of course, Mrs. Mudd may go upstairs.”

“Samuel...” the plump woman started to say.

“Go!” interrupted Mudd with force. She started, looking at him fearfully; Samuel Mudd obviously ruled his house with a rod of iron. Without another sound she scurried across the floor and disappeared up the stairs.

“Now, repeat for us what you told Lieutenant Betz,” said Clay in a soft, emotionless voice.

“It is as I said. Last night two men I had never seen before come knocking at my door near midnight. The older one complained of his left leg being broken. I cut away the boot, and found he had a clean fracture of the fibula. I splinted it, let he and his companion spend the night, and they rode away this morning. Later in the day, I went into town, and heard for the first time about the assassins being in the neighborhood.. I thought that they might be the men who came calling at my house, so I told the first Provost patrol I could find. Lieutenant Betz and his men were sent out, and I've been held a prisoner in my own home ever since."

"Did you recognize either of the two men?" asked Bierce.

"Never seen either in my life," announced Mudd with emphasis.

"Describe them," asked Clay.

In an exasperated tone of voice, Mudd replied to Clay. "As I have said before, two men of average height and dark hair, both clean shaven, one about thirty, the other twenty."

"Did either of them sport a mustache?" asked Baker.

"No, both were clean-shaven."

"One would expect Booth to have removed his adornment as a simple act of disguise," murmured Clay. "Still, his appearance is quite distinctive, and he would remain easily recognizable to anyone who knew him even slightly." Clay paused, and then forcefully asked Mudd, "You are certain you did not recognize the man with the broken leg as Booth?"

The doctor emphatically shook his head. "Of course not! The word had already got around about the assassination. If I had known him, I would have denounced him immediately."

"Would you now?" asked Bierce in a cynical tone of voice. He gestured to encompass the dilapidated house and the surrounding farm. "Looks like the homestead has seen better days. Must have been quite hard to keep your head above water; especially after Lincoln freed the slaves. You might not have been entirely...hostile to a man who struck down the emancipator."

Mudd's features showed a trace of fear for the first time, but only a trace. "It's no secret folks hereabouts weren't keen on the

Republican cause. That doesn't make us assassins, or the friends of assassins."

"I imagine you go frequently to Washington," said Clay suddenly. "It is only thirty miles or so."

"From time to time," replied Mudd with a puzzled frown. "Get most of what I need from the crossroads store."

"Still, you probably cannot get everything you need there," continued Clay. "A man with your farming commitments, especially a man with a medical practice on the side, would need to make a trip now and again to a large city; and Washington is much closer than Baltimore."

"I suppose I go into town once a month or so," came the grudging response. Mudd was not unintelligent, and suspected where this line of questioning was leading.

"You are an educated man, Dr. Mudd," said Bierce. "Two college degrees. Living in Maryland tobacco country must leave you starved for intellectual entertainment."

"I have my books, and my family. That is enough."

"Come sir," continued Bierce. "I am sure that on your trips to the city you are unable to resist the lure of cultural stimulation. The Library of Congress, the Smithsonian...the theaters."

"Of course my family and I give ourselves an occasional treat." It might have been the warm humidity of the room that caused tiny beads of sweat to break out on Mudd's forehead.

"But the theater," continued Bierce. "Ah, the theater. Shakespeare especially. An educated man like you must enjoy viewing a good performance of Shakespeare. Still, good performances are hard to come by. Very few actors can do the Bard true justice. However, there is one, one who has done Shakespeare repeatedly in Washington. A very skilled actor, with a very distinctive appearance. It seems unlikely that someone would forget that actor, once having seen him."

Mudd said nothing; he could not quite meet Bierce's amused gaze.

"You knew," said Clay in a quiet, almost conversational voice. "You knew it was Booth. You had already heard Booth was wanted for the murder of the President. And yet, you attended to his wound, and sent him on his way, undoubtedly with your best wishes for a job well done."

"I swear, I did not recognize him as Booth," replied the doctor in a high voice. "I mean, his mustache was shaved..."

Like a rattlesnake striking, Clay lunged forward and backhanded Mudd across the face with such force that he tipped over, chair and all, crying out as his head struck the wooden floor. Bierce and Doherty each grabbed one of Clay's arms, while Baker shouted "Clay, don't kill that traitor! He may be able to lead us to Booth. Cousin Lafayette wants part of the reward, and will have my hide if we lose the assassin."

With a burst of furious motion, Clay shook off Clay and Doherty, grabbed Mudd by his shirtfront and rammed him against the wall, the doctor's feet not touching the ground. "I will not kill this piece of offal," commented Clay in his conversational voice. "However, if he does not tell me where Booth has gone, he will wish he were dead."

"I don't know!" stammered Mudd.

"Pity. I am a hard man to convince." Clay kneed Mudd in the groin, to the utter shock of the other officers, who had never imagined the cultivated-appearing Clay could behave thus.

"Stop!" came a piercing female wail. All froze and looked to the top of the stairs where a wild-eyed, weeping Mrs. Mudd stood, flanked by a boy and a girl who fearfully clutched her skirts. "Please stop! Don't hurt Samuel any more. I saw which way they went. I will tell you. Only please stop hurting him, in the name of God!"

"Don't tell...bastards...anything," slurred Mudd, almost semi-conscious from the pain.

"I don't care what happens to Booth!" screamed Mrs. Mudd, more to her husband than the Federal officers. "He murdered a man in front of his wife! He's not going to make another widow in this house!" She turned toward Clay, and spoke in a more normal voice that was still ragged with fear. "They rode off on the main road to the southwest; I could just tell they then turned on a side-road going due south. There is nothing especial in that direction, so they could only be intending to reach the Potomac and somehow cross the river into Virginia. I have no idea what they intend after that, nor does Samuel. I swear on my hope of salvation before God that neither he nor I know anything else that could help you."

Clay looked at her for a long moment, then released his grip on Mudd, who slid down the wall to a sitting position. Clay continued to look for nearly a full minute at the tearful woman and the two terrified children beside her. Then he strode over to Lieutenant Betz and said, "Take charge of Dr. Mudd and deliver him to Colonel Baker in Washington." There was a pause, and Clay seemed about to turn toward the three figures on the stairs. With visible effort, he restrained himself, and spoke directly to Betz. "He is to be treated as a prisoner, but is not to be mistreated in any way." Then he walked over to the door, saying over his shoulder, "Captain Doherty, I am afraid you must tell your men to saddle up again. Minutes are precious; we will stay on the trail this entire night, if possible."

Clay was out of the door before any of his companions could say anything. Bierce shrugged and addressed the captain. "We better do as he says; Clay generally gets his way."

*****

Captain Doherty's troopers were sprawled in exhaustion about the large fire that burned in the clearing, holding back the nighttime darkness lurking in the ghostly second-growth timber that surrounded them. For nine days Clay had driven them mercilessly on Booth's trail, refusing to allow more than a few hours sleep snatched from time to time. Several times they had been near to giving up the hunt as hopeless. Mercilessly, Clay would not permit them to give up, and always seemed to come up with some further indication of where the assassins had been. These clues had often been provided by recently-freed slaves, who were more than happy to aid the troops pursuing the man who had slaughtered their liberator.

All of the pursuers were sleeping, save for Clay and Bierce. Clay was talking quietly at the edge of the forest with an elderly black man; Bierce lay close to the fire, and watched Clay with curiosity. Everyone else in the party, including Bierce himself, was filthy and unshaven, not even having had an opportunity to change their clothes. Clay had permitted no time for the luxury of personal hygiene, and during their brief, rare stops, sleep took an absolute priority. Bierce felt a growing sense of awe at how Clay seemed to have acquired only a faint sprinkling of dust on his uniform and a slight downy stubble on his face; it did not seem possible, but it was true.

Clay finished his murmured conversation with the elderly black man. The colonel extended his hand to the informant, and something in the hand glistened yellow in the light from the bonfire. Slowly shaking his head, the elderly man, turned, and melted into the night without taking the proffered reward. Restoring the coin to his pocket, Clay went over to where the sleepless Bierce lay watching, stopping only to shake Captain Doherty and Luther Baker awake. The captain and the civilian staggered over to join Clay and Bierce, knuckling the sleep out of their red-rimmed eyes.

"It is time," Clay announced quietly, a disturbing predatory look on his face. "My informant tells me two strange white men are guests at a farm less than half a mile down the track, and that one of them appears to have a game leg. The farm is owned by a Rebel veteran who has just returned to his family, Richard Garrett."

"We will sweep him and his family up also," responded Baker grimly.

"Probably not necessary," responded Clay. "My informant says the black grapevine hereabouts indicates Mr. Garrett is less than pleased with the presence of his guests. He wants them gone, and will not let them sleep in the house; he has made them bed down in an old tobacco barn."

"If he is not in league with Booth, why hasn't he turned the murderer in?" asked Baker.

Clay emitted one of his barking laughs. "You have seen the country hereabouts over the last several days. The war may be over, but there is hardly a sign of Federal authority to be seen. The countryside is filled with former Confederates, some of which would undoubtedly respond with violence toward anyone turning Booth over to the hangman. No, I suspect the Garrett family will give us little difficulty, so long as we remove Booth from their farm without making it appear to be their doing."

"So, how will this go down?" asked Doherty, a note of eagerness in his voice.

"These are your men, Captain," responded Clay. "If I may be allowed to suggest the following: divide your men into three groups of eight, have your lieutenant take one of the groups and Mr. Baker into the plantation house, securing the Garrett family. You will take immediate leadership of the second group of eight, and position yourself on the house side of the barn so that you can easily cover both sides. I will take Bierce, your Sergeant Corbett and the final eight men to the far side of the barn, covering the other two sides."

"Will we wait for dawn to attack?" asked Doherty

"We will not. We are under a disadvantage in that we need to take Booth and Herold alive. They are under no such compunction as to us. The boards of the tobacco barn undoubtedly are loose, and have many gaps. My informant assures me that between the two of them they have at least one Spencer repeating carbine and two Colt revolvers; perhaps more firearms that could not be observed from a distance. If we wait for daylight, they will have clear shots at us from cover. Once everyone is in place, I will move forward and set fire to the barn. They will not choose to burn alive, I am certain, and unable to see us clearly in the dark, we should be able to secure them with little risk to ourselves."

Nodding to Clay, Doherty shouted, "All right boys, up and at 'em! The murderer of our president is half a mile away, and we are going to finish this thing before the sun rises!" The exhausted men lurched into consciousness with surprising speed; grinning to each other, they began gathering the horses from where they had been tied. As the men began to mount their steeds and fall in, Doherty took Clay aside.

"Clay, I want you to be careful with Sergeant Corbett. He may need watching."

Clay frowned slightly. "Over the last ten days the man has performed his duties efficiently and correctly. He does seem to keep to himself, and read his Bible to excess during rests, but those things are far from sins."

Doherty grimaced. "Oh, Boston Corbett is a good soldier most of the time, but occasionally he goes plain crazy, for no good reason."

"Why haven't you had him discharged?"

Doherty's stolid Celtic face assumed an expression of sorrow. "We kind of carry him, in the company. You see, he served his country, and suffered more than he should; more than if he had died."

Bierce had been following the conversation with interest, and interjected, "How so?"

Doherty looked at the young major, and finally responded. "He was captured, and sent to Andersonville." A chill went through the three officers at the mention of the hellish Confederate prisoner-of-war camp, where over ten thousand Union soldiers had entered, never to emerge.

"Things were...done to him, in Andersonville," continued Doherty. "Things that most folks would refuse to believe. Done by both Rebs and turncoat prisoners who sold their souls for crusts of bread. He was one of the few who escaped. He won't talk about it; but the word is he hid in a pile of bodies for two days before they were taken out of the camp to be buried, killed a guard once he was out, and walked over a hundred miles to Union lines. By the time he got there, he was starved down to less than a hundred pounds, and crazier than a bedbug." Doherty hesitated for a moment, and then continued. "I hear that when he was recovering in the hospital, he raved that he had deserved the things done to him; that his own sinfulness had caused God to allow...unspeakable things to happen to him. I'm no alienist, but maybe that was the only way he could reconcile his faith in God with what was done to him. Anyway, when the doctors weren't around, he took a scalpel, heated an iron, and...castrated himself, cauterizing the wound before he passed out from the pain."

Although Bierce looked revolted, Clay appeared to be merely thoughtful, saying "Interesting. In Roman times, the followers of the cult of Cybele often engaged in such self-mutilation. I admit it is surprising to see the practice recur in modern times."

"Be that as it may, poor bastard should have been sent home," continued Doherty. "But he insisted God meant him to see the Confederacy punished, and that it was the only way he could 'purge his sins.' No one had the heart to send him home. He does his job, and can be a good leader under fire; but sometimes he gets a bit..." Doherty trailed off, using his forefinger to make a circling motion at his temple. "So just keep an eye on him, Colonel."

Clay nodded. Then the three officers mounted their steeds and led the column of troopers down the rutted road dimly lit by a moon in its last quarter.

* * * * *

"So far, so good," murmured Clay to Bierce. The two friends lay on their bellies, observing the dilapidated barn in the faint moonlight; behind them the eight cavalrymen led by Sergeant Boston Corbett lay prone, nervously clutching their Spencer carbines. Clay's plan had gone smoothly. The Garratt family had been awakened without undue commotion and secured; although the sight of Union soldiers had made the ex-Rebel

Richard Garrett surly, he seemed more relieved than not that his unwanted guests would shortly be taken off his hands. Doherty and his men were in position at the front of the barn. Everything had been done with a minimum of noise, and there was no sign from the barn that the fugitives knew anything was amiss, or even awake. The next move would be Clay's. He turned his head and murmured "Sergeant, please come here, and bring the oil lantern we took from the house."

"Sir," whispered Corbett in a voice louder than was necessary. The emaciated, wiry sergeant stood and scurried forward, the lantern in one hand, a Colt revolver in the other. The moonlight was very faint, but Clay's night vision was astonishingly good, and he noticed with some unease the wild-eyed, ecstatic look on Corbett's face.

"Give me the lantern, Sergeant. You stay here with Major Bierce."

"Colonel, please let me go with you," said Corbett in an agitated, raspy voice. "In that barn is the murderer of Lincoln. It means more than my life for me to be in at the end."

Clay shook his head. "Starting the fire will be the most dangerous moment. If Booth and Herold are alert, they could easily kill whoever sets the fire through one of the chinks in the boards, even in the dark. It is senseless for more than one to expose himself. As it is my plan, I must be that one."

"Sir, you must let me share the risk," replied Corbett in a desperate voice with a faint note of hysteria. "If you only knew what I have endured for the Union, you would grant me this favor."

Thanks to Doherty, Clay did know. After a moment's hesitation he said, "Very well. Carry the lantern for me. Remember, no noise. Above all, we must take Booth and Herold alive. If you must shoot, shoot for the legs."

"Thank you, sir," replied Corbett eagerly. "It means the world to me."

"Come then." Clay crouched low and led the way, walking as softly as his expensive boots allowed. In moments the pair had crossed the twenty yards of barren earth leading to the barn. As they reached the wall, Clay could see that his fears had been justified; the decrepit structure had gaps of an inch or more between several of the boards. There was no light from inside, but that did not mean the assassins were not silently waiting to shoot them, once Clay and Corbett blocked their view of the night sky through the gaps.

Silently, Clay scooped up random bits of dry straw and leaves that were near the wall, forming a small pile of combustibles in direct contact with the ancient planks. Wordlessly, he gestured for Corbett to hand him the unlit lantern. The sergeant did so, keeping his cocked revolver in his right hand swiveling back and forth, as if searching for a target. Clay uncorked the oil reservoir of the lantern, and thoroughly soaked the pile of straw and leaves. Then, after carefully placing the empty lantern on the ground, he took a friction match from his tunic pocket, struck it with his thumb, and applied it to the pile. Waiting only to make sure that the fire had truly established itself, he silently gestured to Corbett to follow him. The two quickly scurried across the yard and threw themselves prone on either side of Bierce. None of them said anything; there was nothing to say as they watched the fire grow.

In less than five minutes the fire had clearly spread to the wall, and was making quick progress through the dry, ancient wood of the structure. Muffled voices and sounds of movement inside the barn were suddenly audible over the crackling of the flames. Deciding that the time had come, Clay stood, and spoke in a voice that was surprisingly deeper and louder than his normal speaking voice.

“John Wilkes Booth and David Herold! You are surrounded by over twenty Union cavalry, all armed with Spencers. Escape is impossible, and you will burn to death if you stay where you are. Throw out your weapons, and come out with your hands high in the air!

The muffled sound of voices came from the barn. Although the words could not be distinguished, it was obvious that an argument was taking place. Suddenly, the barn door was jerked open a couple of feet, and a soft-looking, frightened David Herold emerged. The light from the growing fire made visible the tears in his eyes and the wet stain down the front of his trousers, mute evidence of the childish terror of the youth who sought to change history through violence. Captain Doherty and Luther Baker darted forward, grabbed Herold by the arms, and roughly pulled him away from the barn; as they did so, the door was slammed firmly shut. Clay, Bierce and Corbett rose to dash over to the sobbing prisoner, Clay pausing only to gesture to the remaining men to stay where they were. The three quickly reached the place where Doherty and Baker were swiftly confining Herold with heavy iron handcuffs, the kind that in the recent past had been used for recalcitrant slaves. Herold was a pathetic sight; quaking with fear, reeking of his own urine, blubbering like an infant. Many would have been moved to pity by the spectacle. However, all of his captors knew the choices Herold had made to bring him to this place, and felt no pity, least of all the stony-hearted Clay, who had seen Abraham Lincoln die with his own eyes.

Captain Doherty viciously backhanded Herold, saying venomously, “Stop your whining, traitor! Tell us, what weapons does Booth have, and will he surrender without a fight?”

The blow had shocked Herold into silence. Sniffing slightly, he whined, “Tried to tell Mr. Booth it were no good, and that we should give up. He said if I wanted to hang on a Yankee gallows he wouldn’t stop me; but as for himself he would take a couple of blue bellies with him. Guess he could; he’s got a Spencer and two Colts, and knows how to use them. Told him I couldn’t stand burning, and would take my chance on the gallows.”

“You do that,” replied Doherty with a snarl. He turned to Clay. “Well Colonel, what now? We need Booth alive, but it seems like he intends to shoot anyone going through the door.”

“Eventually the fire will drive him into our hands,” replied Clay. “It takes a special kind of man to endure burning to death, and I do not believe Booth is that kind of man. The trouble will be when he comes out of that door firing. Good men will likely die taking him alive. Now that the interior of the barn is well-lighted, I think I need to make a reconnaissance and see if there is any possible way or opening by which we could surprise him."

"That is extraordinarily dangerous," said Bierce. "Booth is desperate and armed. Ask for a volunteer, or let me go. You have risked too much already in this war."

"I am sorry, Bierce. I must do this. The plan is mine; a Clay must take the consequences of his actions, not some well-meaning volunteer, much less a friend." With that, Clay spun on his heel and ran a zigzag course to the burning structure. It took Bierce a moment to realize that for the first time in the more than two years they had known each other, Clay had referred to him as a friend.

Clay reached the outer wall of the barn and peered in through one of the gaps, the interior well-lit by the rapidly-expanding fire. Inside he could see John Wilkes Booth, clearly recognizable despite the absence of his distinctive mustache. A makeshift crutch under his left arm, a Spencer carbine tucked clumsily under his right, he stumped around the interior of the barn, sweating profusely from the heat of the fire, eyes darting about wildly, looking for an avenue of escape that did not exist. Clay decided that he would need to cripple Booth if he were to be taken alive without loss of Federal life. Quietly, Clay drew his Smith & Wesson Number 2 cartridge revolver and cocked it, having decided that he needed to shoot Booth in his good leg. Clay was aware that even leg wounds could be occasionally fatal; but the Number 2 fired a .32 caliber bullet, small enough that the damage to a limb was very unlikely to turn immediately fatal.

"Colonel Clay, how are we going to take him?" came Boston Corbett's hoarse whisper from directly behind him. Clay jerked his head around involuntarily, astonished that the fanatical sergeant had followed without, indeed despite, orders.

He turned back to look into the barn, only to find himself staring down the barrel of Booth's Spencer. Too late, he realized that Booth must have heard Corbett's voice, and glimpsed Clay by the light of the inferno that was now casting its rays outward through the gaps in the boards. Clay saw Booth's hate-filled eye over the Spencer's sights, saw Booth's finger tighten on the trigger. Then an explosive detonation went off, seemingly in Clay's right ear, and Booth crumpled to the ground. A furious Clay whirled to see Boston Corbett holding a smoking Colt.

"Idiot!" Clay screamed. "We needed him alive!"

"But Colonel, he was about to kill you," replied Corbett ingenuously. "I couldn't allow that."

Holstering his own pistol, Clay yelled to Doherty and the others. "Booth has been shot! It is safe to go in." Not waiting for the others, Clay rushed to the door, flung it open, and strode into the burning structure. He saw to his surprise that Booth was conscious, laying on his back and making choking sounds as he spat gobbets of blood from his mouth. Something puzzled Clay, and it took him a moment to realize that far from writhing in pain, Booth's body below the neck was completely, lifelessly inert. Then Clay noticed the wound from Corbett's bullet, a gaping hole in the neck. It oozed blood rather than spurted, so the artery was not involved; but Clay realized that Booth's spinal cord had been severed, and the assassin was paralyzed from the neck down.

Suddenly the barn seemed to fill with soldiers. Clay turned to Doherty and said, "He still may live long enough to give us information. Have your men carry him to the porch of the house, and do what they can to keep him alive."

"If you say so," growled Doherty. "Still, if I had my druthers, I'd be putting a bullet in his brain this instant." He gestured to several of his men, who rapidly improvised a stretcher out of an old horse blanket. In a surprisingly short time the task was done, and the soldiers in blue left the burning barn just before it became fully involved, bearing the inert form of Lincoln's assassin.

Booth was settled as comfortably as his wound allowed on the main house's veranda, just as the sky was beginning to brighten in the east. Richard Garrett came out of the house once to look at the scene, a carefully neutral look on his face; one glare from Captain Doherty sent him retreating back into the bosom of his family. It was quickly confirmed that Booth was completely paralyzed from the neck down, and was even having trouble clearing his throat of blood and mucous. As a corporal who had served some time as a hospital orderly did his best to staunch the bleeding from Booth's wound, Clay attempted to question the assassin.

"Booth, I know you did not act alone. This plot was too elaborate for a shallow and vain actor to conceive. And I do not mean minions like Herold or Atzerodt. I need to know who gave you your orders, who made the arrangements for you."

Booth coughed weekly, and uttered the single word: "Water." Clay gave a quick nod of the head to the corporal, who offered Booth a sip from his own canteen. Small as the sip was, Booth choked on it. When he finally stopped coughing he whispered, "Show me my hand. I cannot see my hand." Frowning, Clay lifted Booth's inert right hand into the actor's field of vision. With difficulty, Booth focused on it, then muttered "Useless...useless." With that enigmatic comment, John Wilkes Booth's eyes glazed, and he died.

"He's dead, boys," announced the corporal with no little satisfaction. As the soldiers gathered around to stare at the body of Lincoln's murderer, chattering all the time about how the $100,000 reward money was to be divided, Clay swiftly checked through the dead man's pockets. He found a watch, some odd coins, a large sum in Federal banknotes, several pencils, and a small diary. He handed everything except the diary to Bierce, saying, "Make a record of everything I have taken off the body. It may have some use later on."

Clay then rose, and walked some distance from the house. He seated himself on an upturned bucket, and began to leaf through Booth's diary by the light of the rising sun. At first his reading seemed casual. Then, something caught his eye. He read further and further; as he read, it seemed as if the world began to spin about him.

Ambrose Bierce trudged up to Clay, and said, "We better start packing up. Washington will want the body as well as Herold, and we don't want to be on the road too long. The dead don't keep too well in a Virginia spring." He paused, and noted that the normally well-mannered Clay was paying absolutely no attention to him.

"Clay, you all right? I know it has been a rough couple of weeks, but it is over now. Clay? Do you hear me?" Bierce's puzzlement had turned to concern; Clay showed absolutely no sign that he was aware of his friend's presence. "Alphonso, are you all right? Are you ill?" Bierce gently placed his hand on Clay's shoulder. Clay started, and glanced up at Bierce, who took a small step backward in alarm. It was not any sort of threat that alarmed Ambrose Bierce. Rather, it was the unexpected expression in the face of his reserved, self-contained friend.

The look on Alphonso Clay's face was one of unutterable astonishment and horror.

Chapter 4:
"Let The Hero Born Of Woman Crush The Serpent With His Heel..."

Alphonso Clay and Ambrose Bierce were once again in Stanton's office at the War Department. Aside from Stanton himself, the only other person in the office was Ulysses Grant, wearing a clean yet rumpled uniform of a lieutenant general. Having paused at Willard's only long enough to bathe and change his uniform, Clay gave his two superiors a mechanical accounting of the events of the last ten days, face expressionless, eyes focused on a point somewhere over Stanton's head. Having described Booth's death unemotionally, Clay concluded his narrative.

"In short, I failed in my primary assignment of capturing the assassin Booth alive. This failure is mine, and mine alone, and should reflect on no one else involved in the chase, least of all Major Bierce or Captain Doherty. I feel nothing less than my resignation will meet the case. However, before I resign, I beg your permission to follow up on several leads that came into my possession during the pursuit of Booth."

Grant took a long pull on a freshly lit cigar, slowly expelling the smoke toward the ceiling. "Seems to me you did as good as a soul could. It was Sergeant Corbett who shot Booth."

"I cannot allow the Sergeant to take responsibility," responded Clay. "He is...unwell. I should have taken that into account, and reinforced my instructions that Booth be taken alive."

Grant's mild, sorrowful eyes bored into Clay's. "I did not mean for any blame to attach to Corbett. Seems to me he acted to save the life of a superior officer; it is doggone hard to blame a soul for that."

"I understand you recovered Booth's pocket diary," wheezed Stanton. "I would like to see it."

"With your permission, I would like to defer handing it over. The pages contain some evidence that there were...further ramifications to Booth's plot. I have come here to ask your permission to immediately follow up on the hints of the diary, and at least put my concerns to rest, before my resignation takes effect. I would also need your written permission to call upon whatever resources of the Army that I may need. Although I hope it is not the case, there is a possibility that minutes may count; I will never be able to forgive myself for not having been a single minute earlier at Ford's Theater." Clay paused, and uncharacteristically took a deep breath. "It is possible that extreme measures may be necessary...very extreme. I wish to make certain that I am not impeded. After that, I will take full responsibility for my actions; but the good of this country, and perhaps much more, could require such... extreme actions."

At first, Stanton appeared about to explode at Clay's refusal to hand over the diary, and at his outrageous demand for untrammeled authority. But for some reason, Clay's final words checked a display of the infamous Stantonian temper.

"Might want to give Clay his head," commented Grant to the red-faced Stanton. "Has his own way of doing things, but he generally delivers the goods." The general-in-chief shifted his attention to Clay. "Colonel, I suppose this is like that time, just before Vicksburg fell. The time when you refused to tell me who had been murdering our officers, but swore on your honor that the killer would never again be a threat to the Federal cause. I recall that the killings stopped. Oh, we got the occasional bushwhacker sniping at a picket, but our losses from such causes fell off, and stayed off. Is this that kind of thing, Clay?"

"Yes, sir, it is." Clay looked at Grant, who stared back at him like the muzzle of a canon. Then the general seemed to make a decision.

"Stanton, cut an order for my signature, right now. Make it read: 'By my order, and for the good of the country, Lieutenant Colonel Alphonso Clay shall be able to call on the use of any resources and men of the Department of War.' Give it to me to sign."

As a reluctant Stanton scribbled on a dispatch form, a horrified Clay blurted "Sir, I cannot permit that. Things may go awry. I expected only a vague order to assist me, signed by some obscure Army official. I may have to do...extralegal things; things which could destroy you if they could be traced back to you. Should certain deeds come to light, it was always my intention to claim that I had vastly exceeded my orders, but the way your letter is phrased, everyone will think you approved in advance every one of my deeds."

"And I do so approve," replied Grant, taking the letter from Stanton's slightly shaking hand and scrawling his signature at the bottom. "I am tired of giving orders and having others pay for them; of sending young fellows to die for my plans, my mistakes. 300,000 young Americans died because of my orders; that's not counting the Rebs. If I can endure the burden of that, I can shoulder the burden of whatever you propose to do." Grant leaned forward and handed the document to Clay. "Anything else, Colonel?"

"Yes, sir. Mr. Courtney Delapore was the first to mention Booth's name to me as a possible conspirator. Although nothing less than a Copperhead, he agreed to assist us, providing that the civilians being held without specific charges in the Old Capitol Prison be released. He has honored the bargain; we have an obligation to do the same. I am certain Colonel Baker will not release the prisoners on his own; he has found ways to...profit from their imprisonment, and suffers badly from the sin of avarice. I would appreciate a direct order to him requiring the release of all prisoners not yet specifically charged with actual crimes."

Grant nodded, then looked at Stanton. "Mr. Secretary, you can sign that one." With a few rapid scratches of his pen, Stanton finished the second order, signed it, and thrust it at Clay. Clay stood and inserted both documents into an inner pocket of his tunic. He then clicked his heels in the European manner, saluted smartly, and strode out of the room without a word, Bierce hurrying to keep up. Stanton frowned uneasily, while Grant looked thoughtfully at the space Clay had recently occupied.

* * * * *

Colonel Lafayette Baker stood in his small office at the Old Capitol Prison, reading the brief order for a second time, and spat out a creatively obscene phrase. Bierce glanced at Clay, and noted to his utter amazement that the corners of his friend's mouth tugged upwards into a ghost of a smile; the movement gone so quickly that Bierce could hardly believe that he had seen something so unlikely.

"The Secretary's instructions are quite clear," said Clay mildly. "The people in question are to be released now, this instant." Bierce thought he once again caught the flash of that ghostly smile as Clay continued. "Do not take it too hard, Colonel Baker. You will still have a fair number of prisoners to exploit and oppress. Only now you will be restricted to exploiting and oppressing those who truly deserve it. For instance, you have all of Booth's conspirators; in addition, a number of killers and blockade runners, that sort of offal. No one will object to how harshly you treat such trash, least of all I. In fact, I need to interview one of your prisoners not subject to the terms of the release. I understand you are holding a

Frenchman, Martin Laval, charged with smuggling munitions of war to the traitors."

The angry expression on Baker's face was replaced by a frown of puzzlement. "Yes, I've got the frog. I'm surprised you even know about him; he's a filthy piece of work, even for a Frenchie blockade runner. Had his ship in Wilmington loaded up with cotton and was preparing to set sail when our boys took the harbor. He had already unloaded a cargo of percussion caps, Enfield rifles, quinine, laudanum, everything Lee and Johnston needed to keep our boys dying for a few more weeks. According to the Provost people, he had even brought in French postcards by the hundreds." The coarse Baker seemed uncharacteristically hesitant. "It wasn't just naked women; I'm no Goddamn Puritan. The Provost lieutenant who brought him up here showed a couple to me, and not for a bit of fun. They were...kiddies, kiddies doing things and...having things done to them. Jesus, Mary and Joseph, some were younger than my little daughter! I don't know what is sicker, the degenerate frog who would sell such things or the Reb bastards who would buy them. Anyway, I've had a little fun with Laval. You want to have a go at him too? I can assign a couple of my boys to hold him down."

"That will not be necessary, Colonel Baker. In fact, I must insist on interviewing him alone. Just give me the key to his cell, and you and your men go about releasing those covered by Stanton's orders. Bierce, you go along with him, and make sure that there are no complications."

A look of concern on his face, Bierce asked, "Wouldn't it be better if I were with you? Laval might give you trouble."

"I appreciate your offer, Major, but I must insist on doing this completely by myself. Colonel Baker, direct me to Laval."

"Your party," replied Baker sullenly. He led Clay and Bierce out of the gloomy office into the gloomier corridor, lit inadequately by the occasional anemic gas jet. The light was so faint that the visitors could not clearly make out what occasionally scurried and squeaked along the bottoms of the filthy walls; independently, they each decided that was probably for the best.

After twisting through several dismal passageways, Baker finally brought them to the chamber holding the French blockade runner. Most of the rooms in the Old Capitol had solid wood doors with no locks, so guards could surprise the prisoners at any time of the day or night. However, Baker pointed to one of the very few where the wooden door had been replaced by a locked grillwork. Clay gestured for the key; Baker handed over a heavy iron item, and with a negligent salute Clay wordlessly dismissed Baker and Bierce. They moved off, and in moments Clay heard Baker's harsh voice snapping orders to his men, and the distant sounds of doors being thrown open. Clay waited only long enough to be certain that the sounds did not appear to be approaching this isolated cell before advancing to the grillwork, through which the prisoner was visible. The door had been secured by a heavy padlock. Through the grillwork could be seen a tall, filthy-looking man, dressed in tatters, pacing with nervous energy about the cell. Clay smoothly unlocked the door and entering the cubicle.

Martin Laval looked sharply as Clay entered. He frowned, and in accented but serviceable English said, "My colonel, I am unfamiliar with you. Has the embassy been in touch with Secretary Seward, and has Mr. Seward ordered an end to the farce of my imprisonment? Have you come to deliver the order for my release?"

"I fear not, Monsieur Laval," said Clay, glancing about the filthy chamber, whose only contents were a lousy cot, a rickety chair, a slop bucket, and a gas jet. "My name is Alphonso Clay. I am here to confirm certain facts that have been indicated to me about the cargo you brought into Wilmington, just before your capture. I do not mean the armaments and ammunition, or even the...unusual art that you ran past the blockade."

Laval chuckled ruefully. "Do not tell me you lack sophistication, like your Colonel Baker. He fancies himself a hard man who understands the world, but show him something of the...sophisticated and decadent, and he responds like a provincial Quaker." Laval paused to massage his jaw, where a large bruise was just visible under his stubble, and chuckled again. "Well, perhaps not a Quaker, but like a silly and uncontrolled child. Be that as it may, your civil war is over, and there is no civilian law applicable to me which warrants my detention. I demand you inform your superiors that Napoleon III may respond with hostility to a French citizen being held under these conditions. I do not believe your country would care to face the wrath of France, so soon after such a devastating rebellion."

"I will consider relaying your message," replied Clay. "First, I need some additional information on the material that you personally delivered to Colonel Ephraim Waite, late of the Confederate Secret Service."

Laval started with surprise, and then scowled. "Who says I made such a delivery?"

"John Wilkes Booth. He wrote of it in his diary, which came into my possession."

"MERDE!" snarled Laval savagely. Then making an obvious effort to regain his calm, he said, "The items were of no importance. Personal items that Colonel Waite had asked me to obtain for him in Europe. Surely Booth wrote nothing *more*?" Despite himself, Laval could not keep the last syllable from rising to a kind of pleading question.

"He did write something more. One of his last entries expanded on that. He had become aware that his chances of escape had vanished, and death would visit him sooner rather than later. He even boasted as to how the foolish Italian Professor Felippi Pacini had no idea he had delivered the South's salvation into its hands."

"Idiot! Vain, idiotic actor! Very well then, you know, but your knowledge will do you little good. Monsieur Waite has the packages, and you will never locate them in time. And even if you could, you should not dare to do so. There are...interests involved. Interests far more powerful, and with a far longer reach, than disappointed slaveholders and defeated generals."

Clay said two words. "Starry Wisdom."

The Frenchman's eyes bulged slightly, and he glanced with fright at the open door. "Fool! Never mention that name where others might overhear," he hissed in a strangled whisper. "Their reach is long, and they prefer to operate in the shadows. Even those who serve them do not speak of them to outsiders."

"Oh, I am familiar with Starry Wisdom. I know that they were a prime mover in the tragedy of our civil war, aiming to create a country under their control, a country devoted to inequality and oppression, a country where they could more easily implement their plans than in a nation aspiring to freedom and equality. They have wealth, power and connections developed over numerous generations; yet their obscene practices and aims require them to live in the shadows. I know that they tire of the shadows, and have manipulated good but foolish men into pursuing goals they would never consciously approve. Oh, the Civil War would have happened anyway, but it would not have lasted as long or been as horrific without the pushing and manipulation Starry Wisdom and its minions exercised behind the scenes in Richmond. And now, they have used you in a last-minute plan to reignite this horrible war, and bring more death and destruction upon our bleeding Republic."

"You know much, Colonel," said the Frenchman slowly, not bothering to contradict what Clay had said. "Then you should know that the brotherhood cannot die, no matter what the fate of its individual members. The North appears to have won, but in truth it was on its last legs, and only barely outlasted the South. With the war suddenly reignited, I suspect few Federal soldiers will willingly undertake the horrors of war yet again, especially if the South rises – how do you say – reinvigorated. Join us; you cannot stop us, and if you assist us, wealth and power beyond imagining can be yours."

Clay strolled over to the gas-jet and began to fiddle with it, apparently wanting to lessen the dismal gloom of the cell. While he delicately adjusted the jet, he said over his shoulder, “If this assignment has the potential that you say, I can hardly believe they entrusted this to one man, no matter how trusted. You must have had assistance.”

Laval smirked. “No more than lifting and carrying. No one but I suspected there was anything more than medicines or explosives in the containers.”

“Waite must be a very impressive individual,” said Clay, still fiddling with the gas jet and frowning with concentration. “I would expect his very appearance leaves an unforgettable impression.”

“There you would be wrong, my friend. He is a somewhat burly man of middle age and above average height; nothing truly remarkable about him save an affectation for dressing head to toe in black. Very useful in his profession; if anyone were to give him a second glance, they would concentrate on the clothes, not the face.

“I see,” said Clay mildly. Then, with the speed of a mongoose striking he whirled away from the jet, caught the unprepared Frenchman in a headlock, and twisted mightily. Laval’s neck snapped with a sound not unlike a fresh carrot being broken in half. Clay then let the smuggler flop to the floor, and stepping back, observed his handiwork. Laval was completely paralyzed yet conscious; his dark eyes darted about in horror as he vainly tried to compel his body to take a breath. Clay began trembling all over, and emitted a series of terrifying giggles. In a few moments he brought himself under control and addressed the dying man on the floor.

“I do not apologize for what I have done, Monsieur Laval. Your story must go no further. Even if I succeed in stopping Waite, the mere knowledge by the public of what was attempted could do incalculable damage to my country. No, I do not apologize for the act of killing you. Yet, I must apologize for the fact that it was only partly for the good of the Republic that I have taken your life. I must say, in honesty and in penance, that I hunger to take lives, that I enjoy the act of slaying, and that you have just given me more pleasure than I have had since... well, since I last was with a certain lady."

Clay looked closely at Laval's motionless eyes, and saw the Frenchman was truly dead. Then, moving silently and swiftly, he detached the dead man's suspenders from his trousers and quickly tied them into a complicated knot. He heard steps coming down the corridor, but did not panic; he swiftly looped the knot around Laval's throat, then lifting the large man and boosting him up the wall with surprising ease, he looped the other end of the knot around the gas fixture. Leaving Laval's remains dangling, he turned and strode toward the doorway just as Baker and Bierce appeared.

"A tragedy, Colonel Baker," said Clay, his face now completely expressionless. "Monsieur Laval had apparently hanged himself just as I entered the cell. Pity. Come Bierce, we can learn nothing further here."

As Clay made to leave the dingy cell, Baker angrily grabbed his arm. "Now just a Goddamn minute, Clay! This stinks like last week's fish! I don't mind seeing a blockade-running Frenchie degenerate beaten to within an inch of his life, but there is a limit!"

Clay turned his face toward Baker; behind the wire-rimmed spectacles, the slight colonel's eyes seemed to glow with unearthly light. In the softest of voices Clay said "Unhand me, Baker. I will not ask again." Lafayette Baker was a coarse, insensitive man, but he sensed his danger, and slowly released Clay's arm. Never taking his eyes off Baker, Clay reached inside his tunic, and produced the paper that Grant had signed, handing it wordlessly to the larger man. Baker scanned it, and visibly paled; he was intelligent enough to see he was on the edge of matters where it was dangerous to intrude. He handed the document back to Clay, who replaced it within his tunic, turned, and strode out of the cell, trailed by a troubled Bierce.

The two friends threaded their way through dismal corridors now crowded with gaunt, starved-looking people in lousy clothing , lugging their few pitiful belongings to the front door and freedom, while the occasional guard looked on with frowning bemusement. Once out in the spring sunlight, Clay paused, shuddered, and took several deep breaths, as if to clear his lungs of foulness. Then he started walking quickly in the direction of Willard's; Bierce silently keeping pace at his side. As they approached their destination, Bierce finally spoke. "You killed him in cold blood." It was a statement, not a question.

"I did what had to be done," replied Clay, not quite answering the question. "The man had knowledge that could cost countless lives, if he ever found a wide audience."

"So you sent me off with Baker, so I would not be soiled by... whatever you did."

As they approached the entrance to Willard's, Clay refused to look directly at Bierce. "You fancy yourself a hard man, Bierce, and you laugh at the piety of the masses. You have seen degrading things, and have suffered degrading things. Still, you have emerged from this war with a core of decency. I would not put a stain on that decency for all the world holds dear. This matter is far from over, and at some point I may require you to give up your life for the good of the nation, but it will be in an honorable way."

By now they had crossed the elegant lobby, and were ascending the broad stairs to the fourth floor which contained their rooms. After he had digested what Clay had said, Bierce replied, "I appreciate you taking all of what you perceive to be the...dishonor upon yourself. However, it is my country too, damn it, and I will do anything at all to preserve it. Anything!"

The two were now outside the door to Bierce's room. Clay took his friend by the shoulders. "I know you would. Giving one's life is easy. Any fool can die for his country. It takes a true man to give up his soul for his country. All the more reason for me to shield you from that sacrifice, if possible."

"At least tell me what we are up against."

Clay released Bierce and took the room key from his pocket. As he unlocked the door he replied, "Very well. You will know something, something which the public must never know..."

"And what might that be?" asked Teresa Duval. At the sight of her, sitting casually in a wing chair with Dr. Dee's terrible book lying open in her lap, Clay was brought up short. Then hustling Bierce into the room, the slightly-built colonel swiftly locked the door and turned toward the woman with a frown on his face.

"Miss Duval, I really must protest. I wish you would not demonstrate so blatantly your skill with the lock-pick."

She closed the heavy book, placing it carefully on the end-table while saying "Come, Colonel Clay, we should have no secrets. A little bird told me that you may be leaving town quickly on important business. I wanted to make sure that we had a proper good-bye."

An exasperated Clay turned to Bierce for support, only to see his friend grinning broadly; for some reason, this caused spots of red to appear on the colonel's pale cheeks. "I must tell Major Bierce a tale, a tale which even if Bierce and I are successful must not become public. Anyone who knows of this will carry a burden for the rest of their lives, a burden that may be too heavy for all but the strongest to keep to themselves."

Duval emitted one of her silvery, chilling laughs; Clay suddenly realized that where he had once found that laugh ominous, he now felt it to be rather endearing. "Colonel Clay, I will match you secret for secret. Now gentlemen, take the remaining chairs. We should be comfortable for the telling of such a tale."

Clay hesitated, and then sat stiffly in one of the two unoccupied chairs of the room, while Bierce lounged negligently in the other. Clay slowly, even reluctantly, drew a small leather-bound diary from an inner tunic pocket; a rusty stain was clearly visible on part of the binding. Still, Clay made no effort to open the volume. Instead, he clutched it tightly, as if it were a dangerous animal that could do horrible damage if released for but a moment. Without looking directly at Bierce or Duval, he began to speak.

"The bulk of Booth's diary is taken up with his plans for the murder of Abraham Lincoln and his subsequent attempts to evade justice. If nothing else, it confirms the guilt of those conspirators Stanton has arrested, except for Mrs. Surratt, and that Dr. Mudd did indeed know Booth. However, that is not the true significance of this document. Towards the very end, when he realized he would not be able to evade capture, Booth sought to reinforce his courage. It is in these last pages that he makes clear what I had suspected – what I had feared. The murder of Abraham Lincoln was not a simple, though monstrous, act of revenge; it was the first step in a plan to reignite the war, and give the South one last opportunity at victory."

"Booth was making such intricate plans?" asked Bierce with a frown. "He was a vain and shallow actor, unable to think beyond a dramatic event starring himself."

"That is true. Booth was only an instrument; a willing instrument, but an instrument nonetheless. Others gave him his orders through Colonel Ephraim Waite of the Confederate Secret Service. I have heard rumors of the man; a dangerous antagonist, devoid of honor or decency. Just one instance: he arranged for infernal devices, filled with gunpowder, to be shaped and painted to resemble lumps of coal. He then had one of his minions smuggle them to City Point, where General Grant kept his headquarters during the last part of the war, and add them to the fuel of the boat intended to carry Grant to Washington. It worked; the bombs were unknowingly shoveled into the boiler by stokers, and the riverboat exploded, killing scores of people, including dozens of women and children who had been visiting their men folk. It was the purest luck that Grant had been detained at the last minute. Further, there are even suggestions that his true allegiance lay not to the Confederacy, but to another organization – far, far older, and infinitely more depraved. But that is beside the point. Have either of you heard of Professor Filippi Pacini, of the University of Florence, in Italy?"

Duval and Bierce shook their heads in the negative. A sad, slight smile flashed across Clay's face. "Such is fame. The world knows of dozens of brutal generals, scores of power-crazed dictators and monarchs – but a good, a kindly man working to save thousands of human lives labors in virtual anonymity. Cholera has been Pacini's obsession. He regards it as the greatest current threat to the health of mankind. True, smallpox and bubonic plague have killed more, but vaccination is gradually eliminating the former, while the latter seems to be confined these days to the outer reaches of Asia. Cholera is different: no vaccine, no treatment, able to strike the high and the low, anywhere in the world."

"True enough," said Duval quietly. "I saw many die of it in the hospitals. It was not a pleasant way to die." She did not add that if she liked the patient, she had often eased his path with an overdose of laudanum.

"I think something between 5% and 10% of our boys die of cholera before the Rebs have a chance to draw a bead on them," added Bierce.

Clay nodded. "A truly terrible way to die, without even the glory of having fallen in the service of our nation. Well, Professor Pacini knew what many peasants knew: that if drinking water was kept clear of human waste, and if you did not touch an infected person or his possessions, it is impossible to contract cholera."

Duval nodded. "All the better doctors in the hospitals would only handle cholera victims with gloves, and would insist that the privies be dug far away from the wells." She smiled a chilly smile. "Those doctors who did not insist on such things tended not to last too long."

Clay looked down at the diary in his hands, and then looked up to the others. "I had known of Pacini before I ever saw his name in this diary. He had published papers in several European journals, claiming that he had isolated a microscopically small animal in the waste of infected people, an animal he calls a 'germ.' He believes that a single germ can enter the body of a man, infect him and create many more of its own kind, which pass out of the body in the liquid...discharges from the infected person. Anyone who touches the victim contracts cholera, and even if no one does touch him, the... effluvia enters the ground and eventually the ground water supply. So, it is not human waste that causes cholera, but an animal that lives in that waste, an animal too small to be seen without a microscope."

"That is all very well," said Bierce. "I am more interested in the sciences than your average officer. But what does that have to do with Laval and Waite?"

Bierce glanced over to Duval for support. However, the cold-blooded killer had turned pale. "Jesus, Mary and Joseph," she whispered; the woman who had believed herself unshockable was profoundly shocked to the core of her being.

Clay nodded, a haunted look on his normally placid face. "Yes. Professor Pacini has isolated an especially potent variety of the germ, learned how to make it grow, even how to preserve it for transportation. He is hoping to find a vaccine for cholera, using his concentrated samples of the disease, but so far without success. According to Booth's diary, Waite had the late, unlamented Laval approach the professor, asking for a large quantity of concentrated cholera. Furthermore, not just any cholera. The Italian had gone to great pains to locate and grow a variety from Asia that is unusually dangerous, unusually infectious – invariably fatal. Laval insisted he wanted that variety alone. Pacini did not hesitate, for Laval had forged documents saying he was from Louis Pasteur, the eminent Frenchman who has already shown himself skilled in the area of microscopic organisms. Pacini evidently did not care who made the discovery, so long as it was made. Before he...died, Laval confirmed he had delivered two carboys of the concentrated disease to Waite."

There was a long silence in the room, finally broken by Bierce. "If a cholera epidemic breaks out in the North, and the South is blamed, the Federal Army, officers and men, will be uncontrollable, and the Radicals in Congress will not want to control them. Say good-bye to an easy peace; they will start a march through the South that will make Sherman's look like a picnic. And the Rebs won't stand and be slaughtered; they will fight back, and the devastation of the last four years will seem to be a mere prelude to the main event."

Duval shook her head in disbelief. "Such a thing makes no sense. The South has already been beaten down. If the war restarts, it will be just that much worse for those English-loving bastards." At the use of such an odd obscenity, the two officers glanced sharply at her, but she affected not to notice.

"You are probably right," replied Clay. "However, Southerners with their backs to the wall may not see it that way. And I cannot be certain that they would not achieve the seemingly impossible. Look at their victories over the last four years, against an enemy with twice the population and ten times the resources." Clay hesitated, then went on. "Besides, there are strange currents below the surface of our wounded country right now, and it is hard to estimate their power. There are Radical Republicans unhappy with the easy peace; some of them would be pleased for an excuse to grind the South into the ground, and treat it as a conquered province, not a returning part of our country. Further, there are some...and I suspect Colonel Waite is among them...who would be delighted to see utter chaos reign, no matter who won. His masters would not care if they came to rule a country that had been destroyed from end to end; in fact, they might prefer it."

Bierce looked steadily at Clay. "You think Waite works for the Starry Wisdom bastards."

"What I believe is immaterial. The only material point is that he must be stopped, at any cost. So, are you with me?"

"Certainly," responded Bierce.

"I as well," added Duval.

Clay looked at the woman with some hostility. “Let us have an understanding. You are not accompanying us. This man is far, far too dangerous; and I only have the sketchiest idea of what he looks like.”

Looking crestfallen, Duval rose. “I see. Well, good luck to you both.” Without another word, she swept from the room, slamming the door behind her.

Bierce looked at the still-vibrating door with a frown on his face. “Well, she took that better than I would have expected.”

Clay did not directly answer Bierce. Instead, he stood up and said, “Pack one bag lightly. We will be on the rails in an hour.”

* * * * *

Fifty-seven minutes later, the engine hit its whistle and began to slowly gather momentum as it left the Washington station. Clay and Bierce shared a private compartment in first class. Bierce, reflecting wryly that it was always a pleasure to travel with the wealthy Clay, asked “Are you certain Waite is targeting New York?”

Clay stared out the window at Washington’s dismal working-class neighborhoods, not really seeing them. “Booth’s diary did not mention the specific target, but it must be New York. It is the most populous city in the North, and the wealthiest. Unleashing a plague there would paralyze the American financial and industrial systems, which are to a great extent controlled out of that single city. Furthermore, it is the transportation center of the North. Half a dozen major railroads, not to mention a score of shipping companies, emanate from New York. As the plague frightens the populace, many people who are unknowingly infected will flee, carrying the pestilence to cities throughout the North.”

Bierce sank his chin morosely down onto his chest. “When you put it that way, I can see it. Still, that description you got from Laval doesn't mean much in a city the size of New York. How can we possibly track him down in time?"

"It will be hard, but not impossible. We do have one advantage. I am fairly sure that I know where Waite will unleash his weapon."

Bierce perked up. "You do?"

"Yes. If Waite is intelligent, there is only one place he would choose. The Central Park Reservoir."

"I have heard of Central Park, but why would its reservoir be so important to Waite?"

Clay gave another ghost of a smile. "Most people have been so preoccupied with the war that they have ignored much that is important to our country's future. New York City has long suffered from foul and diseased drinking water; the very cholera that now concerns us has been a regular visitor, along with other diseases. Well, New York has finally addressed the issue. Two years ago they finished the Croton Aqueduct to bring pure, untainted water from high in the mountains of upstate. It is brought to a reservoir in Central Park, then is drawn off through two great pipes into a series of ever smaller pipes, until virtually every structure has an unlimited source of untainted water. No more drawing your water from next to the privy. People admire the vast buildings and bustling factories of New York, but this water system is by far and away the greatest service the city has yet provided its people."

"And the water from the reservoir goes into every building in the city," whispered Bierce, a note of dawning horror in his voice. "This must be stopped; if it is not already too late."

"I suspect...hope...that Waite has taken his time to cultivate additional batches of his germs. He cannot be certain how much it would take to completely poison a city the size of New York. We must go and watch the reservoir for suspicious activity. Of course, it would have helped immeasurably to have a true likeness of Waite, to show around the major hotels, but..."

The door to their compartment slid open quietly. To both men's utter amazement, in walked Teresa Duval, dressed in a simple but expensive walking frock. Batting her eyelashes in an exaggerated manner, she said in a low, throaty voice, "Gentlemen, could you offer a seat to a lady? I feel a fit of vapors coming on." Without waiting for a reply, she smoothly seated herself on the bench next to Clay; across from them, Bierce looked on with amusement as Clay's pale face began to turn faintly scarlet with rage.

"Miss Duval, I expressly forbade you to join us in..." Clay's voice trailed off. Apparently from thin air, Duval had produced a *carte de visite,* the small photograph on a cardboard backing that the wealthy (and vain) were using in place of visiting cards. She extended it negligently toward Clay; his eyes widening behind his spectacles, he snatched it from her hand. The picture showed two men, posing with arrogant smiles as if to celebrate an important occasion. The one on the right was unmistakably John Wilkes Booth. The one on the left was an ordinary-looking, stocky man, dressed entirely in black; in fact, a man who matched the sketchy description given by Martin Laval. Clay handed the card to Bierce, who after a moment spat out an obscenity of amazement.

"How came you by this photograph?" Clay asked in wonder. Duval seemed to positively preen.

"At Mr. Brady's photography studio. I knew that Colonel Baker's men would have seized all pictures containing Booth alone, but would have been less interested in those where he was posing with others. I also knew that Brady would realize the financial value of any image of a Presidential assassin, and would have held such photographs back. Finally, I strongly suspected that someone as egotistic as Booth would want to commemorate his conspiracy, ideally with a picture containing himself and his master. I told Mr. Brady of my connections with the Secret Service, and that we knew he had withheld photographs of Booth. The poor little fool was terrified, and showed me all he had. I found this one, confiscated it, and left him with a stern warning not to impede Federal investigations in the future."

"How could you be sure this photograph would exist?" asked Bierce slowly, handing the card back to Clay.

Duval gave out one of her silvery, chilling laughs. "I could not be certain, but I thought it likely. An egotist like Booth must have hated having a master, any master. By having a picture taken with that master, side by side, they became equals – at least in Booth's mind."

"This will make things immeasurably easier in New York," said Clay. "I owe you my thanks."

"No thanks are necessary, Colonel Clay." Duval then yawned in an exaggerated manner. "Now if you will excuse me. I am very tired, and must be rested and at my best when we arrive in New York." Before Clay could react, she snuggled up to him, made a pillow of his right shoulder, closed her eyes, and seemingly dropped immediately off to sleep. The face of the normally expressionless Clay showed a confusing mixture of emotions: embarrassment, outrage, and confusion. Still, he found himself unable to move, for fear of disturbing her.

Suddenly he heard a wheezing sound from the other side of the compartment. He looked over at Bierce, and was outraged to see that his friend was convulsed with mirth, and the wheezing sounds were what remained of his laughter as it passed his tightly-compressed lips. Clay glared at Bierce, who stubbornly refused to disappear in a puff of blue smoke.

* * * * *

The morning sun was just beginning to peep through New York's smoky haze as the train pulled up to the station with a hiss of escaping steam. Tired passengers quickly exited their cabins, hurrying to lay claim to the few horse-drawn cabs that would be outside the station. In a remarkably short time Clay, Bierce and Duval were the only ones left on the platform, aside from an elderly conductor too distant to hear their discussions.

Clay turned to Bierce. "Major, go locate a cab if you can. I need a few moments alone with Miss Duval." Grinning wolfishly, Bierce saluted, and strolled off, whistling "The Yellow Rose of Texas." Clay then turned his attention to Duval.

"Very well, you are in this. Will you accept my direction in how to proceed?"

"Within reason," Duval replied sweetly.

"There is a critical task I need accomplished in Buffalo. Originally, I had not decided whether to ask Major Bierce to accomplish it while I proceeded alone against Waite. On the one hand, I could very well need his help in bringing down Waite; on the other, to delay the task in Buffalo could bring all our efforts to naught. I would like you to immediately take the train to Buffalo, and perform a task...suited to your temperament. We both know you are more capable of...extreme actions than Major Bierce. He is brave and resourceful, and would give his life without hesitation for his country, but he is more...human than either of us, and his honor might restrain him from doing certain distasteful things. Are you up to the challenge?"

There was no mockery in Duval's voice. "Tell me what needs to be done, Alphonso," she replied, an eager, shining light appearing in her eyes.

Ten minutes later, Clay jumped into a carriage that Bierce had with some difficulty just secured. As they pulled away from the station, a puzzled Bierce asked "Where is Miss Duval?"

"She is undertaking a separate but related matter on my behalf. Now, please instruct the driver that we will need to visit the major hotels closest to the Central Park reservoir."

* * * * *

By the dim light of an oil lantern Courtney Delapore heaved the last of a dozen milk can-sized carboys into the back of the wagon that stood to the side of the darkened, crumbling farmhouse that stood on the still-undeveloped part of Manhattan just north of 77th Street.

From his post on the driver's seat Ephraim Waite hissed, "Careful with that, Delapore. The wax sealing on the lids won't take rough handling. It took a lot of effort to nurture the contents of the first two carboys, and breed enough to fill the twelve we now have. We don't want to lose any of the contents before they can be put to good use."

"No, and we would not care to befoul ourselves with their contents," muttered Delapore morosely as he clambered up beside Waite. As Waite urged the horse gently into motion, Delapore added, "We must make sure that all of this reaches the women, children, the young and the old – make sure that every bit of it goes to causing horrible death."

Waite chuckled. "Cheer up, Delapore. As the first Napoleon said, you cannot make an omelet without breaking eggs. The deaths are a regrettable necessity to creating a glorious future for the Confederacy, a Confederacy everyone is assuming dead and buried. More people have died for less. Besides, I would imagine a Delapore would not cavil at such measures, given what your ancestors did, back in England."

Delapore started, and turned to look at Waite, whose features were now being lit by the gaslights lining the main road leading to the settled parts of Manhattan. "Sir, what do you mean by that?"

Again Waite chuckled. "You think that your little secret died, when your ancestor slaughtered all of his family and fled to Virginia in 1620? I have...associates who have discovered some very interesting facts about the old family mansion, what was beneath, and what your family did there since time immemorial. Oh, the old stories have largely faded away, but I imagine your ancestor had not been able to do much about the caverns, and what they contained. I guarantee that if some experts were told where to look, they would find things reflecting very poorly on the name of Delapore, very poorly indeed. Even after two hundred and fifty years."

Delapore shuddered. He thought of the contents of the ancient letter shown by the head of the family to every male Delapore upon his coming of age; telling of the horror that had caused his ancestor to murder all his family within reach and set sail for the colonies. The letter that told why it was the solemn duty of every Delapore to work ceaselessly to retrieve the family honor. Knowledge of what was in that letter was terrible enough, even after 250 years; to think that Waite could spread that knowledge to the world gave him a certain hold over Delapore.

New York was already known as the city that never sleeps, but even as the wagon moved into the heavily settled portions of the city, the confusing traffic of horses, cabs, wagons and streetcars moved smoothly enough during the hours of darkness, and after a surprisingly short period Waite turned the wagon left into a road that meandered through the still-unfinished Central Park. Waite and Delapore appeared to soon have the park largely to themselves, aside from an occasional quickly-walking figure. Central Park had already acquired a reputation of being somewhat dangerous at night and emptied out at sunset; a fact on which Waite had counted.

As the wagon rounded a copse of trees, the reservoir came into view, its surface shining in the ghostly light of the quarter moon. For much of its circumference the road the conspirators were on hugged the shoreline. Waite followed the road until the wagon reached another small copse of trees; he then urged the horse off the path and under the largest of the trees. Waite leapt off his seat and quickly tied the perspiring horse to a branch; Delapore clambered down from the seat more slowly, with visible reluctance. Delapore suddenly cocked his head at a sloshing, gurgling sound from nearby.

"Waite, is that one of the intakes for the water system?"

"Very astute, Delapore." Waite glanced around, seeing no one near enough to clearly observe what they were doing. "Very well. Let's unload six of the containers and empty them as quickly as we can at the inlet, before a late-night stroller comes along. Then we make for the other intake."

Going around to the back of the wagon, each man took hold of a container of mass death, and with much grunting and huffing half-carried, half-rolled them to the point of the reservoir where an enormous, largely-submerged pipe greedily slurped at the pure water of upstate New York. Waite then took out of his coat pocket two pairs of heavy work gloves, throwing one of them to Delapore.

"Put these on. The last part is the trickiest. We must break the wax seals and carefully empty the contents. Not a drop must touch your skin; not if you do not want to contribute your life to the Cause."

"That is quite far enough, gentlemen," sounded a voice that was soft yet oddly penetrating. Waite and Delapore whirled toward the sound of the voice, to observe two uniformed figures stepping from behind trees at the far side of the copse, each holding a revolver in his right hand.

As Clay and Bierce advanced, Waite snarled, "Just what do you mean by pointing pistols and law abiding..." Waite's voice trailed off, as he recognized Alphonso Clay in the pale moonlight. "Alphonso Clay," he said in angry wonderment.

"You have the advantage on me, sir," responded Clay with a slight frown. "I do not believe we have been introduced."

"The people I'm with know a great deal about you."

"It's over, Waite," interrupted Bierce in a harsh voice. "A clerk at the Fleur-de-Lys Hotel recognized you from a picture we showed him. We followed you discretely from the hotel to the farm near Harlem, observed where you brewed up your poison through an imperfectly curtained window, watched you load your deadly cargo, and followed you here."

"I didn't see anyone flowing us," growled Waite.

The Federal officers by now were quite close to the two conspirators and stood covering them with weapons that did not waiver in the slightest. Clay said "Let me introduce my companion, Major Ambrose Bierce. He has seen much action behind enemy lines as a scout – a spy if you will – and knows how to follow without being noticed. I simply followed his lead." Clay turned his attention to Delapore. "I am truly disappointed to see you participating in such a monstrous conspiracy. I had not taken you to be that kind of man."

"It was not my choice," replied Delapore, striving to keep a note of whining out of his voice. "I am ashamed to admit that I had deceived you as to the extent of my participation in Confederate espionage; it ended up far more extensive than I had intended. When I indicated my reluctance to participate in this...plan, Colonel Waite made it clear that he would see to it that my treason became widely known; my treason, and a terrible old family scandal that would blight my family's name forever."

"And you think your participation in this unspeakable atrocity will not so blight your name?" responded Clay in wonderment.

"At least there would have been something to show for it," answered Delapore in a voice so low that it was almost a whisper. "Freedom for people oppressed by a tyrannical government, proof that power exercised outside the bounds of the Constitution cannot prevail."

Bierce growled out a number of choice obscenities, before saying, "You idiot! You think men like Waite care about rights and the Constitution? All they care about is power; not just power over the blacks, but power over all, including the precious clan of Delapore!"

"That will be enough, Bierce," said Clay calmly. He turned his attention back to Waite. "It is now necessary for us to go to a quiet place, perhaps your farmhouse, where I will determine to what extent you can implicate Jefferson Davis and other leading Confederates in this atrocity. Your ultimate fate will depend on your usefulness to us; so I strongly suggest full co-operation. Gentlemen, please be so good as to load those containers back into the wagon, and use the utmost care in doing so."

Waite nodded, and stooped to pick up the can in front of him. Then quick as a lizard, in two hops he had landed in water up to his ankles, just beyond where the swirling water indicated the presence of the intake pipe. Before either Clay or Bierce could react, he had turned the can so that its lid was pointing downward at an angle of 30 degrees, his powerful, meaty left hand grasping the handle of the lid, only the thin wax seal keeping the liquid death from flowing into the pipe that fed water to half of Manhattan.

Waite laughed cruelly. "Now, gentlemen, I know you can shoot me dead, but do you care to wager a hundred thousand lives I won't be able to break the seal with my dying breath?"

The lenses of Clay's spectacles glittered strangely in the moonlight. "There is not enough in that one container to cause an epidemic," he replied slowly, his gun not wavering. "You yourself planned to release six such containers into each of the two intakes."

"That was merely caution. I think one may very well be enough. Shall we see?" Waite paused for a long moment to see the reaction of the Federal officers; as they took no action, Waite laughed again. "I thought not. Now, surrender your weapons to Delapore, or I release the cholera!"

"Why should we do that?" responded Clay. "Then you will simply kill us, and release the cholera anyway. The former is a secondary issue, we cannot permit the latter."

Suddenly Delapore spoke up. "Colonel Waite, it is over, and it is for the best. Do the sensible, the humane thing, and give up."

"Oh hell, the cowardly bastard is bluffing!" exclaimed Bierce suddenly. Revolver at the ready, he began striding to where Waite stood. However, before he had covered half the short distance, a small pocket Colt appeared in Waite's free hand. Bierce hesitated, still fearful of causing the release of the cholera. Waite felt no such hesitation, in a smooth motion he cocked and fired the weapon...

Just as Courtney Delapore's body hurled across his line of fire. With a sound more like a sigh than a cry, Delapore collapsed to the ground at the feet of a shocked Ambrose Bierce. In the same instant, the crack of Clay's .32 caliber Smith & Wesson sounded. Waite's left eye disappeared in a spray of blood; his ruined brain caused his hand to relax from the handle of the can as he collapsed into the shallow water. Holstering their weapons as they ran, both officers leaped toward the container. Bierce reached it first, and began to gently turn it upright.

"Let me handle that," commanded Clay. "The fall may have ruptured the wax seal; it might be death to touch it."

"You just saved my life," replied Bierce, sounding calmer than he felt. "The least I can do is shoulder this particular risk." After a moment's examination, a relieved Bierce announced "It appears to be unbroken."

Meanwhile, Clay had knelt by the inert form of Courtney Delapore. Turning him on his back, he saw with some surprise that Delapore was barely alive, breathing raggedly. With his right hand he feebly toyed with the wedding ring on his left; the ring symbolizing the marriage to his long dead wife. A faint smile crossed Delapore's lips, and then with a shudder he died.

A police whistle sounded. The two friends spotted several figures in the distance, hurrying in their direction; apparently gunshots excited comment, even in Central Park.

"Quickly Bierce!" exclaimed Clay. "You take one container, I the other. Onto the cart and away before we are taken with evidence we dare never explain. And we still need to recover our hired horses and tie their reins to the back of the wagon before we can leave the park altogether."

"Where are we headed?" puffed Bierce as he loaded his container gingerly into the wagon."

"Waite's farmhouse," replied Clay as he untied the horse and leapt into the driver's seat, viciously jerking the animal's head in the direction of their horses.

* * * * *

The first glimmers of sunshine were filtering through the tattered curtains covering the windows of the crumbling farmhouse. Waite had apparently converted the parlor to a crude laboratory; scores of containers, most with unknown contents, were scattered amongst the retorts, beakers, and distilling apparatus. It had been obvious to Clay and Bierce that everything in the farmhouse presented some risk of unleashing a deadly plague; it was equally obvious to them that there was only one way to deal with the threat. As Bierce lugged in the last of the twelve big cans from the wagon, Clay finished emptying the last of the two gallons of whale oil he had found in the barn about the parlor, being especially careful to soak the equipment and containers.

"That's the last of them," Bierce said, wiping sweat from his forehead with his tunic sleeve. "Is there anything else to do before we put this place to the torch?"

Clay removed a batch of papers from the side pocket his tunic, and threw them onto the oil-soaked work table. A puzzled Bierce asked "What were those?"

"I found them when I first entered this room, in plain view, while you were securing the horses and wagon. I only glanced at papers, but that glance was enough. A lengthy manifesto proclaiming that the cholera epidemic was just punishment for what the North had inflicted on the South, signed by Courtney Delapore."

Bierce frowned. "Delapore seemed to be a reluctant participant in Waite's scheme. Why would he put his name to a document that would damn him in the eyes of posterity?"

"He did not do so," replied Clay. "There was a suicide note, also signed by Delapore – as forged as the rambling proclamation. It was Waite's intent to murder Delapore, make it look like a suicide, and fade into the shadows." Clay withdrew a friction match from an inner pocket, struck it with his thumb, and tossed it onto the work table, which with a whooshing sound quickly burst into flames. “Delapore probably sensed it. That may have been the reason he chose to take the bullet meant for you.”

“Or he may have genuinely repented, and wished to make amends,” replied Bierce with a surprising lack of his usual cynicism about human nature.

Clay shrugged, as if the matter was of little importance. “I wish we had been able to take Waite alive. I believe that with vigorous...inducements I could have made him implicate the Richmond government concerning Lincoln’s assassination, without raising the matter of this monstrous plot, which must never come to light.”

“That would have been very difficult, especially with a slimy bastard like Waite. Perhaps it is best he died.”

“Perhaps. Still, I would have so loved to tie the traitors in Richmond to Lincoln’s murder.”

The fire was spreading from the table, greedily licking at its oil-soaked surroundings. Bierce said “We had better go; soon this will spread to the whole house, and people will start to come with questions we would rather not answer.”

Clay nodded. The two friends walked quickly through the kitchen and out the back door, where they had left their rented horses. Smoothly mounting, they trotted the short distance to the main road and turned south toward the smoke-wreathed metropolis that was just being illuminated by the rising sun. They rode along in silence for some minutes, the traffic becoming thicker the closer they approached the developed portion of Manhattan.

Finally, Bierce ventured a question. “So, once we have returned these nags, what next? Do we go and join up with Duval, wherever you sent her?”

“No. I believe she will need no help, and there is still more to be done in Washington before our matter is concluded. Much more.”

“Jesus, Clay, will this ever end? How deep does this treason go?”

“Deeper than Americans will ever dream, or at least that is my hope. Still, I dare to hope we may succeed in keeping the lid on this matter. When we started, I feared it was the longest of long shots. Now I dare to hope the odds are fifty-fifty.”

“Fifty-fifty of what?”

“Of suppressing a scandal that if ever known would utterly destroy the chances for lasting peace.”

A thoughtful Bierce could think of no response to that comment. The two friends rode through the thickening traffic toward the bustling city.

Chapter 5:
"He Is Sifting Out The Hearts Of Men Before His Judgement Seat..."

John Surratt slouched dejectedly in the tattered armchair set before the one window in the farmhouse's cramped parlor, a disordered pile of newspapers on the table to his right. He stared out the window, seeing nothing of the weed-choked yard, oblivious to the faint, distant thundering of Niagara Falls, thinking only of what the newspapers had announced. There had been no civil trial for the survivors of the Lincoln conspiracy; Washington remained a largely Southern town, and the Johnson Administration feared unanimous guilty verdicts would be impossible to obtain in a civilian trial. Instead, using the excuse that martial law still applied to Washington City, a commission of military officers under the stern abolitionist General David Hunter had been established to determine their guilt and punishment. The latest papers had announced the verdicts, arrived at with shocking speed. Dr. Samuel Mudd: guilty, sentenced to life imprisonment; it would have been death, but according to the papers some colonel had argued passionately before the tribunal for mercy for the doctor, and it had been reluctantly granted. George Atzerodt: guilty, sentenced to death by hanging. David Herold: guilty, sentenced to death by hanging. Lewis Powell (or as he now claimed, Lewis Payne): guilty, sentenced to death by hanging.

Mary Surratt: guilty, sentenced to death by hanging.

Surratt kicked the wall under the window, swearing viciously and damning all Yankees to Hell. He was in this farmhouse on the outskirts of Buffalo at the express order of the late John Wilkes Booth, charged with helping any Confederate agents or refugees sneak into Canada, assisted by the farmhouse's longtime resident and agent of the Confederate Civil Service, Nathan Tollafson. When Surratt had learned of Booth's death and the subsequent trial, he had been of two minds, and he continued to be of two minds. Part of him wanted to cross the border to Canada, and from there place an ocean between himself and Federal vengeance. The other part was reluctant to abandon his innocent mother to the Yankee executioner. *'Bad enough that his brave comrades would hang'*, thought Surratt. *'But to execute a blameless woman, a woman who had known nothing of the plot, whose only crime was to run a boardinghouse where Booth and the comrades met'* – he found it hard to believe that even the Yankees would stoop to such a crime. Yet there it was, in the newspapers.

He had argued most of the morning with Tollafson. He had told the older man that he should offer to surrender himself to the Federals, in exchange for his mother's life. Tollafson had laughed harshly and called him a fool, pointing out that the national government had never yet hanged a woman and was not about to start now; some states had occasionally executed a member of the fair sex, but never Washington.

Surratt was startled back into awareness of his surroundings by a polite but insistent knocking coming from the back kitchen door. From one of the bedrooms emerged the stringy figure of Nathan Tollafson, who scowled at Surratt. "Never mind about the door; I'm up already. Probably one of the neighbors, trying to peddle eggs or milk again." The grumbling man stomped into the kitchen, and Surratt heard the door open.

Surratt suddenly frowned. The door had clearly been opened, but not a word came from the kitchen, either from

Tollafson or some stranger. The puzzled young man half-turned in his chair to face the entrance to the kitchen, and was started to see his companion slowly walking backwards into the parlor, hands high in the air. He was followed into the room by a lithe, black-haired beauty, smiling broadly, pointing a small but deadly-looking Sharps pepperbox at Tollafson's chest with her right hand, holding a small burlap sack with her left. She glanced at Surratt, and smiled even more broadly.

"Mr. John Surratt, I am very happy to see you here," said Teresa Duval, breaking into one of her silvery, chilling laughs. "It would seem that the information my friend obtained from Mr. Pinkerton's agency was quite correct; even so, it could have taken much longer to find your exact bolt-hole. Luck was on my side. You will please stay seated in that chair." She turned her attention back to Tollafson. "And who may you be?"

"That's none of your business," growled Tollafson. "Just who are you and what in hell are..."

Duval fired. Her bullet shattered Tollafson's left elbow. As the stringy Confederate fell howling to the floor, Duval commented, "Well, it is not important who you are. It is important that you understand I am very serious. That wound will be very painful, but not fatal. You should be able to do a lot with your right arm; in fact, you better do exactly as I say, or your bollocks are the next to go." She threw the sack on the floor in front of Tollafson; it clanked heavily when it hit. She glanced at the heavy parlor table, and nodded to herself. "Mr. Surratt, get up very slowly; then take the armchair you are in, move it toward that table, and sit down. Please no sudden movements; they tend to make my trigger finger twitchy."

As the now thoroughly terrified youth clumsily did as he was told, Duval told Tollafson, "In the sack you will find four pairs of handcuffs. They are currently open; even with one useful hand you should find it possible to handle them. Once Mr. Surratt is seated, please use one pair to handcuff his hands behind his back, then another to shackle his leg to the leg of the table."

Despite the searing pain in his left arm, Tollafson was tempted to spit defiance at the strange woman. Nonetheless, one look at the blue eyes above the smiling mouth, and another glance at the rock-steady Sharps in her hand, convinced him he should do as she said. Lurching about clumsily, moaning with pain, Tollafson managed to do as he was told. Meanwhile, Surratt thought about making a break for freedom, but something in the terrible, beautiful woman's smile seemed to mesmerize him, like snakes were said to mesmerize birds.

After Surratt was secured, Duval spoke. "Good. Now, scoot the other chair over to the stairs leading to the second floor. Sit down in it, and use the third pair of handcuffs to secure your feet together." The scowling, pain-wracked Tollafson did as he was told. Duval took the final pair, and ascended a few steps. From behind him Tollafson heard her speak. "Please raise your right arm." Slowly he did as he was told; with a lightening-swift motion she handcuffed his good arm painfully to the banister. Duval descended to the parlor floor, looked around at her handiwork, and made the small pistol disappear.

"You gentlemen will not be going anywhere," she commented sweetly. "Just give me a moment while I bring some things in from my gig." She glided into the kitchen and out of sight.

"Just who is that bitch, and what does she want?" Surratt asked in a low, urgent voice.

Grimacing with pain, Tollafson replied, "Hell if I know. Not Secret Service or Provost, that's for sure. They wouldn't have sent one man, let alone a woman."

"No, I am neither from Colonel Baker nor the Provost," replied Duval entering the room with several obviously heavy packages that she carried with surprising ease. "I should set up the darkroom first. Preparation is everything. Don't you agree? I caught a glimpse of a spare room off the main hall with the heavy curtains; that should do for the developing." Leaving the two largest packages in the parlor, she glided into the spare room. Various sounds, including the clinking of heavy bottles, drifted into the parlor. An increasingly terrified Surratt whispered "Nathan, what are we going to do? She's crazier than a March hare."

Tollafson, pale from shock and loss of blood, grunted "Don't see much we can do. Maybe we can buy her off. You've still got that money that Booth gave you..." He trailed off, pain momentarily forgotten, as he stared at the woman who had glided gracefully into the parlor.

Teresa Duval was stark, jay-bird naked; yet there was not the slightest self-consciousness about her. Both men gaped at her, not entirely from lust; the spectacle was so utterly unexpected that for a few moments they literally could not think. Meanwhile, smiling at their discomfiture, Duval padded barefoot over to the remaining packages on the floor. Stooping and placing a gleaming razor on the floor, she opened them and with surprising speed assembled from their contents a photographic camera and box of glass plates, with a newspaper oddly left over.

"You gentlemen must wonder at my lack of clothing. Purely professional, I assure you." She scooped up the newspaper, padded over to the table where Surratt was shackled, and after rearranging some brick-a-brack, positioned it so that the blaring headline concerning the conviction of Booth's accomplices faced the camera. "You see, things are going to become a bit – messy soon. I have only one good dress with me, and would rather not have to depart Buffalo with stains that might excite remark."

Duval scooped up the razor from the floor, and flicked it open with a casual motion of her wrist. Such a shame, she thought to herself. That warm, erotic feeling was spreading through her lower belly; if only Alphonso were here to participate, she thought, the pleasure would have reached undreamed-of heights. Her mind only partly on the task at hand, she approached Tollafson and went to work.

The screams began immediately. Tollafson attempted to speak, attempted to beg for his life, but the unendurable pain rendered him inarticulate. The shrieks of the agonized Confederate made the walls of the farmhouse vibrate, but there was no habitation close enough to hear the sounds of his tortured voice.

Surratt began screaming as well, even though untouched. The sight of what was being done before him was unbelievable, unbearable, and yet he could not avert his gaze, could not even close his eyes. All he could do was scream continuously with horror, pausing only to fill his lungs with air to continue his howling. In his terror, Surratt had not regulated his breathing well; hyperventilation combined with emotional shock made him pass out after a few eternal minutes. Even unconscious, the horror of what he had witnessed gave him snatches of nightmares, nightmares where he seemed to be fleeing a nameless, unseen horror through a deserted city made of ancient, Cyclopean stones, where the angles all seemed strangely wrong. Suddenly, an overpowering odor of ammonia filled his nostrils, and he returned, reluctant and choking, to the waking world – only to witness a monstrous sight.

In front of him stood the naked, blood-streaked form of the strange woman, casually waving a small bottle of smelling salts under his nose. Surratt looked over to the chair where Tollafson had been handcuffed, only to see a blood-drenched scene that belonged in a slaughterhouse. He then turned his attention to the table in front of him, where several objects had been placed to the side of the carefully positioned newspaper. Surratt began to sob, tears streaming from his eyes. The woman frowned, and slapped him with stunning force, the shock making him stop his weeping for the moment.

"That will not do, Mr. Surratt. You are an English-loving traitor bastard, yet at the same time still a child, who wanted to play in the adult world. You did not realize that when you began the game, it would be for table stakes, nor just how huge those stakes would be. Try to at least mimic the bravery that the English and Rebels claim for themselves, and face your fate like a man."

"You are going to butcher me, just like you did Nathan," Surratt said in a quavering whisper.

The woman tilted her head and assumed a reflective expression on her beautiful face. "That is indeed possible. However, it is also possible that you will escape with your life, both from this room and from the Federals. It will depend on the reaction to a photograph I am about to take." The naked woman padded over to the camera, swiftly opened the box of unexposed plates, removed one, and quickly went to her darkroom. Surratt heard some liquid swishing sounds, and then the woman dashed from the room and inserted the dripping glass plate into the camera. Then, putting her head under the silk cloth at the back of the camera, she began to make fiddling adjustments while she continued to speak in an agreeable voice.

"I am only now beginning to appreciate the truth in what Mr. Brady says, that photography is more of an art than a science. Arranging the elements in a photograph is just as important as taking the photograph itself. The newspaper headline, the objects on the table, and the terrified expression on your worthless face – all are essential. Please keep your eyes on the table, and hold as still as possible. It is essential that I capture a look of abject terror on your face." A shapely arm snaked around the camera and removed the lens cap. After about a quarter of a minute, the cap went back in place. In a movement almost too quick to follow, the woman took the plate from the camera, and in three leaps was in the darkroom, slamming the door behind her. Once again Surratt heard the swishing of chemicals. There was a long pause, then a satisfied sigh from the room. He heard the door open and the woman padded quickly through the parlor to the kitchen, saying as she went "Very good, Mr. Surratt. I feared a number of exposures would be necessary, but the first will do." He then heard the kitchen pump being worked, and after an interval a splashing of water into the sink; further splashing indicated the woman was cleaning the gore from her body. She emerged from the kitchen and strode straight back into the ground floor bedroom. In a few minutes she returned, now fully, demurely clothed, holding a small brown bottle in her right hand.

"The glass plate should be fully dried by now. I must very carefully package it to guard against any breakage, then go into Buffalo proper and arrange for an express company to ship it south posthaste. The trouble is that I will have to leave you alone for a considerable time, and as secured as you are, it is just possible that you might manage to free yourself. Normally, I would kill you at this point, but I promised my friend I would keep you alive. Therefore..."

With the speed of striking rattler Duval seized Surratt's hair and jerked his head backwards, causing him to gasp with surprise. Before he knew what was happening, Duval had poured a few drops from the brown bottle into his mouth; then placing the container on the table she pinched his nose shut with one hand while holding his mouth shut with the other, forcing him to gulp the liquid. When Duval was certain that he had swallowed, she released him and took a step back. "Laudanum, Mr. Surratt. It will keep you quiet while I attend to my chores. By the time you are yourself again, I will be back. You will then be my guest here for a few days; depending on the reaction to the picture, I will either free you or grant you a quick death."

As consciousness fled from John Surratt, his last sight was of the beautiful, terrible woman's angelic smile; the last sound he heard was her silvery, chilling laugh.

* * * * *

Alphonso Clay and Ambrose Bierce had returned quietly to Washington, not even bothering to report to Stanton or Grant. Instead, they spent two days waiting in Clay's suite at Willard's, never emerging except for brief meals in the restaurant. Clay would not tell Bierce what it was for which they waited, and finally Bierce stopped asking. Instead, Bierce spent his time idly drafting a short story about a man being hunted by an invisible monster, while Clay occupied himself with reading his grandfather's book *Unausprechliken Kulten,*_occasionally making penciled notes in the margins in German. Early on the morning of their third day in the hotel, the monotony was broken by a sharp rapping on the door. Clay leapt up from his chair to answer the knock, and found a burly messenger from the Butterfield Express Company in front of him, carrying a bulky package wrapped in brown paper.

"Lieutenant Colonel Alphonso Brutus Clay?" the man read off a piece of paper.

"I am he."

"Prepaid package from a Miss Brigid Doyle."

Clay showed no surprise at the name, knowing it to be Duval's true identity. Wordlessly he signed the receipt, took possession of the package, and tipped the man a half-dollar. Once the door was closed he rushed to the table and began to tear the package open. The box was sturdy; immense care had been taken to cushion the contents with cotton padding. From the cotton, Clay extracted a single glass photographic plate.

From where he sat, Bierce could not see the photograph. However, he could clearly see the expression on Clay's face. It deeply disturbed Bierce; the expression was a weird, seemingly impossible combination of relief, shock, guilt and hunger. Bierce rose from his chair to approach the table for a clear view of the photograph.

Clay reflexively clutched the glass plate to his chest and said, "Bring the large carpetbag from the clothes press." Bierce did as he was told. Clay placed the photograph carefully inside, never permitting Bierce a clear view. He then began stuffing the cotton from the Butterfield package carefully around the plate, as if it were the most precious and delicate object in the world. When Clay was satisfied, he snapped the carpetbag shut, lifted it with his right hand to test its weight. "Now the waiting is over. We can proceed on the next phase of our assignment. Come with me."

"Where?"

"The Old Arsenal Penitentiary."

* * * * *

The Old Arsenal was marginally cleaner than the Old Capitol Prison. Its looming brickwork walls with armed sentries ceaselessly patrolling the catwalk, and the well-used gallows visible from most cells, gave it an air of hopelessness that even Old Capitol did not have. Here is where the true hard-case offenders were kept; murderers, rapists, child molesters and the like. They generally did not stay long; they were quickly sent on their way, either to a hell-hole prison on a far frontier, or to an appointment with the hangman. Clay and Bierce's papers were carefully inspected at the front gate by a pair of hard-eyed, alert sentries; only when the guards were satisfied was the iron gateway unlocked and thrown open to the two officers and the large carpetbag that Clay would not let leave his hand for a moment. They walked into the hot, dusty exercise yard, to be met by Colonel Lafayette Baker. Clay and Bierce formally saluted, while Baker only scowled.

"What are you two doing here? I got your message about needing to see Lincoln's killers before they hang. You may have Grant's order saying you can do whatever you damn well please, but hell if I know why you need to talk to them. This time tomorrow they will be swinging in the wind. Well, maybe not Mrs. Surratt. I hear Johnson may grant her a pardon. Wouldn't be surprised; Federal government has never hanged a woman yet."

"They will hang this one," replied Clay quietly. "We talked to General Grant and Secretary Stanton before we came here; they in turn promised to go to Johnson and make sure he does not give in to pleas for mercy."

Baker looked openly astonished. "Why would you do that? I thought you Southern 'gentlemen' always looked out for the ladies. Besides, at worse she knew about the plot and did nothing; it wouldn't anger me too much if she cheated the hangman."

"The reason we went to Grant and Stanton has to do with our mission today; and you may not know that mission. Take us to the prisoners. Now."

Scowling, Baker led his visitors past two armed checkpoints, and into a corridor in the bowels of the main building. Baker gestured along the corridor. "They are in the four cells on the right, the most secure in the building. No other prisoners are on this floor; I didn't want any communications going between them to others and through them to the outside."

"Do you have a key that fits all four cells?" At Baker's nod, Clay held out his free hand. "Give it to me. Then leave the corridor, and make sure that no guards come in this area. Matters must be discussed that are not to be heard by you or any of your staff."

Baker seemed to hesitate, so Clay added, "Need I show you the General's letter again? I am to be given all co-operation without any question."

With a muttered obscenity, Baker drew a massive iron key from his side pocket, and slapped it into the palm of Clay's free hand. The security chief then stormed out of the corridor, leaving Clay and Bierce alone with four people who would die the next day.

Clay silently handed the carpetbag to Bierce. The two friends began walking down the corridor. They came to the first cell, a solid iron door with a small observation slit through which the occupant could be viewed. Clay looked in, and spotted George Atzerodt curled in a fetal position on his bunk, frantically muttering in German something that sounded like prayers. The officers moved to the next cell and looked through the slit. There the flabby David Herold sat rocking back and forth on his bunk, tears streaming from his swollen eyes. They came to the third cell and looked through the slit. There the massive Lewis Powell (or Payne; no one was quite sure of his true name) sat rock-steady on his bunk, staring straight back at the visitors through the slit, utterly still except for a rhythmic flexing of his heavily manacled hands. Finally, they moved to the fourth cell and looked through the slit.

They saw Mrs. Mary Surratt sitting composedly at a rickety table, writing a letter as calmly as if she were in the parlor of her boardinghouse. Clay took Baker's key and opened the door. Followed by Bierce, he quickly strode into the cell, and briefly looked around. The heavy brick walls and iron door gave the chamber a dismal air, despite the sunlight streaming in from the barred window, through which the top of a gallows could be glimpsed. Aside from the table and chair where Mrs. Surratt sat, the room contained only a small bed bolted to the wall, a pitcher of water, and a foul-smelling bucket for human wastes. Mrs. Surratt calmly set aside her pen and looked at her two visitors.

"Gentlemen, do you come from Johnson with my pardon?"

"No, Mrs. Surratt, we do not," replied Clay.

Clay and Bierce remained standing; there was no place in the cell for them to sit save the bunk, and they did not care to sit on a bed with a lady present, even one awaiting execution.

Surratt's calm did not desert her; instead, her dark eyes acquired a hard look. "Very well, I had hoped not to force the issue, but to rely on Johnson behaving as a gentleman. I see that is too much to expect from jumped-up white trash such as he. I want you to carry a message to the President..."

"That a high-ranking Federal official was involved in the assassination of the President, and if your life is not spared you will be screaming the man's name from the gallows," completed Clay.

Both Surratt and Bierce looked at Clay with wide-eyed astonishment. The ghost of a grim smile tugged at the corners of Clay's mouth. "I recovered Booth's diary, and he was quite explicit, although he never named the official. You originated the plot, at the orders of the late Colonel Ephraim Waite of the Confederate Secret Service. You needed conspirators to implement the plot, but feared that they would not follow a mere woman in such a desperate enterprise. So while on the surface you continued in the role of a politically uninvolved, likable landlady, you recruited Booth – it matters not how – to be the 'official' head of the plot. I congratulate you to that extent; a well-known, charismatic Confederate sympathizer, too stupid to do anything but what he was told."

Mary Surratt was quiet for a few moments, then folding her hands and placing them calmly on her lap, she replied, "And too stupid to not put anything in writing, even though I had warned him repeatedly to leave not a scrap of documentary evidence. I see now it was a mistake to recruit an actor; they have such egos, and must preen before the public, one way or another. Well, it does not matter whether you have his diary. The threat is not affected; I will scream the name of the man who helped us from the gallows, and all Booth's diary will do is give it credence. The scandal could very well disrupt the Federal Government itself, destroy Northerners faith in it, and give the South a chance to rise again."

"You would give your life for a chance to hurt the Union, to bring yet more death and destruction on the country?" asked Bierce in wonderment.

Surratt lifted her chin proudly. "I am not afraid to die; especially in support of the Cause."

Clay shook his head. "You will go to your deserved execution without uttering a word. We will not reveal the true extent of your treason; you can die consoled by the idea that many will regard you as an innocent woman, unjustly condemned. However, die you must. You will tell us the name of the Northern traitor, but utter it to no one else, even from the gallows."

Mary Surratt laughed scornfully. "And just what makes you think I will do that? Do you intend to torture me in this cell for the name, and murder me here? I think not."

Clay nodded. "You are correct. Such actions could not be concealed, and could create more troubles than they solve. Yet you will do as we wish, without any force being used." He gestured to Bierce to place the carpetbag on the table before Surratt. Clay then stepped forward, snapped open the top of the soft bag, and carefully extracted the photographic plate, which he held before the woman's eyes. For a moment, Surratt could make no sense of the image. Then suddenly her eyes widened with horror, and her hand flew to her mouth as if to stifle a silent scream. Bierce edged around and finally got a close look at the glass plate. His response was different; the survivor of the horrors of Chickamauga and Kennesaw Mountain blurted a vile obscenity, then staggered over to the waste bucket and was noisily ill. Clay ignored his companion, focusing only on the terrified woman.

"I regret the necessity of this, but like you, I serve a Cause for which I would sacrifice anything – even my honor. I quickly realized a mother's love for her son would give me the lever I would need to gain your co-operation. Why else would Booth have ordered one of his most fervent supporters off to Buffalo on a trivial assignment just on the eve of the assassination? Of course the answer was obvious: you expected most if not all of the conspirators to come to grief, and wanted your son clear of danger. Is that not so?"

The stricken woman slowly took her hand away from her mouth, but could not take her gaze off the photograph. In a slight whisper she replied, "Yes. What have you done to my son? What are you going to do to him?"

"For the moment, he is safe enough. As to the future, that will depend entirely upon you, Mrs. Surratt. As you can tell, my...associate has demonstrated a capability for extreme violence; note the objects beside the newspaper. Undoubtedly they are from the Confederate agent you sent your son to assist. The newspaper itself shows a date of three days ago, proving your son was alive, at least as of that time."

Bierce had finished being sick. Wiping his mouth, he stammered, "Sweet Jesus, Clay, what did you tell that sick bitch to do?" Clay silenced the shaken Bierce with a sharp motion of his hand and continued speaking, never taking his eyes from the woman's face.

"Your son is among the living, Mrs. Surratt; the headline on the newspaper testified to that. Whether he remains among the living depends on you giving me the name I require, and maintaining silence during tomorrow's...ceremony."

All trace of color gone from her face, Surratt replied, "You are lying. Those...things on the table are not what they appear to be."

Clay favored her with a shark-like smile. "Oh, they are what they seem to be. Let me draw your attention to the expression on your son's face. Do not think my associate will not take considerable time over him, if necessary. Your son's life was in our hands from the moment he decided to help murder the President."

To that, Mary Surratt had no answer. After a few moments, she whispered, "How can I trust you to release Johnnie unharmed after I am...gone?"

"You can trust me because your son is too small, too insignificant to be any threat to the United States. You can also trust me because I have already compromised my personal honor beyond any point I had thought possible. I will not compromise it further, unless the survival of the nation requires it."

Mary Surratt considered what Clay had said for nearly a minute. Then, she uttered a name. Bierce spat out one of his creative obscenities; Clay merely lost what little color that remained in his features.

* * * * *

Washington in 1865 was in many ways a small town. Waiting only long enough for a mounted messenger to receive a brief instruction from Clay and to have the man deliver a terse reply took less than half an hour. Clay and Bierce decided to walk to their next destination rather than ride. Some minutes passed before Bierce finally broke the silence.

"How could you let her do that? Clay, how could you, with all your talk of 'honor'?"

Staring straight ahead, Clay responded. "I asked her to track Surratt down, frighten him, take a photograph showing he was alive, but at our mercy. I did not tell her to frighten the young man in the...excessive way that she chose."

"Clay, you may not have said the words, but let's be straight with each other: you know as well as I what she is capable of. Yet you turned her loose like a rabid dog."

Clay sighed. "Yes, part of me suspected she would go beyond the bounds of what was necessary. Still, I did not know how long it would take us to stop Waite; I needed the capture of John Surratt immediately. All I learned from Booth's diary and from Pinkerton's men was that he was somewhere in the vicinity of Buffalo. You answer me, Bierce: was there anyone else to turn to, with the combination of skills and ruthlessness necessary to do this as quickly as it needed to be done?"

"You should have used anybody else."

"I could not replace her with anybody; I needed *somebody,* somebody with the requisite skills, and that somebody was not to be found." He paused, and then continued somberly. "Who am I to judge her barbarity, when I have myself behaved unspeakably on so many occasions?"

Bierce frowned as they walked. "You mean that New Orleans business? That was long ago."

"Not so long, Ambrose, not so long. I am many unpleasant things, but a hypocrite is not among them. We are here."

The two friends looked at the brick townhouse before them. The windows were open in deference to the summer heat; through them came the soft murmur of voices, and a piano cheerfully sounding a piece by Mozart.

"Alphonso, are you sure this is the time and place to take the traitor down? What if the Surratt bitch was lying?"

Clay shook his head. "She was not lying. The only thing she values more than her Cause is her son, else why did she send him away at the climatic point in the conspiracy? As for the traitor, it is not enough to take him, or even to kill him; a few important people must know the truth, so he is not made a martyr." Without further ado, Clay marched up the steps to the front door and loudly beat the knocker; somewhat more reluctantly, Bierce ascended the steps behind him.

The door was answered by a neatly dressed, alert-looking black maid; friendly in demeanor with none of the falsely groveling manners of so many Negro servants in Washington.

"Yes, sirs, may I help you?"

"We must speak to your master immediately," replied Clay curtly.

The woman's smile disappeared, to be replaced by a thoughtful frown. "I know that many have important business with him. However, he is not in good health lately, and this is one of the few social occasions he has allowed himself this year. Truly, your business cannot wait?"

"Your concern does you credit. However, it is truly vital."

The woman nodded. The music from inside had stopped, followed by a patter of applause. "Very well; but at least wait until Miss Smith has finished with her next song. He is so proud of her, and things being what they are, it is so seldom he can display his pride."

Clay thought of his love of long ago, gone forever, and gave a brief nod. The maid showed Clay and Bierce in; then with a sketch of a curtsey, she bustled down the hall to the kitchen. From the spacious front parlor a man announced, "And now my friends, for your entertainment Miss Lydia Smith will sing that wonderful song by Julia Ward Howe, 'The Battle Hymn of the Republic', accompanying herself on the piano."

As Clay placed the carpetbag carefully near where coats were hung, a melodious four-bar introduction issued from a piano, followed by the first verse of the tune that was currently sweeping the nation.

Mine eyes have seen the glory of the coming of the Lord;
He is trampling out the vintage where the grapes of wrath are stored;
He has loosed the fateful lightening of His terrible swift sword;
His truth is marching on.
Glory! Glory! Hallelujah! Glory! Glory Hallelujah!
Glory! Glory! Hallelujah! His truth is marching on.

Clay and Bierce stood in the doorway and took in the scene. At the piano sat a beautiful mulatto woman, in late middle-age but lithe and poised, clearly enjoying the music she performed. Next to her the radical Congressman Thaddeus Stevens sat in an armchair, resting both hands on his heavy cane, his grim features softened into something like adoration as he watched the woman perform. Clay and Bierce both realized that the performer must be Lydia Smith, the rumored black mistress to Stevens; the woman whom polite society only talked about in whispers but whom the iconoclastic Stevens treated as his wife rather than his mistress, ignoring the legal and social barriers of miscegenation. As Lydia Smith continued to play, Clay thought of his long-dead Arabella, and for a brief moment his stony heart felt a genuine admiration for Stevens in defying society's conventions.

I have read a fiery Gospel writ in burnished rows of steel;
'As ye deal with My contemnors, so with you My grace shall deal';
Let the Hero, born of woman, crush the serpent with His Heel,
Since God is marching on.
Glory! Glory! Hallelujah! Glory! Glory Hallelujah!
Glory! Glory! Hallelujah! Since God is marching on.

Seated in the corner by a window was the majestic-looking Senator Charles Sumner. The elegantly-dressed Sumner seemed to be trying to pay polite attention to the music, but his vague, unfocused eyes indicated his mind was elsewhere.

He has sounded forth the trumpet that shall never call retreat;
He is sifting out the hearts of men before His judgment seat;
Oh, be swift my soul to answer Him! Be jubilant my feet;
Our God is marching on.
Glory! Glory! Hallelujah! Glory! Glory Hallelujah!
Glory! Glory! Hallelujah! Our God is marching on.

On the sofa were the remaining two people in the room: Benjamin Butler, just retired from the Army and dressed in civilian clothes, and his hot-gospeler former chief of staff, Alan Phillips. The cross-eyed, frog-like Butler seemed genuinely interested, and Clay suddenly remembered he had married a professional singer. The lean, lantern-jawed Phillips made no pretense of being interested in the music, his eyes showing he was focused upon some bleak inner landscape.

In the beauty of the lilies Christ was born across the sea,
With a glory in His bosom that transfigures you and me;
As he died to make men holy, let us live to make men free;
While God is marching on.
Glory! Glory! Hallelujah! Glory! Glory Hallelujah!
Glory! Glory! Hallelujah! While God is marching on.

The others broke into enthusiastic applause. Stevens used his cane to leverage himself to his feet, in obvious pain yet with a smile on his face. He limped over to Smith, bent over and gave her a gentle kiss on the forehead. “That was beautiful, my love. But of course, I would expect nothing less.” He glanced about the room defiantly, daring anyone to show any discomfort for his show of affection to a black woman. His eyes came to rest on Clay and Bierce, still standing in the doorway.

"Colonel Clay, Major Bierce. It has been some weeks since we met in Stanton's office. What brings you to my home?"

Clay and Bierce bowed, Clay saying, "May I complement Miss Smith on her performance? I am not a devotee of the arts, but I have personally never heard better playing or more melodious singing, and their equal but once." A puzzled look on her face, Smith nodded her head slightly in acknowledgement of the complement. Then Clay addressed Stevens.

"Sir, I have just come from Old Arsenal Prison, where I have interviewed Mrs. Mary Surratt. As you know, she is to hang tomorrow, along with Powell, Herold, and Atzerodt."

Stevens shrugged negligently. "I can't say that bothers me. She must have known something about the plot to assassinate Lincoln. What is of more importance is that Johnson is showing even more reluctance than did Lincoln to grant our black brethren their full rights as citizens. Pressure must be brought to bear on him."

"You seem to be organizing for it already," commented Bierce. "After all, sir, you have more influence in the House than does the Speaker himself. Senator Sumner can do pretty much what he wants with the Senate. And I understand that General Butler has somewhat changed his ambitions, and is now running for an open seat from Massachusetts; he will enter not as a normal freshman, but with an existing and powerful network of political and economic supporters behind him. All of you are radical abolitionists, powerful enough to convince the rest of the Government to go along with your wishes – providing there is no interference from the Executive Mansion."

"Yes, I imagine a former slaveholder like Johnson would be slow off the mark on such issues,"added Clay. "Even Lincoln seemed to prefer a lengthy transitional period before freed slaves were accorded full rights. Still, you might find it easier to work your will on the somewhat...unreliable Johnson, rather than the iron-willed Lincoln."

"Damn straight!" exclaimed the ungainly Butler. "He never would see that with the darkies immediately freed and voting, Republican domination of the country is assured for generations..."

"And you expect to be a Republican President some day," interrupted the dignified Sumner in measured tones. "This is not about power, but about justice."

"Can't have justice without power," responded Butler with impeccable logic.

Clay cleared his throat; although not a loud sound, all eyes turned immediately to him. "Representative Stevens, perhaps you would care to ask Miss Smith to leave the room. I shall need to discuss unpleasant subjects."

The beautiful Lydia Smith glared at Clay, then possessively took Stevens right hand in her own. "I am not to be ordered out on a matter affecting the Congressman. I have heard secrets before, and know how to keep them."

Clay did not seem offended in being contradicted; in fact, he gave a slight nod of approval. "Very well, then. In my interview with Mrs. Surratt, she admitted to a somewhat greater role in the conspiracy than the general public believes. Furthermore, through...inducements, she volunteered that two high-ranking Federal officials had been participants in the conspiracy."

"You dare!" exclaimed Smith, leaping to her feet. Stevens restrained her with gentle pressure on her shoulder. He then said to Clay, "You realize what you are saying Colonel? In this room are three of the most powerful men in the Republican Party, men who worked to keep this country united and free the slaves, and you are alleging that two of them are traitors. I think it far more likely that the Surratt woman, desperate to save her neck, would utter a slanderous lie to sow confusion among the loyal."

Clay shook his head sadly. "Although I may not tell you why, I am satisfied as to her truthfulness – in this at least.

Congressman Stevens, Mr. Butler, I must ask you to come with..."

Cursing vilely, Butler lurched up from the couch, drawing a small pistol from his side pocket. Screaming, "No!" Phillips jumped on his former commander, knocking the gun to the floor and pinning his arms behind him. Smith's hand flew to her mouth in horror, while Stevens' grim eyes widened with surprise. Butler cursed with rage.

"Nancy-boy bastard! Butcher! Child killer! You informed on me in New Orleans, and engineered my recall. Now you want to railroad me to the gallows. Well, I'll get out of this, and then you're a dead man, Clay, a dead man!"

Charles Sumner had been watching the spectacle with a somewhat vacuous look on his handsome face. Then he seemed to pull himself together. Slowly rising to his full, considerable height, he spoke in the deep voice that had dominated the Senate for years. "Stop this now. I am the man you want. Let Butler go."

Butler immediately ceased his struggling, and stared with amazement at Sumner. All other eyes swiveled toward Sumner; only those of Clay and Bierce lacked expressions of astonishment. Phillips released Butler, who looked at Clay with angry puzzlement. Sumner walked to the room's bay window, and stared out of it, seemingly at nothing. Clay broke the silence.

"My apologies, Mr. Butler. We of course knew that the Senator was the one we wanted, but needed to demonstrate his guilt before reliable witnesses, else who would believe such a thing? You must really learn to control your temper; it almost placed you in a position of being charged with murder."

"What if he hadn't confessed?" asked a confused Phillips.

"Then we would have gone to another approach," replied Clay. "Fortunately, it did not prove to be necessary."

"This is not possible," said Stevens slowly. "Charles, tell me that this is all some mistake, some sick joke..."

Still looking outside, Sumner silenced his friend with a wave of his hand. “It is true. This is for the best. Since Lincoln’s death, my headaches and...spells where I do not remember where I have been or what I was doing have increased. Perhaps a hanging is the best solution all round.” He then turned to face Clay, as dignified as Roman senator. “Colonel, I am ready to go.”

Clay frowned thoughtfully, then seemed to reach a decision. “The trap I set for you was to see how you would respond to your friends being accused of your crime; from your known character, I suspected you would confess rather than allow an innocent to hang for your actions. I would have quickly ended the charade had you not confessed. However, your confession indicates something that was hinted at by Mrs. Surratt. Tell me in your own words how you came to be involved, and that will determine whether the matter ever leaves this room.”

Sumner turned back to the window and stared, seeing nothing outside of his own mind. “I have always been a proud man. Frankly, there was much in my life of which to be proud. Early political successes came my way, even though I never compromised with evil; slavery was to be abolished, the black man made equal to the white, and the Union preserved. I did my part, long before those views were popular; when in fact they were dangerous.” Unconsciously his hand went to his head and rubbed the scars from his near-fatal beating by Congressman Preston on the floor of the Senate; the scars were largely obscured by his hair, but they could still be glimpsed. “You all may know from the newspapers, and are too polite to comment on, the fact that my marriage has become a travesty. My wife is divorcing me on the grounds of an...inability to perform husbandly duties. This...inability arose at the time of the assault by Congressman Preston. My apologies, Miss Smith, for raising such issues before you; perhaps the humiliation is a just part of my punishment.” Sumner paused, and looked as if he were about to weep. Then with an effort he pulled himself together and continued his story.

"I was at my lowest when I met Mrs. Surratt at a Georgetown reception. She seemed to immediately take a spark to me; I was lonely and..." Sumner made a helpless gesture with his hand. "Somehow, my...inability disappeared with her. Looking back on it, I suspect she gave me some sort of...potion; she was always encouraging me to try the delightful drinks she concocted. At the time I thought it was her, her unquestioning adoration of me that had made the difference. Then one evening I seemed to have one of my spells. When I was clearly aware again, I was in...a place I will not describe. Mrs. Surratt had somehow found me there, paid some money to ensure silence of the...people there, and got me home. My head hurt worse than usual, or I would have suspected something. At the time I did not. Instead, I was filled with shame about my behavior, and gratitude toward her. I told her that I would do anything to show my gratitude. At first, she said she needed nothing; but then, finally she admitted she would appreciate a favor. She told me that her daughter was getting a trial with Laura Keene's company, for one night only. She said she would be forever in my debt if I guaranteed that the president was there that evening, so he could see her performance for himself, and later write a letter of endorsement that would help her embark on her stage career.

"It seemed like such a small thing, and so easy to accomplish. I am good friends with Mary Lincoln, who governed her husband in all things social. Thanks to me, he was certain to be at Ford's Theater on Good Friday. Afterwards, I began to suspect I had been used. I confronted Mrs. Surratt, hoping to be proven wrong. Instead, she laughed at me. She called me a damn Yankee nigger-lover – my apologies, Miss Smith – and said if I valued my life and reputation, I would keep silent. If she were taken, she would tell the world that I had helped her kill Lincoln, because I thought he was moving too slowly on rights for the former slaves. Who would believe that the great Charles Sumner, the friend of Dickens, Hawthorne and Thackeray, would have fallen prey to such an obviously contrived plot? So I kept silent; the headaches got worse and worse, but I kept silent." Sumner's massive head sank until his chin rested on his broad chest, and he began to silently weep.

Absolute silence reigned in the parlor for a full minute. Then Stevens limped over to Sumner, placed a hand on his shoulder, and said, "My poor old friend." Then he turned to Clay. "Colonel, must this be made known? I doubt a jury would find him guilty of murder, but his career would be utterly ruined. He has done much good, and there is still more good for him to do."

"How could you possibly keep this quiet?" growled Butler. "If nothing else, the Surratt bitch will scream his name from the gallows."

Clay seemed lost in thought. Finally, he responded to Butler.

"I have guaranteed that Mrs. Surratt will not implicate him. With her in the grave, only those of us in this room know the truth. I am satisfied that Senator Sumner is guilty of nothing more than foolish weakness, and that justice will not be perverted if the law does not become formally involved. If we will all swear on our honor to keep this secret that should be enough."

"But there should be some punishment for me leading him like a lamb to the slaughter," said Sumner in a low voice, still not looking at the other occupants of the room.

"You will be punished, every day, for the rest of your life, by that most implacable of judges: your conscience."

"My spells continue," replied Sumner. "What if in another one I commit some other folly as bad, or even – God forbid – worse?"

At this point the lean Alan Phillips stood up, and began to speak in an oddly formal manner. "Senator Sumner, I have followed your career for most of my life, and have had nothing but admiration for you standing up against the evils of our time. You have been injured in taking those stands. There is no shame in that; no more shame than in the need of Congressman

Stevens to use a cane. Let me be your cane. My family business is now back on its feet, and will require little attention from me; I will ask for no salary. Let me be your unpaid private secretary. Should your honorably incurred injuries ever lead you toward an injudicious course, I will be there to steer you in the direction you would have wished to go."

Sumner looked intently at the Phillips. "You would make that sacrifice for me?"

Phillips looked at his longtime superior Butler; something like a look of disgust flitted across his face as he recalled the corruption in which he had been forced to participate. "I volunteered for the Army intending to fight for the holy causes of Union and emancipation. In my position with General Butler, it did not always work out as I had hoped. Let me make supporting you in your work my contribution to the causes for which we both live. No sir, it will be no sacrifice at all." While Butler glowered, Phillips strode across the room and offered Sumner his hand; after only the briefest of hesitations, the senator took it.

"Remember, not a word to anyone, not a record in the most private of diaries," said Clay to the room in general. "This matter dies with Mary Surratt." Everyone nodded their assent; everyone had the strongest personal motives for keeping their promise. Clay bowed to the room, clicked his heels in the European fashion, and led Bierce out of the parlor, smoothly sweeping up the carpetbag as he went.

* * * * *

Stifling July heat had descended on Washington with a vengeance; it was even more hellish in the exercise yard of the Old Arsenal. Four shackled figures, hands tied behind their backs, shuffled out of the main building, and slowly ascended the gallows where four separate nooses and four separate trap doors awaited them; they were to be hanged simultaneously. Dozens of soldiers walked the catwalks, alert for any diehard attempt to breach the prison's defenses and rescue the condemned. Scores of soldiers milled about the parade ground in front of the gallows, anxious to see justice done; Colonel Baker had tried to keep them away, but the normally well-disciplined men silently disobeyed, and Baker decided it was not worth the effort to try to shoo them away. At a strategic position on the catwalk, one of Matthew Brady's men had set up his camera and associated equipment; he would take a series of photographs that would become grimly famous. At the very base of the gallows stood Clay and Bierce, the former still clutching his carpetbag.

The hangman and his assistant began their preparations. First was Atzerodt, who seemed to be in shock; glassy-eyed, he continued muttering prayers in German as the hangman slipped on the noose, carefully arranging the large knot behind the right ear, and slipped a black hood over the condemned man's head. Next the same arrangements were made to the sobbing David Herold. The two executioners paused hesitantly before the massive Lewis Powell; even with his hands tied, they feared what he might do. However, stoic to the end, Powell submitted to the preparations without a sound or a movement, a slight sneer on his face. Then the hangman and his helper turned to Mrs. Surratt.

The proud Surratt submitted to the preparations with haughty disdain. She ostentatiously looked away as the two men carefully tied her skirts together at the knees; in the strange sensibilities of the times, a woman could be hanged, but it was impermissible for swaying skirts to display her bare legs to the witnesses. As the hood was being prepared for her, she glanced down at the exercise yard where hundreds of witnesses milled; she started at the sight of Clay and Bierce. Haughty features twisted instantly into a mask of hate, and she opened her mouth as if about to shout. Solemnly, Clay raised his carpetbag so that she could see it. She swallowed whatever she was about to say, content with glaring at Clay. Then, just before the hood covered her still-handsome features, a hint of a triumphant smile graced her lips. Her head disappeared under the black silk.

Clay frowned at that smile, but had only moments to ponder its meaning. The hangman wasted no time; he strode to the single lever that controlled all four trapdoors, and gave it a vigorous pull. The four figures disappeared through the openings, and three almost simultaneous snaps were heard as three necks broke. However, beneath the gallows all could see Lewis Powell writhing in agony, desperate animal sounds escaping from the hooded man's throat; his massive neck muscles had prevented his neck from breaking, and now he was slowly strangling. For some moments the crowd watched in fascination; then, as the animal sounds became more desperate, as Powell's body voided itself of waste, most turned away in disgust, if not pity. However, Clay and Bierce watched unwaveringly. They remembered the horrific injuries inflicted on William Seward and his son, and the trauma of Seward's teenage daughter. Both friends knew that although all three victims would live, they would never be the same again, and owed a lifetime of pain to the man strangling under the gallows. After what seemed to be an eternity, Powell's motions and sounds began to decrease; but they did not stop altogether until ten minutes had passed.

Only at that point did Clay wordlessly turn and walk swiftly to the prison gate, followed by Bierce. As they gained Pennsylvania Avenue and began walking in the direction of Willard's, Ambrose Bierce became puzzled at Clay's silence. Finally, he felt compelled to ask his friend about it.

"Why the long face, Clay? It is over. The traitors are dead, New York saved from a plague, an honorable senator's name protected, and no excuse to restart the war."

"I cannot forget that smile of hers, just as the hood went over her head," replied Clay. "It is as if she knew she had somehow outwitted me."

"You make too much of it. The woman was about to die; that can cause all kinds of facial tics."

"I wish I could be sure."

After a perceptible hesitation, Bierce asked, "Are you going to have Duval release Surratt alive?"

"She has orders to do so once she has news of Mrs. Surratt's execution. Best not to put too much in writing, on matters like these." Clay shook his head as if to clear it. "Well, you are undoubtedly right. Now all that remains is to tidy up of a few things, and resign my commission. Then I will be free to seek out Nathan Bedford Forrest. He may have survived the war, may have been paroled; but now that my duties are done, he will not survive me."

Bierce shuddered; he knew what was behind this. Before he became a skilled, ruthless Confederate general, Nathan Bedford Forrest had been a millionaire slave trader. He had sold an accomplished, mulatto woman to a family in New Orleans, who abused her to the point where she took her own life. The woman, Arabella Lot, was the daughter of Clay's uncle by a slave, and Clay's earliest love. After the war began, he tracked her down, only to find her dead. An insane, bestial Clay had done a terrible thing to the family he blamed for her death, and had only held off tracking down Forrest for similar treatment on the direct order of Ulysses Grant.

"Clay, let it go. It is time to make a future for yourself. Let it go."

Clay stopped walking, forcing Bierce to do the same. He turned to Bierce, who noted with concern that the pale blue eyes behind the spectacles seemed to glow with unearthly light. "A Clay cannot forgive or forget such a wrong. *I* cannot forgive it. In the name of our friendship, which I value, please do not try to dissuade me."

Bierce saw it would be useless. Instead, he changed the subject. He gestured at the carpetbag.

"What are you going to do with that photograph? It would seem to have outlived its usefulness."

Clay said nothing. Instead, he placed the bag on the sidewalk, opened it, and removed the fragile glass plate.

Oblivious to the occasional passerby, he stared intently at it for nearly a minute; the hungry, longing look on Clay's face chilled Bierce to the bone. Then without warning, Clay's face convulsed into an expression of loathing, and he threw the plate down the ally beside them; they both heard the plate shatter into what must be hundreds of pieces. Then, without a word Clay picked up his bag and resumed walking toward Willard's, followed by an uneasy Ambrose Bierce.

* * * * *

The days had been one continuous nightmare for John Surratt. The terrible woman kept him regularly dosed with laudanum, so he would be easy to control. He stayed handcuffed to the chair, the woman tending to his wants without ever releasing him, feeding him like a baby, holding up glasses of water to sip; even managing to help him to void himself into a bucket without loosening his hands, to his shame and embarrassment. Yet he was glad for the doses of laudanum; although the woman had removed the awful objects from the table in front of him, Tolafson's butchered remains were still in the corner by the stairs, beginning to smell something awful, a constant reminder of what the woman would do if he attempted any resistance. Partly through the effects of continuous terror, partly through the effect of the drug, he spent most of his time in a trance-like state, and was unable to be sure what was real and what was a dream.

Just like that morning when he thought he saw the little Willis girl from the farm down the road, the tyke who had been peddling eggs and milk to him since he first arrived, peeking in through a gap left in the dirty curtain of the parlor-room window. The little girl's eyes suddenly went wide as she took in what was in the parlor. Surratt almost cried out to her for help; the woman was gone into Buffalo, and this might be his only hope of rescue. However, in his drug-addled mind it occurred to him that the woman could be back at any moment, and discover the child. Surratt had no doubt what she would do to the little Willis girl. Summoning what strength he had, he shouted. "Run! Run fast as you can! Don't stop!"

The wide-eyed girl heard him clearly even through the closed window, and was off like a rabbit. Five minutes later, Teresa Duval did in fact return, tethering her gig out back and entering through the kitchen door carrying a local newspaper. She paused to look at Surratt, who was now again in an opium-induced sleep. She frowned slightly; the newspaper contained her signal to release Surratt, and she knew Clay would be highly displeased if Surratt died from a drug overdose. She threw the newspaper on the table and strode over to Surratt, lifting an eyelid to inspect his pupils. Nodding to herself, she removed from her pocket a small vial, opened it, and held it under his nose. With a gagging cough, Surratt came instantly awake. Cheerfully, she held the newspaper before his eyes, so he could see the banner headlines announcing the death of his mother and the other conspirators. With a soft wail, Surratt began to cry. Still smiling, Duval slapped him viciously, shocking him into silence.

"None of that, Mr. Surratt. You mother said nothing on the gallows, so you are free to go." She swiftly went to the back of his chair and unlocked the handcuffs with a small key. Still dazed, Surratt remained seated in the chair, massaging his wrists. With unexpected strength Duval jerked him to his feet, then stuffed a large wad of greenbacks into his shirt pocket.

"Time to depart, Mr. Surratt. The money I gave you is enough to get you into Canada, and from there to Europe. Go there, and stay there; if I ever hear of you returning, the Federals will be the least of your problems." She hustled him to the door, opened it, and shoved him so hard he tumbled down into the dusty front yard. With a look of abject horror, Surratt scrambled to his feet and began unsteadily stumbling toward the main road. Laughing her silvery laugh, Duval shut the front door, then went to her room to pack her belongings.

In a quarter of an hour she brought her carpetbag into the parlor and looked around, checking for the last time to see if she had left anything that might be traced to her. Satisfied she had not, she walked over to the now stinking remains of the Confederate agent Tollafson, and considered what to do. Burial would be troublesome, she decided; best to burn the place down. The bones might be found, but the police would think some vagrant had been killed in an accidental fire, and that would be the end of their curiosity. She remembered there were friction matches in the kitchen, and walked to the side of the pump where she had last seen them.

As she picked up the box, the locked kitchen door flew open under the force a powerful crushing blow. Framed in the doorway was a massive, powerfully-built man of about thirty, oddly lacking his left arm, dressed in the blue double-breasted tunic of a policeman. However, his right hand held a Remington .44 pistol pointed steadily at her chest, and behind the sights she saw cold, gun-metal grey eyes looking at her unwaveringly. Behind him stood a younger, thinner man, nervously clutching a Colt. The one-armed man spoke. "Well, Jesse, looks like the Willis girl was telling the truth."

Thinking quickly, Duval assumed an air of panicked fear. "Oh officer, thank goodness you are here! I came here on a visit, only to find the most terrible, awful crime had been committed..."

"Police Sergeant Amos Kendall, miss. Please back into the parlor, and make no sudden movements."

"But Sergeant..."

Kendall cocked the big Remington "Move."

Slowly she did as she was told, calculating the odds against her. If it had been only this man, she might have had a chance of killing him. However, there were two men, both armed and alert. She decided to wait her chance.

"Jesse, come round and handcuff her," said Kendall. The nervous younger officer did as he was told; Duval realized her chances of escape were sinking rapidly. Only when she was handcuffed did the officers turn their attention to the horrible remains by the stairs. Kendall spoke again.

"Only thing I ever saw that bad was after Gettysburg, where I lost my arm. I saw lots of bodies blown to bits by shell or canister shot. However, that was something that happened in an instant, and was over. Time was taken over this poor bastard; lots of time, by someone who enjoyed his work." He then turned to address Duval. "Pretending you just came across this won't wash. We spent some time peeking in, between the gap in the curtains. We both saw you walking back and forth as if you hadn't a care in the world; no lady coming unexpectedly on such a scene would do that. Jesse, check her pockets."

Duval tensed; but with her hands handcuffed behind her back, and Kendall armed, any action would be hopeless. The young man searched her gingerly, seemingly embarrassed by close contact with her, but in a few moments he had produced a large wad of cash, her Sharps pepperbox, and the straight razor that had come to mean so much to her. Jesse sniffed the gun, and then opened up the razor. He looked at his superior and said "Amos, this here gun's been fired recently; and there's some blood stains on the razor."

Teresa Duval now felt fear for one of the very few times in her life. His grey eyes boring into her with the implacability of death, Kendall spoke. "Well now, if the coroner finds a gunshot wound, or that the cuts were made with a razor, looks like Buffalo is going to have itself a hanging."

* * * * *

Once again, Clay and Bierce were in Stanton's office, seated in chairs directly in front of his massive desk. To Stanton's right sat Ulysses Grant, puffing on one of his ever-present cigars.

"The terror promised in Booth's diary has not happened, and now never will," said Clay as he continued his debriefing.

Stanton frowned. "So you still will not give me details of the plot. How do I know there even was a plot?"

Clay shrugged negligently. “You will have to take my word on it. In any event, now that my task is done, I am tendering my resignation. I have personal matters to attend to that have long been deferred.” Clay reached inside his tunic and brought out a folded piece of paper, which he laid carefully on Stanton’s. Surprisingly, it was Grant who reached for it, glanced over it, and then slowly tore it into quarters.

Pale blue eyes glittering behind his spectacles, Clay spoke quietly. “Sir, as a volunteer officer I have the right to resign at any time after the cessation of hostilities. You have no right to hold me in the Army.”

Expelling a mouthful of cigar smoke at the ceiling, Grant replied, “There are three reasons why your resignation is unacceptable. The first is that as we begin to reconstruct the South, your...unique skills will remain more needed than ever. The second is that I know very well you intend to kill Nathan Bedford Forrest. No matter how...personal your motives, such a death at the hands of a former Federal officer would be regarded by many as an act of policy by this government, an act violating the letter and spirit of the terms of surrender. However, the last is the most important reason.”

“And what reason is that, sir?”

“That once I explain how remaining in the service is vital to our country and to me, your personal honor will not permit you to resign. To show the country’s appreciation and my own, I am appointing you major in the Regular Army; technically a step down, but as we demobilize the volunteers, some generals will be dropping back to captain.”

Clay made no response, his blank expression giving no sign that he was seriously considering Grant’s words.

Bierce decided to add his own argument. “Clay, kill Forrest and you not only end your own life, you end your usefulness to the country. General Grant is right.”

After what seemed to be an eternity, Clay finally responded. “Very well, sir. I will do as you suggest, on one condition: that if

Nathan Bedford Forrest himself ever violates the terms of his parole, he is mine, to do with as I will."

Grant looked at him for a long moment, then nodded his assent. He then turned his attention to Bierce. "I have a lieutenant's commission for you in the Regulars, if you want it."

Smiling his cynical smile, Bierce replied, "I appreciate the offer, sir. However, I must decline. My dream has always been to write. A friend in New York wrote to me that I can have a reporter's job anytime I want. I must see if I can make it as a newspaperman."

Grant did not seem disappointed; in truth, he did not care much for Ambrose Bierce. Rising from his chair, he offered his hand to Clay. "Well, take a month's leave. You have earned it. Come back after you are restored and taken care of any personal matters, and we will discuss your future duties in more detail." The General gave Clay a warm handshake, and a more perfunctory one to Bierce.

Stanton also rose, shook their hands, and then seemed to remember something. "Clay, I'll thank you for Booth's diary now; it is the property of the United States."

Clay shrugged negligently, produced the small volume from an inner pocket of his tunic, and with a bow handed it to Stanton. "Of course." Both Clay and Bierce saluted smartly, turned on their heels, and marched out of the office of the Secretary of War.

Grant then strolled over to the open window and looked out at nothing in particular, still working absently on his cigar. Stanton opened Booth's diary and began to scan idly through it. Suddenly, something toward the end caught his attention. He began furiously flipping the pages at the back of the book, and then looked up with rage-filled eyes.

"God damn Clay! He's torn pages out of the diary; they were numbered, and at least 18 are missing. What was on them? We'll never know what was on them! God damn Clay!"

Stanton's rant was interrupted by a soft but insistent sound from near the window. He turned, and saw with amazement that Ulysses Grant was laughing so hard he could barely catch his breath.

Chapter 6:
"Mine Eyes Have Seen The Glory Of The Coming Of The Lord..."

Clay and Bierce walked through the lobby of Willard's, the former in uniform, the latter in crisp new civilian clothes.

"So you are off to San Francisco," commented Clay as they exited onto Pennsylvania Avenue.

"After a few days here to look up some acquaintances," Bierce replied jauntily.

"Do you have any concerns about your new career?"

"You know, I believe that I don't. My writing is excellent, and I should have no trouble becoming established in journalism."

Clay permitted himself a small smile. "Modesty was never your strong suit."

"He who toots not his own horn, the same shall not be tooted. Besides..." Bierce trailed off. Clay had stopped dead in front of a newsstand, eyes riveted on the front page. Bierce could tell that his friend had read something that shocked him, from a distance of a yard; for the hundredth time Bierce was amazed at the acuity of Clay's vision, despite his spectacles. Suddenly Clay snatched the two-cent newspaper, threw a quarter down on the vendor's table, and rushed away, not waiting for the change due him. Bierce rushed after Clay, who had stopped at the street-corner, intently scanning a below-the-fold story. Bierce peeked over Clay's shoulder and read the following:

Shocking Butchery in Buffalo; Woman to Be Charged in Atrocity

> We are informed that a woman giving the name Brigid Doyle is to be charged with a murder that has terrified all upstate New York. Miss Doyle was found alone in a farmhouse with the remains of a man who had been brutally slashed to death. The arresting officer, Sergeant Amos Kendall, has adamantly refused to discuss the nature of the fatal injuries, but our sources in the Buffalo Coroner's office have described them to us. Delicacy forbids revealing the nature of the injuries in a paper that may be read by the fair sex; but our readers can be assured that they are of a nature that brings the perpetrator's very sanity into question. We are informed that Miss Doyle's trial will commence in two days time before Judge Elijah Pabodie, who is notoriously stern with wrongdoers. Therefore, we can assure our readers that Miss Doyle will not be able to rely on her sex to avoid the ultimate penalty...

Clay turned to face Bierce, shoving the paper into his hands. Bierce was startled by the pallor of Clay's face; normally pale, what little color it had was gone, and the small officer's features resembled more those of a marble statue than a living being. Bierce was even more startled by what Clay announced.

"I must go to Buffalo now, this instant. You must do me a great favor. Contact Allan Pinkerton. He employed Duval and respected her. Now he has organized a national detective agency. Tell Pinkerton I am on my way to Buffalo, and to have whoever he has in Buffalo drop whatever they are doing and gather information on Elijah Pabodie. Cost is literally no object. Please send the telegram; I must go by the next train north."

Bierce looked with concern at his friend. "Have you considered that this may be for the best? She may have served the country, but she is evil and dangerous. Should you not let justice take its course, and remove her from this Earth?"

Clay gave Bierce a hard look, blue eyes sparkling dangerously behind his spectacles. "I know that she is all you say. However, you forget what she knows of the Surratt business. She will undoubtedly try to negotiate a deal with the judge to save her life; the price would be that information. It would blow this Government to pieces, and trigger undying hatred of the North for the South. I am going to Buffalo to prevent that. Promise me you will send the telegram!"

Bierce silently nodded his assent. Without a word Clay turned and dashed toward a nearby cabstand, leaped into an unoccupied two-wheeler, and shouted to the driver to make all haste to the train station. Bierce looked after him sadly, murmuring to himself, "All you said is true; but that is not why you are going to Buffalo."

* * * * *

Teresa Duval was going through her morning exercises, rhythmically straining every muscle in her body through a series of pushups, sit-ups, stretches and running in place. So far no opportunity for escape had presented itself, and it looked increasingly unlikely that it ever would. Sergeant Kendall had told all the jail staff what he had found, and as a result fearful care was used by all who approached her. Still, if fortune favored her with a chance, she was determined to be fit enough to make the most of it. She completed her routine, her breathing only mildly elevated. Hands on hips, she looked over her cell carefully for the hundredth time. Three of the walls were solid brick, containing not so much as a barred window;

the fourth wall was a very solid iron grate with both a key lock and an outside dead bolt.

She was becoming resigned to her fate. She had not given her current name, and dared not try to access the considerable sums of money she had in secret accounts to buy the services of a skilled, experienced defense lawyer. Contacting Jay Gould for help was out of the question; she smiled grimly to herself at how quickly Gould would arrange for her permanent silence, even in this jail, should she threaten a hint of connection between him and what had happened at the farm. She thought longer about Alphonso Clay, but acknowledged to herself that he dare not appear to help her; that would lead people to trace a connection to Grant and Stanton, and people would never believe she had not done what she had done with their approval, much less their knowledge. No, Clay's sense of duty would require him to sacrifice her, to protect the country and his commanders. The thought crossed her mind of threatening to reveal in open court the whole tangled scandal unless she were freed, bringing chaos on the country in general and destroying the careers of Grant and Stanton. Even as she mulled the idea over in her head, she realized to her own surprise that she could never do that; for it would hurt Alphonso Clay, and although she was prepared for the country and Grant to go to Hell in order to save her own life, she would die before she would destroy Clay. She laughed bitterly, and damned the thing called love.

The door to the corridor was suddenly thrown open, and the one-armed figure of Amos Kendall appeared, followed by two hulking guards. He approached the cell, threw back the bolt, and with his one arm deftly unlocked the grate. He did not enter, but dove his hand into his side pocket and produced a pair of handcuffs which he threw at her feet.

"Put those on Miss Doyle, or whatever your real name is," he said in a voice filled with quiet menace. "Judge Pabodie is waiting for the preliminary hearing. You are in luck; he has cleared his docket, will have you formally charged within the hour, and appoint one of our fine, experienced public defenders to represent you, since you apparently do not have much money of your own." He chuckled grimly, and Duval understood all too well how mediocre her defense counsel was likely to be. Sullenly, she placed the handcuffs on her wrists.

After he finished his quiet laugh, Kendall continued. "You are really getting the express treatment. Pabodie expects to impanel a jury this afternoon, and start the trial tomorrow morning. Given the evidence, you will be in for the high jump by the weekend. Oh, and by the way, I didn't hear the handcuffs latch." He stared with grim amusement at Duval; with a resigned shrug, she clicked the handcuffs she had carefully left almost closed into place.

With an exaggerated bow, Kendall indicated she should go in front of her escort. Sighing to herself, she did as indicated, mentally canceling her half-formed plan to grab Kendall's revolver, a plan which the handcuffs would only partly have hindered. A walk down several long corridors and through a side-door led her into a whitewashed courtroom. The room was not large; the spectator section could hold only about twenty and was already crammed to bursting, which was why the bailiff had already closed the main door. Two tables stood in front of the judge's bench. At one was a young, sharply-dressed man with oiled hair, obviously the prosecuting attorney; Duval caught his hawk-like eye, and immediately pegged him for dangerously intelligent. She was brought to the second table by Kendall and his men, who then left her to stand with her manacled hands for everyone to see; she held her head high, affecting not to hear the hostile mutterings from the gallery.

Suddenly the bailiff shouted. "All rise! This court is now in session. The Honorable Elijah Pabodie presiding."

As the spectators rose to their feet, the dark-visaged, grey-haired Judge Pabodie entered from the side door in a swirl of black robes, swiftly taking his seat. Banging his gavel once, he glared at Duval and said in a quavering tenor, "We are here to consider the case of the State of New York versus Brigid Doyle.

The district attorney's office has asked to bypass the impanelling of a grand jury to seek an indictment. In view of the evidence and the demand of the community for justice, he has asked for a summary proceeding to indict and proceed immediately to trial. Miss Doyle, I assume that you have no representation. Do you choose to represent yourself, or would you prefer to claim indigence and have the court appoint counsel for you?"

Before she could answer, she heard a familiar voice from the spectator's section. "Your Honor, I represent the defendant." The voice caused her heart to skip a beat; she whirled around and saw Alphonso Clay, his uniform freshly pressed, striding down the aisle toward the bench, a thin portfolio tucked under his left arm. He bowed slightly to Pabodie. "Your Honor, I am Lieutenant Colonel Alphonso Clay, United States Volunteers. I am admitted to the practice of law in my native state of Kentucky, as well as the states of Massachusetts and New York. I have evidence that will make the proceedings against Miss Doyle unnecessary. May I have permission to approach the bench?"

Startled by this development, Pabodie looked at the prosecutor to see if he would raise objection. The ambitious young district attorney saw no advantage in making trouble for a high-ranking Federal officer so soon after the victorious conclusion of the war; he had higher ambitions, and voters might object to his harassing a boy in blue. Slightly shaking his head, he busied himself with his notes and filings. Pabodie then made a curt gesture indicating Clay should advance. The slight officer came up to the bench, opened his portfolio, and placed it before the judge, announcing in a loud voice, "These papers will show that Miss Doyle not only did not commit murder, but that she has rendered valuable service to the Union in ways that can never be acknowledged."

The spectators' voices became an angry buzz. Clay's voice suddenly dropped to a murmur, audible only to Pabodie and himself. "These papers are depositions from two of the young people – children, really –whom you have defiled over the years. Because they were poor and helpless, and because they knew the establishment would believe you over them, they have never before come forward. However, via various inducements they have now executed the depositions you see before you. I am sure with more time I can find more victims of your unnatural lusts."

In a few moments, Pabodie seemed to visibly deflate, all color draining from his face. "Nobody will believe these," he hoarsely whispered.

"Many will not," Clay whispered back. "Many will. Your wife, for instance. Also, I understand you have an ailing, elderly mother. Such accusations could be a grievous blow to a woman in her position."

Pabodie had seemed to age a decade over the last minute. "God damn you, Clay. What do you want from me?"

"The release of this woman in a way that will guarantee she will never be bothered again in this matter. Then you will have this documentation, and nothing further will be heard of sick indiscretions. If it salves your conscience, the unidentified man found in the farmhouse was a Rebel spy, whose life was forfeited the moment he was caught."

"What if...the people who signed these documents choose to follow up on the matter?"

Clay favored Pabodie with a look of withering contempt. "I am a realist, and know, as they know, that although they could destroy your career and reputation, you would never serve a day in jail. You have too many high-ranking friends who will refuse to believe what you have done. On the other hand, I am a man of property, and will pay your victims for their continued silence. Money will never make up for what you did, but at least it will allow them to crawl out of the grinding poverty that would otherwise be their lot."

Pabodie's eyes drifted down to the papers, which he had clutched in his hands. Without raising his eyes, he suddenly shouted "Bailiff! The case against Miss Brigid Doyle is dismissed with prejudice. Prepare the order!"

The bailiff looked amazed, but quickly recovered himself, went to his small table, and began preparing the papers for the judge's signature.

The prosecuting attorney was made of sterner stuff. Face reddened with outrage, he jumped to his feet "Your Honor, I protest! Dismissal with prejudice means no charges may ever be brought against the accused on this matter, regardless of what additional evidence is produced! In the name of the public and the state of New York I must..."

"The case is dismissed with prejudice!" Pabodie shouted back. "This court is adjourned!" Ignoring the angry buzzing from the spectators, he scrawled his signature on the papers the bailiff had placed before him. He then rose slowly, clutched the papers given him by Clay with both hands, and with staggering steps exited the courtroom, eyes never leaving the papers in his hands. Taking Duval's arm, Clay led her through the same door, obviously anxious to avoid an incident with a hostile crowd. Pausing in the corridor, they heard Pabodie's heavy steps as he slowly ascended the stairs to the second floor.

The door to the courtroom opened again, and they were confronted by the one-armed figure of Amos Kendall. Glowering at the pair, the policeman spoke in a voice charged with menace. "Don't know what hold you have on Pabodie, but it has let you get away with a crime the likes of which I have never seen, and may God grant I will never see again. Now I put you both on warning. This is my town, and the people here are my responsibility. I want you gone by sunset. If I ever see either of you again, you will not be leaving this town – ever. Understand?"

Clay nodded his assent. However, Duval was unable to let it go at that. "Sergeant, I believe you should remove my handcuffs. They chafe." Glowering at her, he deftly produced the keys with his remaining arm, and unlocked the manacles on his first try, stuffing them into a side pocket of his uniform.

Duval rubbed her wrists to restore circulation, and then spoke sweetly. "You have some property of mine. I would appreciate it if you gave it back."

Kendall's eyes narrowed, but with only a slight hesitation he did as he had been asked; producing from another of his tunic's pockets first a wad of cash, then a Sharps pistol, and finally a Wilkinson straight-razor. Duval made them all disappear into pockets of her dress, saying, "I especially appreciate the razor. It has come to mean much to me over the years." In her mind's eye she saw her burning childhood home, an image of the night she had acquired the razor, and given it its first taste of arterial blood.

Clay touched her elbow. "Time to go," he said quietly, as he guided her to the rear of the courthouse, while the one-armed Kendall stared at them with implacable grey eyes.

As they passed through the back door, Clay pointed at a small carriage. "Quickly, into the gig. We must make haste and be on the next train to New York City." He handed her up into the passenger seat, then untied the horse from the hitching post and jumped into the driver's seat. As he took the reigns and put the gig into motion, Duval placed her hand on Clay's right arm.

"I did not expect you to come," she said, smiling broadly at him. "I would have understood if you had left me to hang, given what was at stake."

Clay spoke while continuing to look straight ahead. "It was necessary for the Union. I could not be certain that the fear of imminent death might have led you to implicate Grant and Stanton through me."

"I see," replied Duval, a smile on her lips, a predatory gleam in her eyes. Feeling suddenly tired, she rested her head on Clay's shoulder; Clay stiffened, but did not object. "I see," she repeated.

Through an open second-story window of the courthouse, a muffled gunshot suddenly rang out. Clay and Duval were already too far down the street for them to notice the sound.

* * * * *

The couple worked their way through the crowds to the platform where the train from New York City to Washington waited. "You must give the credit to Allan Pinkerton," Clay said, responding to a complement Duval had paid him. "I could never have gathered the information about the judge so quickly on my own. He is assembling a truly impressive national organization."

"Still, it was you who thought to go to him, you who hired him." Duval held Clay's arm even more possessively, to her own surprise; the last thing she would have considered herself was a "clinger."

Clay suddenly stopped, forcing Duval to do the same. "Why, that is General Halleck," he commented with genuine surprise, pointing to a blue-uniformed officer slowly working his way along the platform. Then in a louder voice he called "General Halleck, sir!"

Henry Halleck came to a stop, and swiveled his bulging eyes in Clay's direction. Then he shuffled over to Clay and Duval, the former saluting, the latter making a sketch of a curtsy. "Colonel Clay, I hear congratulations are in order," he said, absently scratching his elbow. "You are to become a major in the Regulars."

"I have that honor, sir. May I introduce my friend, Miss Teresa Duval? She has been of invaluable service in my recent assignment."

Halleck turned his watery blue eyes toward Duval, and nodded. Duval came to the same conclusion as had Clay earlier: that the general was a habitual user of some opium compound.

"My pleasure, Miss Duval." He turned his attention back to Clay. "At the risk of impoliteness, I must be leaving immediately. My train from Washington was late, and if the steamer to Panama is on schedule, I have only a bit more than two hours to get to the docks. It is fortunate that my family and luggage have already gone ahead."

Clay frowned. "Panama?"

"It is the quickest way to San Francisco. The ax has fallen; Grant and Stanton have removed me as chief of staff, and are sending me to California to head the Military Division of the Pacific."

Although not tender-hearted, Clay felt a pang of sympathy for the fallen general; the Military Division of the Pacific sounded grand, but it was in fact a backwater command with few troops, who easily handled the occasional difficulties with the Modoc Indians.

"I am sorry to hear that, sir," replied Clay.

"No need. My headquarters will be in San Francisco. Not only is it a delightful city, but I have nothing but fond memories of it. Did you know that before the war I was not only the most successful attorney there, but the best architect in California? I even constructed a building people said could not be built in San Francisco: an office building that was fireproof and earthquake proof. They said it could not be done, but I did it. I had nothing but praise and success, before the war. Then I rejoined the army, and...well, I know that history will speak ill of me. That is why I like to remember my accomplishments before the war." His eyes had drifted from Clay and Duval, and it seemed as if he were talking to himself. "They said it could not be done, that the ground was too unstable, the materials too expensive, but I did it and made it pay. It will stand for more than a century. Symmetry was the secret; perfect symmetry in the load-bearing walls, the foundations, the fixtures. Symmetry left no weaknesses." He refocused his attention on Clay.

"That is what always bothered me about the Booth conspiracy. There was a lack of symmetry about it. Attacks on Lincoln, but apparently none on Grant or Stanton. Attacks in the North, but none on our commanders in the South. Perhaps that is why I failed as a general; I was expecting symmetry, when war involves individuals who do not apply the laws of engineering." Halleck seemed to blink some self-pitying tears from his eyes. "My apologies; I am rambling. Clay, congratulations on a job well done. Good day to you both." With a slight nod, Halleck turned and shuffled toward the front of the station where the cabs waited.

Duval smiled grimly as she watched him disappear into the crowd. "However did such a fool come to hold such a powerful position?"

Although her question was rhetorical, Clay gave her a serious answer. "Because until the war he did indeed seem a remarkable man, succeeding at all he did. When he faced a job where he could not succeed, it broke him." Clay drew out his watch and consulted it. "We must make haste or we will miss the Washington train."

In less than a minute they had found their train, boarded it, and entered their first-class compartment. Just as they seated themselves, the train lurched into motion with the scream of a whistle and the hiss of steam; there had indeed been little time to spare.

The events of the last few days had taken much out of Duval. Without so much as a word, she placed her head on Clay's shoulder, and promptly went to sleep. Clay frowned upon such intimacy in a public place, even if that public place was a first class railroad compartment, but found to his surprise that he did not have the heart to disturb her. Feeling exhausted himself, he made himself as comfortable as he could without disturbing her, and began to doze.

In his fitful sleep, the events of the last few days flitted through his dreams, recognizable yet distorted in the way of dreams. His dream-self was puzzled by the way two scenes in particular repeated several times.

In one, Henry Halleck was a schoolteacher, dressed not in uniform but in a frock coat. Clay seemed to be a little boy sitting at a desk, and to be the only one in the class. The dream Halleck paced back and forth before the blackboard, addressing Clay. "I have kept you after, young Mr. Clay, because you do not understand the vital importance of symmetry." He stopped his pacing and glared down on the dream-Clay disapprovingly. "I am disappointed in you, young Mr. Clay. Every animal, every plant on this planet is symmetrical. When you look into the skies, you see that the stars are distributed symmetrically. And yet you do not appreciate the importance of symmetry."

This would then be replaced by a dream of Mrs. Surratt's hanging. In the dream, instead of the brightly-lit exercise yard and the hundreds of witnesses, the gallows stood on a vast, dark plain, with not a soul in sight except for Surratt, the hangman, and Clay. As the hangman started to place the silk hood over her head, the dream-Surratt smiled; the same triumphant smile he had glimpsed at her actual execution. As the mask went over her head, she said, "You did not appreciate symmetry, and that is why you will fail." Several times this particular dream ended there. However, in one final repetition the hangman threw the lever, Surratt fell through the trap, and a sickening snap jarred Clay awake.

The start of his body awakened Duval. She looked at him sleepily; then seeing the look of horror on her lover's face, she came fully awake. "Alphonso, what is it? What is wrong?"

"Damnation! Symmetry! A plan of this nature would have symmetry. Why were all efforts at rekindling the war focused on the North, when there was such bitterness and resentment in the defeated South? Because there are indeed efforts in the South! The goal was to restart the war, it mattered not how or on what side."

"But what could be done to cause the South to rise up again as a whole, after all the death and destruction they have endured?"

"I know of only one way certain to do so. I will take immediate action, and pray that I am not too late. I will drop you in Washington, and proceed."

"Alphonso Clay, you are not going into any lion's den without me. You know I can cover your back as well as any man. Now, where are we going?"

For a long moment Clay looked at her; then with an odd combination of emotions flitting across his face, he said one word.

"Richmond."

* * * * *

Robert E. Lee walked so softly into his wife's bedroom that she did not notice his arrival. She lay flat above the covers, restlessly making small movements to adjust her spine to some position marginally less painful. Lee looked sadly at his wife's hands, twisted by arthritis into a parody of what they had been when he had first met her, more than thirty years before. He glanced at the cumbersome wheelchair beside the bed, the prison in which his wife lived when she was not lying on the bed. He walked over and sat on the bed beside her; she turned her face toward him, the lines of pain softened by a look of the purest love. He bent forward and gently kissed her forehead.

"The pain is no better today?" he inquired, already knowing the answer.

She smiled weakly. "It is no worse, Robert. Any word on our sons?"

He smiled a genuine smile. "Custis, Rooney and Rob are well. They plan a rendezvous with our daughters, and are coming to see us in a few days' time."

Mrs. Lee's smile broadened. "We have such fine children, do we not, Robert? Especially the boys. They fought so hard and so well for the Cause; I thank God for His returning them to us whole."

Robert Lee struggled to keep a look of melancholy from his face. If his wife's prayers had been answered, God had been deaf to the prayers of so many other mothers of young soldiers. He felt he must not show his sadness and bitterness; his wife had so few pleasures these days, and he was determined never to detract from any of them.

"If they have become good men, it is entirely your doing," he replied. "I was around so little while they grew; whatever is good in them must be from you."

Mrs. Lee placed her crippled hand lightly on that of her husband's, and continued smiling. "Never underestimate the influence you had on them. They knew you were away because of duty; and they could see you always did your duty, always kept your honor, no matter what the cost."

"Still, as I look back I realize what it must have been like for you, all those years I was in Mexico or on the frontier, running the plantation and raising the children. It was wrong of me."

"It was never wrong, Robert. You were always my knight in shining armor; and a knight cannot spend much time in his castle if he is to be a true knight."

Lee chuckled ruefully. "Some knight I have been! The castle is gone. Arlington has been seized by the Federals, and turned into a cemetery for their dead. It will now never be returned to us; we can never go back to the place where we spent the happiest times of our youth." He gestured around them. "Here we are, guests in the house of an admirer, who has given up his home to us; no servants except the washer-woman who comes every other day. I wish I could give my beautiful princess more."

"We are together; that is enough. Still, we cannot impose on your friend for long. What will we do for money? Will you accept the offer from the Khedive of Egypt to head his army?"

Lee shook his head. "I will never order young men to their deaths again. Never. As for how we will live, today's mail brought an offer from Washington College to be their president. The salary is not great; but the position comes with a house and servants."

Mrs. Lee laughed softly. "You, a teacher? How could you stand the boredom?"

A melancholic expression came over Lee's face. "Looking back on my military career, I now realize I was happiest during the short time I headed West Point. The army was a duty;

education was a pleasure. Yes, it may be boring, but I want to spend the remainder of my days being bored with you."

"Then we will go to Washington College." She hesitated, and placed her gnarled hand on her husband's arm. "Robert, I know that you disapprove; but I really do need more medicine for the pain."

Robert Lee kept his tone light, although his heart was breaking. "Now, you know you have already had a dose this afternoon. Another would send you to sleep for the rest of the evening."

The withered hand clutched harder. "I know it is weakness; but the pain is especially bad today, and I would rather sleep than be awake with it."

With a heavy heart, Lee rose from the bed and went to the dressing table by the window. He picked up a spoon and a dark brown bottle, uncorking the latter as he walked back to the bed. Carefully measuring the drops of laudanum into the spoon, he then gave the narcotic to his wife, hating the necessity, hating himself for feeding his wife's addiction.

"Thank you, Robert," she said. Then as the narcotic began to take immediate effect, she sleepily murmured, "I will dream of better times, when we were young," then closed her eyes.

Tears blurring his vision, Lee stumbled from the bedroom and into the large parlor. All the doors and windows of the house were open, and a slightly cooling breeze wafted through the front door. Lee stood in front of that door, letting the wind dry his tears. He noticed some women across the street, looking his way and talking among themselves. The sight depressed him; they were undoubtedly talking about him, about their glorious temporary neighbor, and what a noble and great man he was. They could not imagine, they would not believe, what the slaughter of the last four years had taken out of him.

Suddenly the women stopped talking, looked down the street, then quickly split up, going to their respective homes lining this street, one of the few upper-class streets in Richmond that had survived the fire. Lee turned his head and saw that a lone rider was coming into view. Lee's vision was not what it had been, and not until the rider reached his house and turned his mount into the carriageway could he tell that it was a burly, clean-shaven Federal in a captain's uniform. That explained the sudden departure of the upper-class housewives, Lee realized; the very presence of a damn Yankee could be contaminating.

The massive officer dismounted and tied his horse to the hitching post beside the front porch. Lee watched the captain take a deep breath, then slide a Spencer carbine out of the saddle's scabbard. Then the stranger began striding to the door, chambering a round as he went. A thoroughly alarmed Lee retreated several steps into the parlor, uncertain as to what this meant, and what he should do. Was this an insult being offered by the occupation authorities, trying to humiliate with a show of force? Was it something worse? Lee had no weapon within easy reach, and would not run to find one. Resolutely, he took a position at the entrance to the hallway that led to his unconscious wife's bedroom.

The large, clean-shaven man entered the parlor, saw Lee, and hesitated. The man seemed familiar, but Lee could not remember where he had seen the intruder before. With no fear for himself, concealing the terror he felt for his wife, Lee addressed the man. "What is the meaning of this outrage, coming armed and without permission into my house? How dare you, sir!"

"I dare because there ain't no other way," said the man in a deep, drawling voice. "All the sacrifice, all the blood – it can't be for nothing."

Lee's eyes widened with shock as he finally recognized the voice. "Not you. It cannot be."

"I wish there was another way; but things went wrong up North," replied James Longstreet in a sad, mournful voice. "I even told Colonel Waite I would shoot Sam Grant to get the war back going; Sam is the best friend I ever had. But Waite told me it could only be you; only your murder by a Yankee would cause the beaten South to rise up and go at the North again. If Grant died, the North would be outraged, but the South wouldn't really feel the spur to rebellion that they would if it were you."

"You are working for Ephraim Waite? The man is an uncivilized butcher. I told Jefferson Davis repeatedly to dismiss Waite from his position."

"And Jeff Davis never did," replied Longstreet. "Davis may be a fool, but he and I agree on one thing: after all the blood that has been spilled, we must do anything to gain our independence. Anything. With the North blamed for your murder, the South will rise as one, and fight to the very last man, woman, and child. It may take ten years, it may take longer; but sooner or later Washington will grow weary of bushwhackers and partisans, and we will win."

"So Waite told you to murder me."

Longstreet seemed to square his shoulders. "I volunteered. It was the last thing I would have liked to do for the cause; so it was my duty to do it. I owe it to my boys; the boys who died at Gettysburg, the boys who died in a dozen battles, big and little, for the Cause."

"Can't lead from behind," said Lee softly, repeating Longstreet's famous motto.

"That's right. So I shaved off that rat's nest of a beard I grew during the war, so I wouldn't be recognized by bystanders. I got a Yankee captain's uniform that would fit, and a Yankee carbine that I will leave here after...I'm done. I made sure your neighbors saw a Yankee officer entering the house."

Lee briefly closed his eyes, and had a vision of a century of partisan warfare, countless bushwhacking, countless cavalry raids on civilians, fire and blood steadily sweeping across the South until it was another Ireland or Poland, full of oppressors and oppressed equally brutalized, equally devoid of Christian humanity. A South become a sick perversion of the land that he so loved. He opened his eyes, and saw Longstreet had pointed the carbine at his chest, and was squinting over the sights.

"Pete, for myself I do not care; but for the South I beg you, do not do this. I know more about Waite than do you; he is worse than a beast, and never served the Confederacy as much as he served masters who do not care about our land. He is corrupt, and is trying to create a land where his corruption will flourish."

Longstreet said nothing; he simply continued to point the weapon at Lee. Lee knew Longstreet could fire at any second, so he made one last appeal to reason.

"Pete, you and I did terrible things for the Cause. We felt badly about them, but we did them. But we never did murder. Killing in battle is one thing; as horrible as it is, it does not degrade a cause. However, what you are doing now is simply murder. Has the Cause come to the point where it can only be saved by murder? Pete, I know that you are good man. Look inside yourself, and ask yourself if the Cause, any cause, is worth such means to achieve. If the answer is yes, then fire, and do not be ashamed."

Lee looked calmly at Longstreet, as unafraid and dignified as a Roman consul. Longstreet seemed frozen in position, squinting down the carbine. The two stood as still as statues for nearly a minute, until Lee broke the silence.

"Let me make the decision easy for you. I am going to come and take that gun away from you. If you are going to ever pull the trigger, now is the time."

Lee crossed the distance between them in four measured steps; Longstreet remained motionless. Slowly, Lee grasped the barrel of the Spencer, gently directing it toward the ceiling. With equal gentleness, he disengaged Longstreet's hand from the trigger; Longstreet still did not move. Lee carefully placed the weapon on a sofa. Still holding his position, Longstreet finally spoke.

"I couldn't pull the trigger. God damn me, I couldn't pull the trigger. My mind said to do it, but my finger wouldn't move. It's over, all over. The Cause is lost forever." Quietly the man who had suffered three serious gunshot wounds in his life without a tear or moan of pain began to cry.

Lee walked over to Longstreet and hugged him, as a parent would a desolate child. Suddenly, Lee heard the sound of horses galloping down the street to his house. Through the open door he saw a young, blond officer with spectacles slide off his mount without bothering to tie it up; the man began running to the house, drawing a revolver as he ran. More amazingly, he saw a lithe, attractive woman, who was shockingly riding astride, gallop up, vault off her animal, and run with equal speed right behind the man, a small pistol somehow appearing in her hand. The two burst into the parlor, and skidded to a halt. Lee could tell the intruders were swiftly taking in the strange sight of a grey-haired gentleman consoling a hulking brute in uniform, and the Yankee carbine lying on a sofa. The man was the first to speak.

"Mr. Lee, I am Alphonso Clay. There is good reason to believe that an attempt will be made on your life, with the intention of making it appear to be the work of the Union." He looked meaningfully at the large man in the blue uniform. Lee separated from Longstreet, who brought a hand to his face in an attempt to hide his tears.

"That is nonsense, Colonel," replied Lee. "Even my good friend General Longstreet fell for such rumors. It explains why he is currently wearing a Union uniform. He had some silly idea that the sight of a Federal officer in my home would discourage an assailant. I was just assuring him that his fears were groundless. Is that not so, Pete?"

Not trusting himself to speak, Longstreet merely nodded his assent.

Clay looked hard at the two Rebels, then at the carbine, then back at the men. Slowly holstering his revolver, Clay replied "I see. I suppose the threat is past. Do you concur, Mr. Longstreet?" The large man nodded. Clay shrugged, and turned to Duval.

"I suppose then that we should..." Clay trailed off. Duval still had her Sharps pepperbox in her hand, pointed straight at Lee's heart. Clay could see the strangeness of her eyes, and suspected she was not entirely in this room, but back in Ireland, where dignified men with drawling accents had caused terrible things to be done to her parents. With a flash of intuition, he realized that for the moment she did not see Lee, but some long-dead English soldier. Clay carefully placed his hand on her arm, and spoke in a low voice. "Teresa, there is no need. It is over. All of it is over. What you are thinking of never makes it better. Never. Believe me, I know."

She started, and looked directly into his eyes. Suddenly the small gun was gone as if by magic. Clay turned to the now puzzled generals, bowed slightly, clicked his heels in the European fashion, and without a word strode from the room, closely followed by Teresa Duval.

* * * * *

Duval was luxuriating on one of the massive, comfortable sofas contained in Clay's impressive library, drinking coffee and holding polite conversation with Mr. John Rockefeller, the young oil magnate with whom Clay was a silent partner. A fire burned in the grate; although still late summer, Kentucky was going through a cold spell, and Clay always made certain his guests were comfortable. Clay had said he needed time to himself; he had not specified, but Duval knew that he was spending time at the tomb of his mulatto cousin Jeremiah Lot, born of a liaison between a dissolute uncle of Clay's and a slave. There was also a tomb for Lot's sister, Clay's love from before the war; there was no body for the tomb to receive, but Clay had constructed it nonetheless.

Rockefeller finished his coffee, and placed the cup on the tray on a nearby end table. "I appreciate your hospitality Miss Duval. However, I must get to Louisville within two hours if I am to make the train to Ohio." He stood and made a slight bow to Duval. “My business with Major Clay is concluded, and I said my goodbyes before he went out this morning. Please thank him again for his hospitality.”

Duval also rose, and executed a graceful curtsy. “It has been a pleasure, Mr. Rockefeller. I know that despite his desire for his investments with you to remain anonymous, he has the highest regard for you, both as a businessman and as a gentleman.”

“And I have the highest regard for him, especially for his farsightedness. America’s need for oil is growing by leaps and bounds, but every year the whales become fewer and fewer. The only substitute for whale oil will be petroleum distillates. Those like Clay who see that future will reap the greatest rewards. Do not trouble yourself by seeing me out; the stable boy already has my gig prepared. I hope we meet again.” With quick steps the rail-thin young man strode to the door, retrieved his hat and stick, and closed the massive front door behind him.

Duval walked over to the fireplace and stared into the flames, a thoughtful look on her face. Clay’s house was elegant and gracious; his landholdings enormous; his wealth skillfully finding its way into the businesses that would find favor in the decades to come. It would be so easy to make herself mistress of all this, she thought; the prudish Clay was uncomfortable with their relationship being unsanctified by marriage, and it would not take much to maneuver him into a proposal. Yet to her continuing amazement, she knew she would not do that. Partly that was because she fiercely valued her independence, and found even the theoretical submission required of a wife to be distasteful. More importantly, however, she realized that she wanted Clay to marry her because he wanted to, not because he felt he should.

She heard the rear door open and close, and the click of approaching boot heels. Clay entered the room, a desolate look on his face; Duval could guess the reason for that look. He walked over to the fire and stood beside her, staring into it. The silence continued for nearly a minute before it was broken by Duval.

"I have had a letter from Mr. Pinkerton. He wishes to employee me as a roving investigator in his agency, to be given the most delicate cases. The salary he offered is $250 per month, plus expenses." She did not add the she expected to still take well-compensated assignments from Jay Gould on the side.

"He must appreciate your worth," Clay responded. "A factory worker is lucky to get a fourth of that. Will you accept?"

"I believe I will. After all, a single lady must find some way to support herself."

"What does this mean for us?" Clay asked, not looking at her.

"That will depend on you."

Clay finally looked directly at her, pale blue eyes glowing weirdly behind the lenses of his spectacles. "There is so much you do not know about me. You may think that you know it all, but you do not. If you knew it all, you would flee my presence."

"I have fled no danger in my life. In fact, I rather enjoy danger. Tonight, tell me all. Tell me what you think is so dreadful about yourself. You may be surprised at how little it will matter to me."

Clay looked deeply into Duval's eyes. "Very well, tonight you will learn all. You have earned that right. However, remember what you learn, you will not be able to unlearn." Then something seemed to occur to Clay. From an inner pocket of his tunic he drew eighteen crumpled pages, pages he had torn from Booth's pocket diary, pages with the potential to blow the just-reunited country apart forever. He threw them onto the fire, and carefully watched as they all blackened, shriveled and turned to ash.

"What was that?" asked a puzzled Duval.

"A record of things that never happened," replied Alphonso Clay.

AFTERWORD

This is a work of fiction, where massive liberties with the historical record have been taken for reasons of plot. To name just one instance, Lafayette Baker did not have the complete control of Washington security that I indicated in this story. Nonetheless, a surprising number of incidents in this tale happened as described. For instance, by the time John Wilkes Booth's diary came into the possession of Secretary of War Stanton, eighteen pages had been obviously torn away; to this day, there is no proof as to what was on those pages or who removed them. With the exception of Clay's presence, the pursuit and killing of Booth happened much as described in this novel. The assassination of Secretary of State Seward was partly thwarted by the unexpected arrival of two soldiers, who have never been clearly identified. Finally, the Confederate Secret Service did plan a number of terrorist attacks, some involving attempts to introduce disease into northern cities; the attempt to murder Ulysses Grant with a bomb . disguised as a lump of coal occurred as described; and there were attempts to start fires in crowded cities of the north, which fortunately came to nothing.

HISTORICAL CHARACTERS

The following are brief descriptions of some of the historical characters in ***THE BATTLE HYMN OF THE REPUBLIC.***

Lafayette Baker (1826-1868) was probably the most despised Union officer of his rank. Through underhanded maneuvering he succeeded in having Allan Pinkerton dismissed as unofficial head of Union intelligence and took his place. The rumors of corruption and abuse of power that surrounded him were ignored only because of his cold-blooded efficiency in countering Confederate agents and spies. Although not present during the chase of John Wilkes Booth, he and his cousin obtained a significant share of the $100,000 reward, and Baker was promoted to brigadier general. However, shortly thereafter President Andrew Johnson discovered that Baker was spying upon him, for the benefit of the Radical Republicans. Johnson dismissed Baker, who died shortly thereafter of what was supposed to be meningitis. However, recent tests on Baker's remains have shown he died of arsenic poisoning. At this distant date it is impossible to prove who was the murderer; Lafayette Baker was hated by so many people.

Ambrose G. Bierce (1842-1914?) was not in Washington at the time of this novel. However, I needed a sardonic scout for the plot; and Bierce was nothing if not sardonic. He had miraculously survived being shot through the head during the Atlanta campaign; within two months he had returned to combat, despite being plagued by blinding headaches and vertigo that would be with him on and off for the rest of his life. Some people attribute his black view of life to damage from this head wound; but the evidence was abundant that he was a strange and difficult personality long before a Confederate bullet injured his brain. After the war he earned his living as a journalist, working much of the time for the young William Randolph Hearst; on the side, he wrote fiction on the supernatural and the all-too natural horrors of the Civil War. His greatest moment of glory, aside from the Civil War, was when he directed for Hearst the public relations campaign against the Southern Pacific Railway's attempt to sneak through Congress a bill forgiving some $70 million in back taxes owed to the Federal Government. The then-head of Southern Pacific, the old robber baron Huntington, was nothing if not direct; he personally accosted Bierce on a street, informing him that every man had his price, and bluntly asked what Bierce's price would be. Bierce's reply is reputed to have been: "A check for $70 million, made payable to my good friend, the Treasurer of the United States;" eventually, that check was written. From this point, his life slid downhill, due as much to his own flawed character as anything else. By 1913 he was 71 years old and in constant pain; divorced by a wife he had genuinely loved, who could no longer tolerate his repeated infidelities. One beloved son had murdered a friend in a sordid fight over a girl, before turning the weapon on himself; another had quietly drunk himself into an early grave; his daughter wanted nothing to do with him. Telling some people he intended to go to Mexico to join a revolution, and others that he intended to throw himself into the Grand Canyon, he disappeared; no trace of his fate has ever been found. He would have undoubtedly been amused by the mystery he left behind.

Boston Corbett (1832-1894?) was a strange, tormented man. Although his self-castration occurred before his imprisonment at Andersonville, not after as I have stated in the novel, his experience in the living hell of that Confederate death-camp eliminated what little normality there may have been in his character. He did in fact fire the shot that killed John Wilkes Booth; despite acting against orders, he was ultimately hailed as a hero, even being awarded $1,653.84 of the reward money. He then left the army, and spent the following decades in increasingly bizarre incidents. At one point, having been appointed doorkeeper to the Kansas legislature, for no reason he emptied a revolver at the astounded legislators, fortunately without causing any injury. Finally confined to an insane asylum, he escaped and wandered north to Minnesota, where he is presumed to have died during the Great Minnesota Wildfire of 1894.

Ulysses S. Grant (1822-1885) was born Hiram Ulysses Grant; a clerk at West Point made an error in recording his name as Ulysses S. Grant, and he never bothered to have it corrected. His initials of U. S. Grant led to classmates calling him "Uncle Sam," later shorted to "Sam." Throughout his career, everyone noted the absence of foul language in Grant, all the more puzzling in that he seems never to have formally joined a church; his foulest epithets really were "darn" and "doggone." Isolated from his family after the Mexican War, he commenced heavy drinking, and was forced to resign from the army. During the Civil War, there is only one documented instance of his being drunk; despite all the rumors, it would seem that when he had a task, or when he was with his wife and children, he simply did not have an overpowering need for alcohol.

Controversy over his political career has obscured the fact that most modern military historians rate Grant as one of the three greatest American generals (for those who are interested, Winfield Scott and Douglas MacArthur are usually considered the other two). It is clear that he was not happy with his military profession, the only career in which he was completely successful; one does not need to be Freud to see the significance in his refusal to eat meat unless every sign of pink was cooked out of it, or to eat chicken because he "could not bring himself to consume anything that walked on two legs." Although often denounced by political opponents as a mindless butcher interested only in attrition, he in fact was supremely skilled; he lost fewer men in completely defeating Robert E. Lee than his predecessors had lost in repeated abject defeats at the hands of the Confederates.

His Presidency is usually considered a failure. However, recent historians have been revising his political reputation upward, although it will never equal his military reputation. The corruption of his administration was exaggerated by his political enemies; in fact, when he learned of illegal practices he moved against them relentlessly, even if it involved his own relations. The group called the "Liberal Republicans" criticized him as incompetent and dictatorial, and since many then-famous writers were members of that group, their hatred has tarnished his political reputation to this day. However, it should be noted that they meant to be "liberal" to the defeated Confederates, and were angry at Grant for using martial law to put down the Ku Klux Klan and to enforce the political rights of freed slaves. If Grant's successors had continued his policies, the civil rights struggles of the 20th Century would have been unnecessary. In 1884 his savings were completely wiped out by the failure of a fraudulent Wall Street firm in which he had been persuaded to invest. At the same time, he discovered he was dying of throat cancer; a 20-cigar-a-day habit had caught up with him. His family still dependent on him for support, he knew the only thing he had to sell was his memoirs. Assisted and encouraged by his postwar friend Mark Twain, racing death, unable to eat solid food, refusing more than low doses of pain killers in order to keep his mind clear, he finished the book the day before his death, gaining his family $500,000 and winning his last battle.

Henry W. Halleck (1815-1872) was a man who had almost all the gifts; his ultimate tragedy was that people *expected* him to have *all* the gifts. He was a soldier so scholarly that his fellow officers dubbed him "Old Brains." By the time of the Civil War, he was admired and respected by all that knew him.

When California was annexed to the United States, he was its first Secretary of State, presiding over its Constitutional Convention and re-organizing its land laws, all while performing his full-time duties as an Army captain. Resigning from the Army, he decided to become a lawyer. Starting from scratch, within a year he was one of the highest-paid in

California, and its acknowledged expert on Mexican and American land law.

While carrying out his legal practice, he also managed North America's largest mercury mine, and constructed the first earthquake-proof building in California, a multistory office structure that when finished was the largest building on the West Coast; it stood until the late 1950s.

His reputation was such that when the Civil War broke out, he was promoted straight from a civilian and former captain to a major general's position. He arrived in the East to discovery the ultimate irony; the only career at which he did not excel was the Army, the one for which he had been trained. After a dismal performance as a field commander, he was transferred to the desk job of chief of staff, where he did better.

However, the stress of the position aggravated his health problems, especially his hemorrhoids. He treated them with a remedy containing opium, and was sometimes noticeably under the influence of the drug. He stayed in the Army after the war. Disliked by Grant, he received a series of postings far away from Washington, until he died of a stroke at age 57.

James "Pete" Longstreet (1821-1904) was probably next only to Stonewall Jackson as Robert E. Lee's most able subordinate. As a general he was often considered too slow and deliberate in his movements. However, it can be argued in his defense that he refused to throw his men into hopeless frontal assaults with no hope of success; unlike so many of his contemporaries on both sides. His personal courage was unquestionable; he was seriously wounded three times in his career, and lived by his motto, *"Can't lead from behind."* Despite being born in South Carolina and raised in Georgia, he was unenthusiastic about both slavery and secession, but the pull of family and friends dragged him somewhat reluctantly into the Southern army. During the war, three of his five children died of an epidemic that swept Richmond. After that, the previously outgoing and fun loving Longstreet became increasingly morose and religious. After the war, he became an enthusiastic Republican, endorsing his good friend Ulysses Grant for President, attending Grant's inauguration in 1869. He accepted a number of political appointments under Grant and later Republican presidents, including Customs Commissioner, Minister to Turkey, and Railroad Commissioner. His apparent apostasy caused him to be reviled by most Confederate veterans, even to the point of widespread attempts to portray him as an incompetent commander, and to hold him responsible for the defeats of the sainted Lee. However, Lee must be allowed the final word on Longstreet's ability as a general: although sparing with compliments, he repeatedly called Longstreet *"My old warhorse."*

Dr. Samuel Mudd (1833-1883) was a doctor and planter in rural Maryland, and a known Confederate sympathizer. Without doubt he had met John Wilkes Booth on at least three occasions, and undoubtedly recognized the man whose leg he set as the fugitive assassin. Whether Mudd was actively involved in the assassination is uncertain, but what is certain is that he gave aid to Lincoln's murderer, and attempted to misdirect the searchers. Sentence to life imprisonment by the same military tribunal that gave death sentences to the other surviving conspirators, he was sent to serve his sentence at Fort Jefferson in the hellish Dry Tortugas. In 1867 yellow fever broke out at Fort Jefferson, killing a number of prisoners and guards, and the prison doctor. Volunteering to take the doctor's place, Mudd aided the sick with genuine courage, saving a number of lives. The guards were so grateful that they petitioned President Johnson to pardon Mudd, which he did in

1869. Samuel Mudd returned home, cheered by Confederate sympathizers, but soon faded into the private life of a struggling farmer. Still, for many years after his death, he was not forgotten; for decades, when someone had done something dishonorable, it was said that *"His name was Mudd."*

Edwin M. Stanton (1814-1869) was one of the best trial attorneys in the country at the time of the outbreak of the Civil War. Consulted by a number of high Government officials, he was rather surprisingly elevated by Lincoln to Secretary of War when the corrupt Simon Cameron was forced to resign. It was one of Lincoln's best appointments. Stanton could be politically devious, but he was incorruptible when it came to money and the public trust. Working for ten hours at a stretch at a stand-up desk, he made it a point to give priority to low-ranking petitioners over congressmen and generals, for most of whom he had undisguised contempt. He was known for a vicious, even brutal temper to subordinates, which was often followed by some sort of indirect apology; if he sometimes blew up at people, it would be as much at Lincoln as those who worked for him. Furthermore, he was not without consideration. When one of his overworked aides was on the verge of a nervous breakdown, he ordered the man to take two weeks leave, and gave orders to the guards that he not be readmitted to the building for two weeks.

Having started the war unsympathetic to emancipation, he was converted to it, and became its most vigorous champion. Inevitably, this caused conflict with Andrew Johnson after the war; the new President had been a Union-loyal Tennessean, but was utterly opposed to equal political rights for blacks. Johnson tried to dismiss Stanton, in contravention of a statute (passed over Johnson's veto) requiring Senate approval for the removal of Cabinet officers, as well as their appointment. This led the House to impeach Johnson, but in the Senate the impeachment failed by a single vote.

At that point, Stanton resigned, tired and sick, determined to make some money for his family while he still could. However, the strain of the war had permanently affected his health; always asthmatic, the continuous congestion in his lungs was so bad that a busy legal practice was beyond his energies. In 1869, help seemed on the way. The new President, Ulysses Grant, nominated Stanton for an open seat on the Supreme Court. Tragically, Stanton died of asthma-induced heart failure before the Senate could confirm him.

Thaddeus Stevens (1792-1868) was a stern, unbending, ruthless Pennsylvanian who never let anything or anyone stand in the way of his goals. It was even rumored, probably without foundation, that as a young man he murdered a pregnant girlfriend by throwing her down a well; whatever the truth, nothing was ever proved. Stevens never married, but lived as if married to a free black woman, Lydia Smith, making absolutely no effort to conceal the relationship. His detractors whispered it was this relationship that caused his interest in equal rights for blacks, but in fact his absolute devotion to equality long predated his relationship with Smith. He served in Congress from 1849 to 1853, and from 1859 until his death. From 1861 on he used his power as Chairman of the House Ways and Means Committee to make him one of the most powerful members of the house, and possibly more influential than the Speaker. He favored the harshest of terms for the South, and was the moving force behind the so-called excesses of Reconstruction. His devotion to rights for blacks continued after his death; his will left instructions that he be buried in a "blacks only" cemetery.

Charles Sumner (1811-1874) was the Senate's most consistent and eloquent proponent of freedom for slaves, and of equal political and social rights for the black man (not necessarily the same thing in those days). A pompous, humorless egotist, he nonetheless won the firm friendship of such people Henry Wordsworth Longfellow, Nathaniel Hawthorne, and Charles Dickens; so there must have been much of merit in his personality. Pompous and egotistic he might have been, but he never, ever, compromised on those issues he regarded as important, and regarded those who did with contempt; whether that is a good or bad thing depends on the reader.

His imposing physical appearance, dignified bearing, and deep, cultured voice made him perhaps the most impressive public speaker in an age of impressive public speakers. As indicated in the novel, in 1856 he was nearly beaten to death by the nephew of a secessionist congressman he had denounced the day before.

Southern hardliners cheered it as a great victory, but it was a victory at too high a cost; for the next three years Sumner's chair sat vacant in the Senate, a mute reminder of the cost of crossing the Southern slaveholders, and their willingness to see a Senator struck down for daring to oppose them. Sumner resumed his duties in 1859, and became unofficial leader in the Senate of the "radical Republicans": those Republicans dedicated to the complete subjugation of the South and equality for the black man. Still, the near-fatal beating had taken much out of Sumner that never returned.

Although not as disabled as I have made him in the novel, he suffered for the rest of his life from blackouts, forgetfulness, blinding headaches, and terrifying nightmares. Although Sumner's single foray into marriage took place after the time of the action in this novel, it was every bit the disaster I have portrayed. His wife openly accused him of impotence during the divorce proceedings, to the amusement of Washington and the mortification of the proud, dignified Sumner. Still, his personal tragedies should not obscure the fact that he left an unambiguous record of work to save the Union and see all Americans equal before the law.

John Surratt (1844-1916) fled to Canada after the assassination, and from there went to Europe, ultimately ending up as a member of the Vatican guard under an assumed name. Recognized and deported to the United States in 1867, he was put on trial, but the jury deadlocked, eight for acquittal, four for conviction, and the case was dismissed. John Surratt spent the rest of his long life in deserved obscurity.

Mary Surratt (1823-1865) was married to a struggling Maryland planter who was an abusive alcoholic. When her husband died in 1862, she found herself in desperate financial straits, deciding the best way to address this would be to open a boarding house in Washington, a city whose population had exploded under the pressure of war, and where lodgings were at a premium. A rabid supporter of the South, her boardinghouse had become a gathering place for Rebel sympathizers, including John Wilkes Booth. She had long known that her son John was a Confederate courier and spy, and Booth's meetings to plan the abduction or murder of Lincoln took place at her dining table when she was in the house. It stretches credulity past the breaking point to believe she did not know of, and approve, the plot. Although many writers have tried to make her a hapless victim of a kangaroo court, it is clear that the military tribunal which heard her case wanted to find a reason to acquit her, but could not believe that she at least did not have prior knowledge of the assassination plot. Unlike how she is portrayed in the novel, she was probably not an active plotter, but she undoubtedly had knowledge of the plot and could have stopped it, choosing not to. Whether she deserved to hang for that is up to the reader's own sensibilities.

Elizabeth Van Lew (1811-1900) ran the most successful espionage network on either side in the Civil War. I have not fictionalized her exploits at all; she and her agents were providing intelligence of critical importance to Washington from the very heart of the Confederacy. When Richmond fell to the Union forces, Miss Van Lew was the first civilian to raise the Union flag. She had exhausted most of her inherited fortune in running the spy ring at her own expense. In an act of stunning ingratitude, Washington refused to reimburse her for her expenses after the war. She was in an especially precarious position; as more became public of her wartime exploits, the more the hostility of her Richmond neighbors grew. However, to this story there is a happy ending. A wealthy group of Bostonian admirers learned of her plight and established a substantial trust for her benefit, allowing her to live in the ease and comfort to which she had been born.

About the Author

Jack Martin

Jack Martin is a life-long Californian; he never set foot outside the Golden State until his 30th year, but has traveled extensively - in his imagination.

Trained in the prosaic fields of economics and law, and earning his living in the corporate bowels of an enormous aerospace company, in his spare time he stretched his mind by studying the wonders of astronomy on the one hand, and the glories of American history on the other. Sonia, his wife of twenty-seven years, was possessed of a brilliant practical business mind; yet she greatly enjoyed Jack's stories of the American past, and encouraged him to write them professionally.

She especially enjoyed his speculation about a "secret history of the United States:" incidents and turning points so vital to our future yet so potentially terrible that knowledge of them was withheld from the American public. With her prodding, he has created a series of novels involving the character of Alphonso Brutus Clay: a Civil War Union officer who will find himself deeply involved in several such incidents that will never find their way into the history books.

Sonia passed away on Christmas Eve 2009 after a brave four-year fight against ovarian cancer, and therefore did not live to see the first of the books that she inspired. However, Jack is convinced that somewhere, she knows.

BLACK SOLDIERS
BLUE UNIFORMS

The Story of the
First South Carolina Volunteers
by Thomas Higginson

"de Fus' Souf" - America's First Officially Recognized African-American Regiment.

While the unit was all black and composed of former slaves, the officers, by decree of Secretary of War Edwin Stanton, had to be all white. The first commanding officer, therefore, was Thomas Wentworth Higginson, who tells its incredible story.

LADY REBEL: THE STORY OF LORETA VELAZSQUEZ

By Loreta Velazquez

The story of a true Confederate hero – only he was a she.

Wife, mother, combat officer, spy... The debate continues to this day as to whether her incredible story is true.

You decide!

Blue, Gray and Red: Two Nurse's Views of the Civil War

By Louisa May Alcott and Kate Cumming

Two Nurses - Two Experiences - One Civil War

Blue, Gray and Red presents the hard reality of the Civil War. There are no stirring bugle calls, only the calls of the wounded. There are no battlefield heroics, but there is also no lack of heroism. It presents the suffering and courage of *both* sides, as written by two people—two nurses—who lived through it.

No understanding of the Civil War can be complete without appreciating this side of the war as well.